mahasena

Kala is the author of two bool
Most Perfect Grammar (2016
Burned & Cindered (2018). Sh
Sathyavak and Totoro aka To
her family of humans and non-humans.

mahasena

PART ONE OF
THE MURUGAN TRILOGY

KALA KRISHNAN

context

cntxt

First published by Context, an imprint of Westland Publications Private Limited, in 2021

1st Floor, A Block, East Wing, Plot No. 40, SP Info City, Dr. MGR Salai, Perungudi, Kandanchavadi, Chennai 600096

ISBN: 9789390679133

10 9 8 7 6 5 4 3 2 1

This is a work of fiction. Names, characters, organisations, places, events and incidents are either products of the author's imagination or used fictitiously.

Typeset in Minion Pro by Jojy Philip, New Delhi
Printed at Thomson Press (India) Ltd.

For
the poetry, grammar, music,
the poets, grammarians, musicians,
&
The God
of Tamizh
&
for Sathyavak,
named for the God

CONTENTS

before

a prelude

— BIRTH —

Ganesha was happy. He was finally going to have a sibling. Have the company of someone other than parents, relatives, collaborators, friends and devotees. His own baby brother. He was slightly disappointed it wasn't to be a little girl, but that was okay. A boy just meant more ego, a little slowness, nothing he couldn't deal with. Besides, if this boy was going to be all that they were expecting him to be, it would be fun, and fun was something Ganesha sorely wished for but rarely, if ever, got.

Everyone, including his parents, had grown used to depending on him for sagacity. Now, after just having completed the gruelling scribing of the 'longest poem ever', he was especially weary of sagacity and dependability. He would so like some baby babble in his ears. Sometimes he felt as if the portentous sound of the 'language of the gods' still clung there, making him want to put a little finger in and ease it out. A baby brother would laugh and clap and talk in a language that had neither grammar nor rules of composition or sound units, or balance of sense and suggestion.

He would gladly exchange the status of Elder God, Leader of the Ganas, for Elder Brother.

He would not be able to see the little boy just yet, though. As soon as he was born, he would be taken away to Bhuloka, the seventh or eighth of the fourteen worlds, depending on whether you were counting from the top or the bottom, to a land with water on three sides and mighty Himavan standing guard at its head. He would be taken to a forest in the south, where his arrival was awaited. The journey was to be a relay, with different people, already selected for this task, carrying the baby, each in their turn. The child would be received and cared for by the six women waiting there, and taught the many lessons he must learn. That was one of the conditions of the child's birth; Father and Mother had agreed to it, as had the two gurus, Brihaspati and Shukracharya, and everybody else, including Ganesha. But that didn't lessen his annoyance.

Ganesha turned to his father, who was seated under his favourite tree, and the sight made him smile. No matter how many times you saw them, tree and man, you marvelled at how grand they both looked, despite being so dishevelled, especially now, in the glow of the rising sun. From his father's head, the jata, bleached red and gold by the sun and wind and cold on this highest mountain in all creation, tumbled down, like the ashen ariel roots of the tree. A thin stream of light, powdery, like fine dust, emanated from the middle of his forehead. Mother, seated beside Father, was leaning towards him, and he knew that their two bodies, at some point, would be so close together, you couldn't tell where one ended and the other began.

They were called by many names: Shiva-Shakti, Shambhu-Uma, Shiva-Parvathy, Gauri-Shankara. Most people thought of them as a single unit; even when their names were said, one seemed incomplete without the other. It was not without some irony that the wise ones called them the Mother and Father of

Creation, knowing that the Father could be motherly, and the Mother just as easily not. They were his parents and the parents of the little boy whose birth was imminent, the baby for whom these uncountable creatures were gathered: two-legged, four-legged, many-legged, fierce, gentle, Gandharva, Rakshasa, Asura, Pishacha, Kimpurusha, Vidyadhara, Sura, Manava, they were all here.

Father Shambhu and Mother Parvathy were engrossed in the birth of their second son, for this was no ordinary birth. Father Shambhu's legs, lean and muscled from years of walking, dancing and climbing the high mountain, were crossed; his back was parallel to the trunk of the tree, not leaning against it. Mother Parvathy sat next to him; her legs were folded at the knee and tucked to one side. His left hand curved around her waist, resting on her hip; his right hand rested on his right thigh, as if to hold himself down, if needed. Mother's right hand was on his back; the fingers of her left curved around a sprig of newly blossomed saffron flowers. Ganesha liked to look at them when they sat like this—they really looked like they had given birth to the endless universes.

Father's third eye was pulsating. Its glow grew more defined, more solid, even as they watched, and the warmth it gave off became more pronounced and spread further. Ganesha looked around at the rows of beings, all waiting; some of them were becoming restless, they shifted from foot to foot, and wiped their foreheads, as the air began to get warmer. Ganesha himself was sweating, so he pulled the green upper cloth off his shoulders. The two lobes of the eye on his father's forehead quivered, they were moving like the twin lips of a fish mouth: open-close, open-close, open-close. When they stilled, only a delicate line remained, trembling and shifting, as if it was an image under water. The light inside seemed to be pressing against it. He couldn't say how long it was before the lids widened and light, fierce and fiery, pushed through, filling the air with a burn that made those gathered there to shift and shuffle and exhale louder. In silent consensus, people moved aside to make place for those who found the heat unbearable and wanted to leave. How right Nandi had been to arrange the waiting crowd in rows, in order of their ability to bear the heat of Father's third eye.

Ganesha looked over at his mother; she was smiling, *of course she was smiling, she was always smiling,* with that heart-warming smile that could change in a moment to glaring anger, to quaking rage that shook the worlds and sent its beings scattering in fear. An anger that could alarm even Father. Ah! So many stories to tell his soon-to-arrive baby brother. Even as he thought this, Ganesha's eyes were viewing another scene, one that would not happen for a long time yet—his baby brother, grown to a man, standing at the head of an army, his face raised to the sky, his eyes blazing, his shoulders squared and his hands holding a lance. That lance would have a name, but the name would be in a language not yet formed—the old language made new by this baby who wasn't even born yet. On that day, he would be accompanied by several lakh battle-ready women and men, who thrust their weapons high in the air and shouted his name. And by his brother's side, there would be a woman, unarmoured, unarmed, in her hands cymbals, on her lips that very language.

Ganesha's eyes narrowed in reflex against the relentless gust of burning air that was now beginning to surge from his father's third eye. Father's other eyes were still shut; Mother's were open, watching the crowd. She would be looking for those who, unable to bear the heat, might need to be led or carried away. Nandi and Uncle were close by, both also looking around.

Then, the moment that they were all waiting for arrived: the third eye was widening, accompanied by a reverberation, like the trailing ring of a cymbal. As the crowd watched—and it should be no surprise that, wherever they were, each one of them could see

Lord Shambhu's face—the eye opened fully, and from it rushed a swirling, many-ribbed curl of blazing light. The musical re-echo grew more pronounced, more defined, and collected into strains; notes tumbled like marbles from a child's fist. After a pause, they resumed, surer, spaced out, rhythmic. They seemed to gather order and concord, and flowed now as music—its eddies and waves lucid. Like an underground stream that breaks through burning desert sand to pool into an oasis, it cooled the air and the breath of those breathing that air. A wind began to stir in the trees; the leaves of the great banyan that grew on Kailasa, unaffected by the cold, quivered and rustled. Sighs of relief rose here and there, blending into the music.

Ganesha was thinking, *Oh, this sibling, he gets better and better*, when his breath stopped for a tiny fraction of a matra—he could *see* the child: a face and hands and legs, dark as ebony; in the face, twin eyes as big and shapely as half-open lotus buds, lips curled in a smile. Ganesha often wished that he didn't need to know everything, but at that moment, though he knew the baby would only be 'born' after he had reached his designated home, part of him wanted to stretch his arms out and pick up the little one. He wanted to kiss him on those cheeks, round like his belly, which had begun to shake—

He was laughing! This boy, yet unborn, could see him! Tiny fragments of the laughter Ganesha was trying to hold in, escaped. Here he was, able to see everything, everywhere, and this little boy had begun to see even before he was born! And already, the two of them were sharing a secret that was invisible to the rest of the universe.

The flame was beginning to get fierce once again. Here and there in the crowd, people fainted and were carried out by beautiful Gandharvas, who could carry whole mountains in the palms of their pink hands, their graceful fingers capable of playing and fixing everything, including broken hearts.

Ganesha stood up, so did his mother, and then Uncle Vishnu moved forward, and the three of them stood under the flame as it sputtered and began streaking back and forth with a lusty ringing, covering the length and breadth of the gathering—no mean distance. The heads of all the assembled beings moved as one, this way, that way, forward, back, sideways. The boy was already playing tricks! Ganesha could see the little one's belly rise and fall as he laughed, his eyes spilling light, his clapping hands sending sparks flying.

Father Shambhu was lost to the world, his eyes closed, all three of them. Sweat was breaking on his forehead, running down his neck and chest. His face looked just like the poets described it: the splendour of a thousand suns, all at once. His body shone like burnished copper, its evening-sky ruddiness dusted over by sun-glow. Father had sighed when Mother's hand left his back and her hip moved from under his hand. Ganesha, noticing this, was reminded of the time one of Father's chelas, wanting to worship only Father, turned himself sliver-thin and tried to slip between them, and they just fused, making the deluded devotee see the foolishness of trying to separate what was inseparable.

A loud crackle snapped him out of his reverie. His head shot up, and there was the little one, grinning at him, his hands waving from side to side, making the light sputter and hiss and fizzle. He smiled, and the boy smiled back. Ganesha raised one hand and lowered it unhurriedly to chest level, and the little one seemed to understand that it was a sign to slow, for the sounds and movements began to settle, and the boy in his crib of flame, he too settled.

The music from the flame started again, more complex now, the notes in a formation, as if the phrases were telling him something. Ganesha's heart surged: this music was for him; it had the slow grandeur of an elephant's gait! It rolled, sped up, charged, slowed, turned around, as if the notes were a ball that the little boy was playing an intricate game with. Invisible and inaudible to everyone but Ganesha, the sound dissolved into the flame, and there was only one thing now: resonant light. The little one continued to look at his elder brother and smile, and as the elder watched, the baby eyelids closed, sleep settled on his face, and the swirl of sound and light settled around his ankles. He was wearing anklets of sound! There was no other way to put it—the notes had taken life and were now sleeping, coiled like a leafy vine around a slender bough. Ganesha's heart pushed against his ribs, tears sprang to his eyes, he glanced towards his mother, and she smiled at him, then turned back to the flame, now still and silent.

1

THE JOURNEY

It had been a unanimous decision: Agni would transport this cocoon of flame—he was the God of Fire, after all. Even for him, it would not be simple, for this was no ordinary fire, but one that held the combined power of Shiva and Parvathy. No one and nothing could bear it unless they had the blessings of the Divine Couple, which Agni did. In addition, Mother Parvathy had promised Agni that if he needed help, he would get it.

Vayu was to accompany Agni in his mission to transport the child to Bhu, for Agni had the worst case of nerves you could imagine, and Vayu, none at all. Agni was always in doubt: he hesitated, he shivered and he shook, imagining that he might flare too much or too little. Unless someone quickly stepped in, he might burn down entire forests, sacrificial halls or homes, or he could leave everything barely singed. In both cases, Vayu, who had to partner Agni's work, blowing at the appropriate strength, would be furious. Knowing that he too would be blamed for the failures, Vayu's annoyance shot out of his mouth in gusts, which just made Agni even more nervous. But that too had been taken care of. Vayu would travel far behind and only approach if Agni called for help.

Which was why Agni was smiling and humming under his breath as he stood waiting while the flame quietened and rolled into a neat ball of glow. When the gods signalled for him to take it, he held out his cupped palms and the ball dropped slowly into them and lay still. There was utter silence as, smiling widely and bowing his head to all, Agni rose up into the air and soared off. When he could no longer be seen, Vayu also took off in the same direction, and he too disappeared from sight.

Agni was calm; he settled into a comfortable glide, the flame in his hands curled up like a baby. They had a long, long way to go. The sky below billowed and frothed, and waves of blue and foamy white rose and settled. It was like opening and shutting his eyes to the same scene, once, twice, and on and on. As he flew, he began to tire, and it wasn't long before the old insecurities began to raise their heads. *Would he fail, like he always did? Would he be able to do this?* Agni calmed himself by humming … the little ball of fire stirred in his hands. Agni stopped humming and looked carefully. *Was he waking up? Had something disturbed him?* The ball settled down once again, and they flew on. Vayu flew at a distance, not once calling out or teasing Agni.

Agni was relieved that Vayu was behaving himself; also, Mother Parvathy's promise had given him confidence. He sighed and relaxed, and dropped lower. He liked looking at the landscape: spreading carpets of green, brown, red and a lot of ochre; *ochre is a forest colour, nowhere else can yellow and black mix so well.* In the endless spread of green, the ochres were like flags. His belly expanded to make place for the joy that was stirring; it bubbled and rose, filling his chest, and darted out of his throat in a flurry of notes, unpleasantly random, spilling untidily into the sky. Agni loved to let his voice soar, singing songs he had heard the musicians sing, repeating the many scales he had heard the students practise. Sometimes, he made up his own tunes. The problem with all of this was that Agni rarely paid attention to what his voice was doing, he didn't care that the tune was being impossibly stretched or that his singing was not pleasing to the ear—he just kept going, like he was doing now. It was a good thing neither Nandi nor Tumburu were around. They would have stopped him, held him still, sung him the notes, and made him repeat after them. Agni could have sung well if he paused and focused, but he was always in a rush.

Ow! What was that? Agni felt a burn.

Agni burning, you ask? Yes, Agni felt a burn, and though the ball of flame in his palms was still, he had seen a spark spring from it and sting him, and there was still a tiny flicker on its surface. It's Vayu's doing, Agni thought, and turned to look for him, but he was not to be seen. Where was he?

'Vayu,' he called. 'Vayu, where are you?'

No answer. It seemed as if Vayu had nothing to do with it.

Agni reminded himself that Mother Parvathy had told him he would have help if he needed it. He could do it, of course he could. La, la, la, sa, ga, ma, ga re sa … *ow! Owowowow! What was that*? He felt his skin sting. He heard a crackle—the ball of fire was crackling, a tiny glow flickered inside. *What was happening?* Agni's mouth shut, his eyes were on the ball, he slowed and drifted with the wind. Then the sputtering and glowing stopped, he heaved a sigh of relief, and continued on his way.

It was morning, the sun was shining, and below him, valleys and mountains, plains and seashores passed by. The air was still cool. Clouds with rain in their bellies passed by and hailed him, birds called, and he thought he could hear voices saying, *That's Agni, carrying the divine child*. Did he hear someone say, *Only he could have done this*? Agni's chest was swelling, his mouth opened, and he began to sing loudly. *Ouch!* He nearly dropped the ball. It was glowing, like an ember about to ignite, it sputtered and hissed. To Agni's horror, tiny beads of fire appeared inside the ball and began to spin. Faster and faster they turned, and Agni's eyes scrunched shut, in a reflex against the explosion that seemed imminent. All his confidence disappeared, he began to tremble, sweat sprouted on his face, his chest was cold and his eyes stung. He couldn't bear it. His hands ached, he wanted to drop the ball and flex his fingers.

Agni was so nervous that he couldn't stop humming, and as his nervousness increased, the low crooning turned into a yodel, scale and pitch and rhythm all forgotten. The ball of fire in Agni's hands grew redder and hotter and began to jump, like grains of rice in a hot pan, popping and leaping. *Oh God, what was happening? What was wrong? What did this child want? Couldn't he just lie still and be carried to his destination?*

Were the clouds looming above him? Was the sky closing in to smother him? He could barely breathe, but he couldn't stop the yodelling; he shut his eyes, and his breath steadied, he gritted his teeth and shouted, 'Vayu, Vayu, where are you? Help!'

In an instant, Vayu was there, next to them. He said, 'What? What's happening?'

Out of Agni's mouth there came a sound that was a mess of humming, yodelling and singing, and as he sang, the fireball jumped and vibrated and rose and fell, while inside it, scores of little beads of fire spun, turning round and round, spirals of fire.

Vayu took one look and guffawed. Through his laughter, he said, 'Agni, stop! Stop!'

Agni stopped flying.

Vayu held his arm and said, 'Stop singing; you're singing tunelessly, it's agitating the child.'

Agni was almost hysterical by now and Vayu had to hold him by both shoulders and repeat what he had said. When he did, the flame slowly stilled and became silent, and returned to its moonlight-like luminescence.

'See,' Vayu said, 'I told you. How many times have we told you not to sing so out of tune?'

Before long, they arrived at the designated meeting spot. They could hear Bhagirathi now, her waves rushing, leaping over rocks and boulders, sounding like peals of delighted laughter. They could smell the fragrance of river mud and the plants that flowered alongside her banks.

Vayu called to her, 'Ganga, Ganga, Bhagirathi, stop, slow down, we have brought him. Stop now, so that we can come down and give him to you.'

Ganga slowed and stopped, the two flying gods descended, and after greetings had been exchanged, Agni handed the flame-ball to Ganga. In her moss-dark hands, it looked like the sun in a bowl of sleepy night.

Agni took leave of Ganga and Vayu, who would accompany her for a small part of the way. When the ball of fire left his hands, Agni had felt as if someone had held him upside down and all his insides had dropped out, as if he was collapsing inwards. He should have been feeling relieved—hadn't good fortune been on his side, letting him carry out his task without too much of a mess? Just a little while ago, all he'd wanted was to hand over this fire-child and return to Kailasa, but now he lingered, flying overhead, above Ganga and Vayu. His eyes filled, tears sprung and flowed down his face, and that's when he heard the music. It was emanating from the glowing ball and rising up into the sky, into his ears. It filled his head and flowed down, into his empty, hollow, tired frame. He felt as if he were a child, back on his mother's lap, and she was rocking him, singing to him. Something was happening to him, though he could not say what. He felt full, full and light, his belly was tingling, his chest was tingling, his throat was tingling; something was moving from his guts, sweeping through his chest, rushing up the tunnel of his throat and out of his mouth: in perfect tune, the notes of a raga he loved. Tears rushed into his eyes as his voice soared, its timbre and tone making the clouds turn and slow and birds call out in joy. He folded his hands, his eyes closed, and he thanked the yet-unborn child for doing something that no one else had been able to do: teach him to sing in tune. He was ready to make the return journey now, he ascended higher and flew on. As he flew, he recalled something that made him laugh through his singing: when he had placed the flame-ball in Ganga's hands, she had staggered, calling out, 'Ow!' He laughed aloud. *So, this fire burns not only fire but even water!*

Ganga surged ahead. With mighty strokes, she covered vast distances, running down hills, winding around mountains, plunging into ravines, tunnelling through mud banks and sweeping along the plains. The terrain, so familiar, felt different, for she had to ensure that the ball of fire in her hands was safe. She needn't have, but Ganga tried to keep to the shade when the sun blazed, to slow when she came to a dip in the land. At one time, she wondered if the child was hungry, then it struck her that she was being silly. She shook her head, tossed out those thoughts, and resumed her customary flow.

When she came to the spot where she was to meet her sisters, they were both there, Yamuna and Sarasvati, waiting for her to arrive. Ganga could flow no further, bound by a promise given to someone who had asked of her that she would never venture beyond this point. So she had sent word to her sisters, asking them if they would undertake the rest of the journey. Yamuna could, but did not want to: she liked the comfort and the daily hustle and bustle of this place. That left Sarasvati. You can't begin to imagine just how eagerly she accepted the task of ferrying the baby god to his secret destination. It meant a lengthy, arduous journey, which in itself was nothing, for both as a river and as the deity in charge of the natyaranga, Sarasvati was used to taxing routines. She was used to deceit and betrayals, you know how the performing arts are! But this was different. She would have to take a subterranean route to the mountains of the deep south of the land; she would have to hide from everyone, for no one, except his elder brother, his parents and uncle and aunt could know where this child was headed.

Going underground was not just a matter of putting her head down and piercing through the earth's surface—she needed the permission of Earth, who would surely object to her children being deprived of Sarasvati's waters. She had to cross the towering Vindhyas, and that would be tough too, persuading him to let her make her way underneath, and then cut through his belly and flow out, towards the southern plains.

These were daunting challenges, but Sarasvati was eager to set off on her task. It's not that she didn't like her work, or that she felt unimportant, it was none of those, but of late, she had begun to tire of the daily chore of purification and blessing, irrigation and transport. She couldn't tell when or how it had started, but every so often, she was filled with an irresistible urge to stop seeing and hearing. She wanted to shut herself away; she wanted to hoe, irrigate and cultivate the mud inside her ribcage. But her duties stood in the way, keeping her constantly journeying along the same routes. This journey she was making now was off course and final; it was the end of one life and the beginning of another.

When Ganga first asked her sisters to undertake the journey, Sarasvati had prayed to Ganesha for guidance with her answer. He saw what she desired and he appeared in her dreams to tell her who the women waiting to receive the baby were; they could tell her if she had made the right choice: the six Krittikas.

Now, the Krittika sisters, whose name meant 'the Cutters', were famed for many things, two of which were their knowledge of the ways of the stars, planets and of fortune, and their ability to read the charts and foretell what was to come. They were called 'the Cutters' because that's what they did: they cut away what was not necessary, and you could no longer turn to anything or anyone other than yourself.

Sarasvati wanted that cutting, she wanted the sisters to cut her free of everything that prevented her from asking the most frightening of questions: *What am I, when I am not doing?*

So she gladly accepted her sister's request to go in her stead on the second leg of the journey. And if truth be told, neither Ganga nor Yamuna wanted to meet the Krittikas. *What if they pointed out Ganga's sense of self-importance, what if they told Yamuna that she had always envied her sister Ganga and that was what made her less than she could be?* Ganga had come prepared to bargain with Sarasvati, but she didn't have to. Sarasvati saw this as a way to legitimise her running off. And thus it was that she left the earth's surface and dove downwards, travelling through the secret passageway that Vindhya had graciously made for her. He had weighed the situation and decided that he would much rather be the hero than the villain of this story.

Sarasvati flowed on towards a forest that ran along the flanks of a mountain range. This is where the boy would live until it was time for him to be transported back to where he had come from.

She looked at the little fireball in her palms; her heart felt bigger in her chest, her eyes filled. Sarasvati crooned to the ball. 'My dear,' she said. 'I can't see you, but I love you. If not for you, I would still be duty-bound.' The fireball rustled and glowed. It was beginning to emit a faint sound, which turned into a hum; she recognised notes and phrases. The music made her pick up her pace, for she sensed that she was close to the designated spot.

The ball was getting hotter. Slowly, it went from red-hot to white-hot. Sarasvati began to feel a little anxious. *Why so hot? Had she missed the spot? What was she supposed to do? Why was nobody here? She had better hurry.* She curved her back and swam furiously. 'Fireboy', as she had begun to think of him, was now a furious white miniature sun, emitting a brilliance and heat that should have burnt her but didn't, just as the intense hum ought to have deafened her but didn't. Instead, she too turned white-hot and resonant.

As Sarasvati raced on, the forest of trees became an unbroken, diaphanous line. Her eyes stung, her head reeled, she had to slow down and stop, and she did, because the ball had abruptly begun to spin and sputter, and sparks shot out of it in all directions. *How did none of them strike her?*

Then, with what seemed to be a kick, the ball exploded. The air caught fire, hundreds of birds took wing, soaring into the sky, calling in alarm. Sarasvati's eyes shut; her ears shut; she could see nothing and hear nothing. She felt nothing.

A sudden stilling of all sounds made her open her eyes. Her ears shook off their temporary deafness and into them flowed the most divine sound she had heard. It was coming from everywhere and everything, and she herself was ringing with the sound. Her hands unclenched and she looked around. She was in a backwater, the shara grew thick, and in between the reed stalks, in six lotuses, there lay six babies, all with the same face, the same smile, their skin the colour of ebony caught in moonlight. They lay there kicking their legs and arms, laughter gurgling out of their mouths. Sarasvati smiled back at the babies. Nobody would know that it was she who had carried them here. Tears streamed down her cheeks, it seemed as if the music was melting into everything, and as if this symphony was being directed by the babies' legs and arms. She wanted to pick them up, all six of them, but as she billowed forward, she heard voices, female voices, running towards the cove of shara. She sighed and held back. Soon, they appeared, six strong-limbed women, whose eyes turned to her, and who smiled as if they were one, a single person. They stopped, folded their hands and bowed to her. They said, in one voice, 'To the secret Sarasvati, the secret is to remain secret. Do not rise up but stay below. Do not return to the lands of the Malaya breeze and the rising devadaru, do not mimic the mountains' upward reaching, but be like the worm that burrows. Stick to the south, for here, death lives and life dies.'

Sarasvati heard the words as if she herself had authored them and someone else was reading them aloud. She reeled, as if air had stormed into her tired lung sacs—the Cutters had affirmed that she was freed of all the things she had feared to leave. She looked at them and they smiled. She, too, smiled and said nothing, turning back instead, the way she had come. As she flowed back, she heard again the peacock calls that had followed them all along the journey here.

Sarasvati flowed swiftly to her new home, hidden, secluded, where she would not be called on to compete or judge or explain herself. And for that she had this child, these children, to thank. Sarasvati's thoughts made her slow. This child's history would not include her, would it? It was Ganga who would be thanked, perhaps they would even name the child, children, Gangeya—Son to Ganga. But so what? She knew, and the boys knew, and surely these peacocks too knew. Why else would they be hailing her so lustily?

2

KUMARA AND HIS SIX MOTHERS

There were few to match the Krittikas in the telling of fortunes and prescriptions for antidotes to life's misfortunes. Many came to them to learn about the fate of things they held dear or dreaded: kings asked if they would return from wars; lovers if they would make and keep a life together; physicians if their treatments would be timely; generals if they might lose courage; the mothers of young women if their daughters' heads would be turned by beautiful but mercurial men. Others came asking for cures: for stubborn wombs that would not bear children, for the impotence of husbands who could not give pleasure, for varieties of harm done by themselves, and by strangers and loved ones.

The Krittika sisters could read your stars, they could draw a chart of your life events, they could read your fate from your hands, your feet, your face, or by touching you—a tip of their finger barely making contact with your throat, the inside of your wrist, your ankle, the underside of your foot, your ear, your forehead—or from what you were wearing, the direction of your entry into their forest, what bird or animal called as you arrived. In short, all things were potential signs and they could read them all. But whether they would tell you what they saw is another matter.

They could offer you remedies for all your misfortunes—a herbal cure, a cure of prayer and speech, of turning inwards, a cure to appease the spirits of ancestors or of the Gandharvas that lived in the trees or the wells, lakes, ponds, flowers around your dwellings. But the question always was, would they? It was difficult to tell why or when they would choose to remain silent because they did not discriminate between seekers on any discernible grounds: wealth, knowledge, species, gender. There was only one thing they consistently refused to do, which was to corroborate or refute suspicions of infidelity: they knew well what such knowing could do, as they knew how desire was sometimes beyond antidotes and righting.

They had gained this knowledge in a time before they learnt to read signs and tell what lay ahead. When they lived in the northern sky, these star-women, a cluster of seven at the time—among them a sister, now gone—were a modest constellation, one among hundreds of others ruled by the Sun. They were married to the Seven Sages, whose names are of no consequence, it is their actions that matter. The tale of how the Krittikas came to be the mothers of these six boys starts up there, in the skies.

The seven star-women went about their days, effective in what they did, happy to be where they were, wanting for nothing, resenting no one. Then, one day, the eyes of a passing god fell on them as they were bathing, and their strong bodies, their lustre, the way they were one despite being seven individual women, filled his head with visions of being in the midst of them as they tended to his lust, fourteen hands, fourteen legs, seven mouths, fourteen breasts, seventy fingers and seventy toes, and seven vaginas into which his organ could go! His loins swelled, his heart expanded, his breath slowed.

He approached the women and made his proposition. He was, he said, so filled with longing for them that he could barely breathe; he wished, he said, in a voice that held no doubt, to lie with them and enjoy them and to give them the enjoyment of his *supreme virility*.

The Krittikas looked at the god and said that they were spoused to husbands whom they would not cuckold or betray, and turned away. The god, knowing all too well the fate that befalls gods who let their lust go to their heads, left, crestfallen perhaps, or maybe scheming to get what he wanted. That, however, is not the crux of the story. It is this: one among the seven, looking on the god and hearing him describe his desire, was in turn filled with an irrepressible urge to participate in it. Her thoughts and dreams and all of her imagination was swept up into a tornado that spun between her and the things around her. The days passed, but not her wish to know the pleasures of lying with the god. And so, one day, she turned herself into six more, approached the god, and said to him that time had not let them forget his desire. Instead, it had entered their bodies and hatched into swarms of eager birds, ready to take wing. He lay with all seven, not knowing that they were but one, and she did with him, not once but seven times of everything. Then, their desire spent, there was nothing left, nothing to say or do, and the seven women walked away from him, turned back into the one, and went home.

She blurted out the truth to her sisters, fearing what it might bring. The six were appalled, angered, saddened and disappointed, but she was their sister, and a partner in the work that they jointly accomplished—they would not betray her. All except one, who said, 'I will not be part of this trickery. She strayed from her path, she deserves punishment. You must not stand in the way of her getting what she deserves.' This one, called Arundhati, was forever celebrated by aftercomers as a paragon, elevating the role of spouse above that of sibling.

All might still have gone on as ever, for it was not as if the seven sages enjoyed their wives' bodies or thought about their own as a source of pleasure. But the god, of course, went about boasting of his prowess, using words like 'irresistible', 'potent', 'chaste', 'travesty', and perhaps also 'cuckold' and 'dried-up sages'. And, of course, word got around to the seven sage husbands of the seven women, and, of course, they came storming in, demanding explanations. Perhaps they took up handfuls of water, readying to curse their wives, but Arundhati stepped forward and offered proof of her whereabouts on the day that 'the sin' had been committed. She went off with her husband, his smirk a template that men to come would mimic. As for the other six, they said to their husbands, one of us could not restrain our longing for the god; one of us lay with him.

Maybe they remembered that the central message of their husbands' wisdom was that fate is unknowable and unyielding, and hoped that they would view what had transpired in the light of this wisdom. Perhaps the women ought to have reminded their husbands of how often they had travelled to the tops of mountains, the middle of deserts, the insides of caves and the bellies of fierce pyres for their austerities, leaving their wives behind. Perhaps the women should have reminded them that they had married to enter wedded life, an equal sharing of all of each other. But they did not. Instead, they waited for the men to speak, and when they did, all six women were disappointed, for all six husbands, as if with a single will and a single voice, demanded to know who had 'erred'.

In that moment, the six Krittikas had proof that wisdom and truth are also mutable, like material things. They no longer wanted to direct heavenly traffic with their light or perform their other duties. They left their places in the celestial lookout and set off, dizzy with the realisation that they no longer had a prescribed route. They had to make their own way.

The gods cursed them for putting themselves above their responsibility to the cosmic order, and for failing to be dutiful wives. They cursed them to wander aimlessly through the universes forever after. However, the Lord of the Ganas, the wise and kind

Ganesha, intervened and decreed that they would wander, but they would gather knowledge as they wandered, and that they would be released, no, that they would release themselves, when the time was right. He instructed the sisters to wait for that time, and when it arrived, to go to Bhuloka. Ganesha promised them that, in the future, at a time when they would not need to be told what lay ahead, they would be given charge of the child born of his parents, Mother Parvathy and Father Shambu. And that was how the Krittikas, stars, beyond Time's sway, wandered through creation as the aeons passed, learning and understanding, till there was nothing left to learn on thirteen of the fourteen worlds, and they made their way to the remaining one: Bhu, Earth.

When they set foot on Bhu, it was as if their bodies woke from slumber. So far, they had felt nothing, but now, torrents of grief, shame, guilt, and a sense of wasted time rushed into their bony, hollow frames. After the day they answered their husbands' questions, the sisters had not spoken of the incident that had caused them to leave their sky posts, their homes and their spouses. Not one among the six brought it up or complained, assigned blame or expressed regret, almost as if it had gone out of their memory. But here on earth, their hearts filled with bitterness, bile rushed up into their throats and made them spit and retch. Their bellies burnt, their guts twisted, their bodies shuddered as if to shake off something that had taken hold. The endless wet of tears had made the skin on their faces and necks wrinkle; their hair grew brittle, snapped and dropped around them; their eyes clouded over; their skin grew dry. Whatever had kept them going without food, water and sleep now left them, and they began to feel the exhaustion that had been silently accumulating over all this time.

But they could not eat, nor sleep, nor rest. They grew weak and wasted, but they neither dropped down in a faint nor fell into slumber. No food would pass their lips nor water stay down. No matter how much they retched up, no matter that they walked day and night to exhaust themselves, no matter that their legs collapsed under them, they were awake and conscious. Sleep eluded them. Sometimes, their bodies seemed to curl in and gnaw at them, but still, no sleep. So, when one of them dozed off, leaning against an arjuna tree, the other five also sat around its trunk, leaning, and they too slept. They slept through several risings and settings of moon and sun, and when they woke, their eyes had stopped running, their bellies felt cool, they were thirsty and hungry, and they looked at each other and saw how thin, haggard and dirty they were.

They went down to the river and immersed themselves in its sun-infused warmth. Fish swarmed around them, nibbling at their dry skin. They scrubbed themselves with the soft mud of the riverbank, they floated their clothes away down the river and sat in the sun to dry. They ate the fruit that hung low on the summer-warmed trees. The six Krittikas thought that their circumstances had now changed, but when they lay down on the soft, mossy forest floor, though there was a cool wind blowing and they slowed their breathing, they remained wide awake. They got up and went to the arjuna tree, which had given them restful, life-giving sleep, and all six of them slept again.

They tried sleeping under a bael tree, a peepal tree, a sal tree, a neem tree, but nothing happened. So, it was the effect of the arjuna, they deduced. They took a leaf, a piece of bark, some seeds, and made a paste of each one, and they each ate of one. They found that they slept with leaf and bark paste but not with the seeds, and between bark and leaves, it was the bark that gave them longer sleep, but the leaves made them wake up feeling happy. So, they combined the two. In this way, they combed through the forest, testing everything, and they found things that tempered their anger, diluted and sweetened their bitterness, that crushed and discarded their sadness, and lit their senses and their speech.

In course of time, nature's ways became clearer to them. They looked around and saw how nature was made of patterns, but also that these were sometimes deliberately broken: animals left their unfit young to die, sometimes they ate them; trees and plants died of their own when they knew they were not strong enough. Yet, sometimes, trees sent out their own fluids to a plant wilting near them, and sometimes a tree's branch bent to let the straggling tendrils of a dying creeper climb; sometimes an animal adopted and stubbornly nurtured the abandoned progeny of another animal. Nature knew what to do, when and in what measure. To the women, it seemed that each plant, tree, animal and creature carried inside it something that let them see forward and act in the moment.

As time went by, and they assessed everything that they had learnt in the many worlds through which they had journeyed, one thing became clear to them. Everything, in all the worlds, stood somewhere in a rippling base that constantly spread out and contracted; if you were attentive, you could see the ripples come close, merge and separate. You could also see how, sometimes, things that were at the merging of two ripples were shifted by its force from one, and joined into another ripple. This knowledge started the Krittikas on their occupation of fore-seeing, fore-telling and fore-stalling what might appear to be unshakeable fate but was just one of many potential paths. As their knowledge grew, so did their understanding of knowledge and knowing. They understood that knowledge is a whetted blade cutting whatever touches it, that to know is to be separated, that knowing slices away the veil between what the knower believes and what *is*. When the Krittikas do not answer a question, it is because they know that the answer will cut the questioners away from their lives, and, left without a life to live, they might choose to die. But, at other times, when someone asks a question, the women remain silent because the questioner needs to answer it himself.

When the sage Dhritiman came to them and asked if his wife had been unfaithful to him, it is said that the sisters, who had not stopped him from entering the forest, said, 'We know the answer, but will not speak. It is there in your heart and you can hear it. Go back and learn to listen to your heart rather than your genitals, which we can see are well developed.' The sage had stood silent, his face burning and his genitals shrinking. As he walked out of the forest, he felt shame, guilt, sorrow. He realised that he had always known the answer to his question: he and she did not match.

It is said that when he turned back, Dhritiman did not walk but ran, and ran so fast he felt he was flying, and collapsed, sweating and panting. He felt like a man who had lived all his life bent over, not knowing that he could stretch. Dhritiman never returned home. His wife married another, who was to her as the light is to the dark, or the dark to the light: an apt match. Dhritiman later wrote a treatise called 'Utsahamarga: The Way of Enthusiasm, a Guide for Conversation Between Those Bound Together in Matrimony'. This is what the Krittikas were known for: cutting away, trimming, roughly slicing away the unnecessary—their lifework corresponded with the meaning of their name, Krittikas, the *Cutters*.

As the Krittikas unerringly guided those who came to them, all the while learning how to step into the swirl of their own fates and redirect its currents, they knew they were ready to take care of the child of Parvathy and Shambhu: everything that they understood hinted at the secret of this birth. They went to Lord Ganesha with offerings of wild fruit, honey, and the porcupine quills they knew he enjoyed writing with. He blessed them and said to them that the child born of Shiva and Shakti would come to them, and that they would nurse him and teach him what he needed to learn.

And they had known without being told that there would be one child for each of them.

The Krittikas stopped briefly to acknowledge Sarasvati and bid her farewell, then waded through the reed thickets towards the babies, who were swaddled in a light that was like sun-glare and moon-glow fused. From the lotuses, music sounded, its rhythm in concord with the things around them: the lapping water, the whistling wind, the scampering of creatures. Then they saw them—six babies, their skin a deep brown verging on black, their faces stretching with wide smiles, their eyes leaping in their faces, their hands and legs beating, as babies' legs and hands are wont to do.

They each picked up a baby, they kissed his forehead, and his little hands clutched at them; they sat down on the bank and put his lips to their breasts, which had become heavy with milk that morning, and he drank, long and deep. In that moment, it seemed to them that everything was listening to the sound of the babies suckling. Their hearts were full of love for the boys, and they remembered that Ganesha had said that the child would love them, that they would be the first people he loved, and that the world would always remember this. Now, here he was, not one but six, and they felt loved.

The six sisters walked back into their forest. They could hear peacocks calling, and all six of them smiled in unison. On the kadamba trees, buds burst into flaming red, out of season, and again, the sisters looked at each other and at the babies they held. There was a faint hum in the air as they passed, as if the kadamba were whispering. Their ball-like flowers fell in a shower, turning the forest floor red. And as they walked, each of the babies had a kadamba nestling on his little round belly. The sisters named the boys Kumara: the boy.

The Krittikas took the babies into the heart of the forest, the one they had picked from all the forests spread across this vast land—at its southern extremity, where it tapered into the ocean, where the rains fell in plenty and the sun shone without fail. Once the Krittikas chose this forest, it had become *their* forest, and word went out through bands of hunters. To them, the hunters who came seasonally and to whom this forest was a place of prayer, it would remain open, always. To everyone else, it was forbidden. In the unlikely event that someone wandered in, they would find a single path that, without their knowing, wound around itself in a loop on the outermost ring of the forest. Their steps would take them over the damp forest floor, dotted with ripe fruit that dropped from the trees with a sound like that of pebbles hitting water, they would see the dream-like birds on the trees and the lotuses in the lake. Their eyes would drink of this beauty and they would go home happy, feeling as if the forest had bent towards them and dribbled drops of green sap on their heads in benediction. But if someone knowingly trespassed, the forest paths would sink into the damp moss, the birds would fall silent, the lotuses would close, the sun would shut his eyes and the wind would sound like an army, marching, closing in. When they were allowed out, they would have grown gaunt-eyed, grey-haired and all a-shiver, and every time they saw a tree or heard the wind blowing, their eyes would dart around in their sockets as if they were blind. The Krittikas made a fortress that was guarded against all things—material and not, living and not, in this time and all times, in dreams and in the lived—which could harm their wards.

On high Kailasa, at the top of the hub of creation, Ganesha sat in his usual place. He could see the six babies smiling, and the six women's smiles. It seemed as if the six little boys were looking right at him and smiling back, but they were only one baby. The baby he had seen in the flames that streamed out of Father's eye. *The imp.* If only he were here right now, he could be singing him to sleep, rather than going over all the grievances and requests that his parents seemed to have palmed off on him, permanently. It was his mistake, he should not have offered to help. Kumara would be his excuse for *shirking* all the tedium he had long wished to say no to: he would take charge of the child. Mother and Father were busy, weren't they? And anyway, they weren't particularly good at this business of child-rearing, as he'd learnt. Not that he minded. He had liked raising himself, he did what came to him, and because he was all-seeing and all-knowing, he simply did what was right. But Kumara, ah, he would bring him up, like a *real* child.

The Kumaras' lessons began right away. The women carried the six babies through the forest in their arms. The babies' heads turned this way and that. The Krittikas pointed out everything around them, naming every tree and creature, and long before they spoke, each of the boys was imitating the sounds of the forest, the birds and animals, the wind in the trees and bushes, the waters gurgling and rushing, the growl of thunder and the drip-drop, drop-drop-drop of rain.

When their necks settled, the Krittikas carried the Kumaras on their hips and showed them the forest's understory, where saplings struggled to stand straight and grow tall enough to catch the scanty sun. The mothers called to the many creatures that lived there—bugs, snakes, big cats, lizards, insects by the hundreds—and they came out, jostling, pushing and nudging each other, to get closer to the children. The boys laughed and kicked and flung their arms out. The sisters sat them down and the animals came to sit around them. The snakes appeared to be the boys' favourites. The large ones slid up close and lay there hissing as the boys laughed, while the little ones slithered over the boys, running over their chests, sliding down their backs, coiling around their necks and on their heads.

When the Kumaras were old enough to sit by themselves, they clambered onto the backs of the tigers, lions, leopards, deer, wolves, foxes and wild gaur that lolled on the forest floor; when they could stand and walk and run, they cajoled their animal friends to run, holding on tight to their necks and backs, and urging them on with volleys of laughter and animal sounds.

Every day, the sisters tied the boys to their backs and climbed the tall trees in the forest's canopy, and quickly, the boys learnt how to climb, at first with a cord of softened ariel roots fastened around one of their ankles, the other knotted to a branch at the top of the tree, so that if their hands or feet slipped, they would hang from the tree by the cord.

The boys understood the forest, and it seemed the forest knew this and became joyous: the wind changed pace and the streams rippled more vigorously, flowers burst open out of time, and animals came charging into the clearings as the boys moved through the forest.

Thus, a year passed, another one started and was now drawing to a close. Soon, the Krittikas would have to return the six Kumaras to their parents. In these two years, the boys had learnt many lessons and the women delighted at how well they had learnt them. But when it came to keeping still, it was another story altogether! They fidgeted, they shouted, they pretended to fall asleep, or be sick. And so, it took a long time and many bribes before they learnt how to turn their backs on the thoughts assembling in their heads and attend to the soft voice speaking in their hearts.

The boys loved everything. Their ears leapt to the sounds of the forest, their noses ran towards the smells that thronged there, their eyes roved and pushed towards the red kadamba flowers, the white lotuses, and the trails left by animals. Their tongues rarely stayed inside their mouths. They tasted everything—fruits, flowers, water, mud; they held their faces close to their animal friends and licked their faces. Even the snakes stuck their fangs out and let them lick. And as for touch, the boys ran their hands over the bark of trees, and leaves, and the backs of animals. They lay on the forest floor and rolled in the mud, they hugged and kissed, and they wanted to be held and kissed. It was as if the five senses had taken up residence in the six Kumaras.

In time, the boys became quieter, and the Krittikas heaved sighs of relief. They reassured themselves that the boys would see that this was not just a lesson in concentration, but that when their hearts joined with their minds, they themselves became different and saw differently. The sisters knew the rewards of a concord between heart and mind, when the two became the heart-mind—it was as if someone picked you up and immersed you in nothing, and when you rose to the surface, you brought with you something from this no-thing. The women watched the Kumaras for signs that they had felt these things, and when their movements and speech stilled, and they began to sit for long periods, just watching and listening, it was a sign that their wards had understood.

The Kumaras loved to listen. They appeared to be able to turn off their eyes, nose, touch and taste, and let their ears see, feel, taste and touch. For the women, even though they knew that sound was to the Kumaras what breath was to others, it was still a source of wonder. They remembered how music had flowed from the six babies in their lotus cribs and fallen over them like garlands. After these lessons of stilling, when the boys walked, it seemed they were marking pace to a beat that you too could hear if you fell in with them; when they spoke, their voices rose and stretched and stepped to some unseen rhythm, and you felt you were listening to song.

Then, one day, Ganesha appeared in the dreams of the six Krittikas and said to them that it was time for the last lesson. This was the lesson that must hint at the secret of the birth of this child of the Parents of the Universes—that secret itself was for a later time. *Not too little, Ganesha said, and not too much, but of a measure that will warm and begin the process. And not, beware, till he asks. Remember the condition: he must seek and question first, so he may uncover that which is in him already.*

So, the women waited for their Kumaras to arrive at the question that would permit them to give him knowledge about himself that would fall into his ears and sink into his chest and become a seed, warmed and waiting to sprout.

They did not have to wait long, for with their new stilling, the boys began to take note of how animals lay down in favourite spots—the side of a tree, as if basking in its shade, or by the side of a young creeper, as if to lend a hold—and never stood up again. When birds, animals, bugs and even plants came to feed on them, the boys no longer tried to chase them away but sat by, watching and making sounds that could have been words in what the sisters had begun to call 'the Kumaras' language'. They often talked to each other in *their* language, and it sometimes reminded the Krittikas of another language they had heard a long time ago, the faint memory of its sounds coming back. The forest seemed to know that something was brewing inside the little boys, and it stilled and waited when the boys were quiet. The little mongooses didn't come streaking through the undergrowth with their loud calls, nor did the snakes slither over them or the ants climb into their hair; the lions, the horses and the giant birds did not make sounds inviting them for a ride. The boys deliberately sought out secluded spots, away from their mothers, where they sat for long periods, as if preparing for whatever was coming, for it was clear that something was.

Their bodies, too, reflected the shift: no longer did they stand with bellies pulled in, chests out, hands on hips, as if to resist whatever was headed their way. Now, they walked slowly, their steps more measured, as if they were looking for something they had dropped or something they had heard scuttling about the forest floor. The sisters missed the thoughtless laughter of the Kumaras, their constant demands to be carried, hugged, kissed, their need to be surrounded by attentive eyes and ears, but they reminded themselves that the time for separation was drawing near. They sometimes held each other and wept, sometimes they laughed at each other for crying, sometimes they walked close to where the boys sat leaning against a tree trunk or lying by the river, and stood watching them and listening to the rise and fall, the sweet murmur of their speech. If all went well, they would see their beloved Kumaras catch their first glimpse of the secret that was contained within them.

As for the boys, when they stilled, everything around them disappeared, and in that absence their un-knowing crystallised and they saw the things they had missed, the questions they had not asked, the answers they had not sought. They learnt to lead their doubts, observations, seeing, hearing, touching, smelling and tasting to the cauldron of their mind-heart and to tip them in, to be boiled and cooked into a broth of questions.

The sisters' wait ended when the Kumaras asked for the name of the thing that made running animals give up running and growing plants stop growing and slowly disappear. They told him its name: mrtyu. Next, when they asked what was the name of the thing that made everything move and grow, they told him that it was known by many names, one of which was 'ojas'. From there began a series of lessons about what makes things as they are, about what sits inside moving things, making them 'alive', and which, when it leaves, makes them go still and 'die', and which, unseen, also lives inside things that are stationary. The mothers explained that this thing that is never destroyed is called the rasa, the sap, and it flows in plants, trees and creatures, and crystallises inside rock and mineral. The Krittikas taught the Kumaras how to distil this physical rasa and refine in into thick, semi-solid rasayana, carrier of rasa, that rejuvenated those who partook of it, strengthening their own rasa and brightening their ojas. When that task was perfected, they spoke of the other, the supreme rasa, the Life Force, the Great Sap, which was what made everything work. And of how, when the wise ones imagined a being who held and nourished all creation, they imagined that being to be this rasa, and to say 'raso vai saha', it is truly rasa. This rasa, the Krittikas said, connected everything. It bound what was in the worlds above to those in the worlds below: when the planets moved and the stars changed position, a similar movement took place inside the bodies of animals, plants and all manner of beings and materials, because everything was part of the same being—the rasa. 'Why then,' asked the boys, 'do different things look and behave differently? Can we make one thing become like another, can the rasa of individual things become like the supreme rasa?'

The Krittikas answered their questions carefully, not imparting to them all that they themselves had learnt, so that the Kumaras would uncover the mysteries themselves.

In all the worlds, there were but a few, including Ganesha himself, who had this knowledge, and none of them could teach it to the Kumaras, because that was one of the conditions laid down by the Asura king, Surapadman, who, too, knew the secret. The child, he had said, 'must gain this knowledge from those who are not of his family, and he must struggle to learn it'.

Ganesha had seen the Krittika women's hearts empty as they gave up their identity as cosmic place-keepers and wives. This emptiness had seemed to him a safe place for the secret of the child waiting to be born.

When he spoke with the Krittikas, Ganesha did not tell them that they would one day be imparted the secret of Life, or how hard it would be to gain this knowledge.

This was how it happened. Soon after the Krittikas came to the forest, they set up a loom, with the help of the hunters, and begun to weave the cotton that fell to the ground from the wild cotton trees. They also acquired styluses, began to cure palm leaves, distil inks, and work with ores in the smithies that the hunters helped them to set up. They made charts and tables, and wrote down the measures and the processes for the making of cures, antidotes, the rasayana and other tonics. They recorded their calculations about the worlds that they watched: of plants, animals, minerals, stars and dreams.

There came a time when, every day, it seemed as if some unseen hand was turning their heads towards some new thing. Flocks of birds that arrived once in fourteen days to perch on a certain tree led them to finding the little nubs of flesh that grew out of its bark; the branches trunked there and milk flowed from there. They found a certain spot where ants congregated, and it revealed to them the warmth rising up from under the earth. They also began to have dreams of majestic beings that called to them from under the earth and offered them gifts of shining rock, of nodules of glowing, jewel-like patches in boulders. They knew well enough that dreams don't come out of nothing, and they knew too that whatever had happened till then was leading to the final part of their work on Bhu.

The Krittikas brought out their palm leaves, on which they had recorded tables, illustrations and listings of all that they had learnt, and pored over what they had put down. They cleared a big square of the forest floor and, with sharpened spikes, drew a map of their learnings. They found there several trails, and all of them converged at one spot, as if culminating in one conclusion. There, they drew two sets of arrows, one pointing upwards and the other pointing down, and around that they wrote, 'as above, so below'. They drew lines whenever one thing on their map was connected to another, and when they were done, there was nothing in the large grid on the forest floor that was not connected to another.

In the days that followed, snakes came out of their hollows, untwined from their perches on the branches of trees, climbed out of the marshes and lay in the clearings and on the paths, hundreds and hundreds of them. They hissed and side-winded for two risings and settings of the sun, and on the third day, when the sun was exactly overhead, all the snakes, in unison, wriggled and stretched themselves out of their skins. The sisters waited, they knew this wasn't over. Then came a great hissing, as if the whole forest had turned into one big serpent, and all the snake skins rose up from the earth. They turned into birds, silvery and sparkling, and with a beating of wings and calls that were unlike any bird call, they soared and flew upwards into the clouds, which in their turn roared and rained down. The hissing grew so loud that the sisters' ears shuddered and tried to close, even as the creatures of the forest joined in. With a lurch, in the middle of that forest of sound, a patch of earth the size of a small cloud opened up, as if a giant creature had sucked it in from beneath. The trees fell silent, as did everything and everyone else. There was no sound, except that of the sisters breathing. They got up and, holding hands, approached the mouth of the opening.

Hand-in-hand, they leapt in and were transported to the first of the seven regions of the netherworld. From one region to the next they went, through Atala, Vitala, Sutala, all the way to Patala. The beings who lived and ruled there welcomed the six Krittikas as if they had been waiting for them. In each part of the netherworld, they were told to ask to be instructed about any one thing, and the sisters, who knew what they wanted, asked for instructions that would bring them closer to the secret that they must learn in order to be able to teach it to the divine child who was to come into their care.

At last, they arrived in Patala, where Anantha, the serpent who holds up the worlds on his ten thousand hoods, lay coiled up. They had kept their last question for this great serpent, who was as old as creation and whom neither Time nor Death could affect, but who could affect everything in creation with the minutest movement of his body. The sisters stood before Anantha, and his face shone in the glow of the jewel that grew in the centre of each hood; it was like standing under a bright sun. They bent their heads and addressed him. 'O Anantha, who sees and hears everything, and from whom nothing is secret, pray instruct us in the secret of the Life Force. Show us how to see it, how to speak to it, how to understand it and teach it to the child whose birth we are all awaiting.'

The serpent, on his throne of crystal, lay still. He was surrounded by trays of fragrant oils, jewels, cloths that sparkled, and barks, leaves, roots, flowers, fruits and the seeds of medicinal plants. In the middle of all this sat trays of stone from which radiated many-coloured rays of light.

'Krittikas,' the sonorous voice of the serpent king filled the room. 'I will tell you once only, so listen carefully.'

Over five days and five nights, he instructed them, and on the sixth, the six sisters were ready to return to earth and await the task that they had undertaken. A portion of this knowledge, imparted to them by Anantha, was the last lesson that the Krittikas taught the Kumaras—because the questions he asked pertained only to that portion.

3

KARTHIKEYA, SKANDA, KANDHAN

It was a day like any other, but the forest was unusually hushed. The sun was just rising over the horizon. The Krittikas had gone down to the river, not just to bathe, but to let their hearts be soothed by the murmur of the river. As the water flowed over them, it slowed and its ripples spread, lingering a moment, as if tip-toeing past. Like the sisters, the forest and all its creatures appeared to know that the boys were leaving today, and that it would be a long time before any of them remembered how to be happy without six little boys calling to them, touching them, pulling them, singing to them in a language that only they understood. They too were hushed.

The sisters waited in the river for the water to douse the fire in their bellies. Eventually, they stepped out and draped themselves in the cloth they had kept for this day—new, and fragrant with the leaves and blooms of wild tulasi and dry palash leaves that they had rolled the cloth into.

The Krittika mothers shook the six little boys awake, picked them up, held them on their laps and suckled them. They let the boys play until the milk settled in their bellies, then took them to the river and bathed them. They scrubbed the stout little bodies with crushed neem and mango leaves and coated them with the clayey mud of the riverbank, they scrubbed them down with softened turai, and finally dried them and rubbed over them the fragrant bahumulaka. After that they brought out the roll of cloth they had woven on their loom. When they first abandoned their clothing in the river, the sisters had gone naked for a long while, letting the light and wind heal their bodies. Then, the hunters came and the villagers sent word through them to ask permission to enter the forest. That is when the Krittikas had built their loom with implements they instructed the hunters to acquire from the town. They gathered the wispy white bolls that burst from the ripening pods of the cotton trees. They wove their own cloth, and they wove and stitched cloth for the new-born in the villages, leaving it on the verandas of homes, rolled up and knotted into forest leaves, redolent with the scent of herbs or flowers that would seep into the cloth, protecting the child.

The cloth the Krittikas had made for the Kumaras was the colour of elephant tusks and had the texture of leaves that had lain on the forest floor so long that only their veins were left. They each dressed their own Kumara with cuts of the cloth, folded twice to make it thick enough to fall well. They held him still and wrapped it around his waist, pulling one end and tucking it in at the waist. They stood back from the little boys and admired them, then they brought out little lengths of another cloth: black-blue indigo, striated with gold and silver thread, and beaded with tiny stones. This cloth would never age, never tear and never grow dull, and everyone who looked at it would feel as if they were looking at the stars in an evening sky from the top of a very high mountain.

They were ready: the six Krittika women and their six Kumaras. The six pairs of little-boy eyes were bright; sometimes their gaze turned towards the sky, at other times they rested on the faces of the women or on the creatures crowding around or rubbing up against the boys. Each of the Krittikas held their Kumara tight and hugged him. They knew that they would not see him again for a very long time.

The Krittikas knew when, exact to the one-thousandth of a matra, the real mother of this child would appear to take him away. She would bless them, they knew that, and bring to an end their self-imposed exile. She would reinstate them to their old positions, held temporarily by others. The Krittikas knew they would not take their husbands back, for that truth no longer was. They had no need for them, or anyone else, for they wanted only to be recognised as the guardians of the six Kumaras. Their chests swelled with a mix of pride and sorrow; their breasts grew full with milk and they wanted to suckle their little boys one last time. As if reading the minds of their mothers, the six boys turned and made the sound they made when they wanted milk. The women each picked up her child, sat down with him on her lap, and each of them fed as they had for two years, their little hands clutching at one breast while they drank from the other, laughing and gurgling. The women's eyes filled and ran over, and they lifted their free hands and wiped the tears before they wet the heads of their wards. When they were done, each of the boys lifted his face, smiled at his mother, sat up and put his arms around her neck, and kissed her loudly. Each of the women embraced their Kumara, and for a moment, they all sat like that, each Krittika star with a little boy-god in her lap, his face pressed to hers. For a moment, the twelve hearts beat as one and the forest heart beat along, and the hearts of all the forest creatures joined in.

The moment was broken by the delicate sound of bells and the fragrance of flowers that wafted in and filled the air. The Krittikas raised their heads, the six Kumaras raised theirs, and all the forest turned to look. And there they were, the mother, father and brother, all on their mounts—Nandi the bull, Simha the lion and Mushika the mouse.

The six Krittikas stood, put the six Kumaras down, folded their hands and looked at the three gods in front of them. The Kumaras grabbed their mothers' hands even before their feet touched the ground. Shiva, Parvathy and Ganesha smiled at the women. Ganesha hailed them, saying, 'Mothers, greetings! Know that our gratitude is yours and that no thanks will suffice for the care you have given the Kumaras.'

The three visitors looked into the forest and raised their hands in greeting, the lion, the bull and the mouse raised cries, and the forest called back in its many voices. Then their eyes turned to the six little boys, who stood clutching the hands of their mothers—six stout, serious-looking boys, their ebony-sheened faces glowing with good health, their eyes wide, thick curls springing from their heads and cascading down to their shoulders, around which was draped what looked like a piece of sky.

The boys examined their family. Father was smiling. Inside his matted locks, some of which were coiled up on the top of his head, there appeared to be a piece of the moon, and it appeared that the moon was peeking out at them. *He uses the moon for a hair pin? Our mothers use pins they carve out of bones lying on the forest floor, or from soft wood.*

A burst of laughter made them turn to their brother. He was tall and delicate, his skin looked like the petals of a flower and his very human laugh, coming out of the mouth of an elephant, was funny, especially when his face was smiling like that. *Did he hear what I thought?* The boys scrutinised the face of their sibling. The elephant head nodded, smiling; the Kumaras smiled, *this was Brother*.

Finally, they looked at the woman who was their real mother—did the boys look at her last because they didn't want to see her, they didn't want any mother other than their six mothers, or because they noticed that she was ever-so-slightly hesitant, a very tiny bit less eager than the other two? This other mother was different from their six mothers; she didn't look like the Krittikas, but like him. Her skin was like his, the colour of mature ebony, while the six mothers' skin was the colour of sandalwood. This mother had hair like theirs—cascades of curls that fell around her face and chest and back; like theirs', her hair was neither braided nor knotted, nor coiled up. The boys thought she was humming till their eyes took in the bees circling around her head, her wrists and waist, around the flowers she was wearing. They saw that she was looking at them, her eyes were full, her face was serious. She didn't say anything. No one said anything, they all waited. The boys' eyes stayed on the group, moving from face to face.

Shambhu wanted to rush forward and pick up the boys, but he waited for Parvathy to make the first move, he knew how much store she set by these things. She had created Ganesha on her own because he had said to her, *let's wait*. He knew that she felt she hadn't been important in this new birthing—the flame had come out of *his* eyes, though it had been formed by both their energies, and then, she had to agree to let the Krittikas raise the boys.

Parvathy looked at the six boys, *her six boys*, their hands clasped in the hands of the six women. She knew how accomplished they were, how much knowledge they had, she knew how well they had cared for her sons, nursing them, teaching them, protecting them. It should have been her hands the boys held on to when they stood up and tried to walk, it should have been her shoulders they lay on when they were sleepy, and it should been her voice singing them to sleep. It should have been *she* who gave birth to them … The cauldron of her belly began to bubble up and boil with anger, resentment, jealousy, helplessness, the cloud of its fumes rose into her throat, clouding her breath, dimming her sight, slowing her hearing … The touch of a hand, cool on her arm, brought her thoughts to a stop; her breath slowed and steadied and her eyes cleared. This hand was always cool, its touch always gentle, this was a kind hand that took the hands of those who were lost and led them back on to paths they had strayed from. It belonged to her son, her beloved firstborn, Ganesha, whose sweetness spread to whoever was around him. He was smiling now as he said, 'Mother, the Kumaras are waiting. The Krittika mothers are also waiting.' In his direct, gentle way, he had reminded her that she was The Mother, it was she that all creation looked upon as its mother.

The Krittika sisters had foreseen Mother Parvathy's state of mind, but they did not know what would come of her anger: they had sworn to never read their own fates, that whatever was to come should come unknown, unheralded. So, when Parvathy relaxed and smiled, they heaved sighs of relief. The goddess raised her folded hands to them. 'Sisters,' she said, 'Shambhu and I, and all the gods, are beholden to you. We thank you for your patience and commitment to teaching our son. Every twelve months, everything in creation will recall this debt to you. That one day will be set aside for you, it will be named after you and, on this day, whenever it falls in the year, they will remember you and our sons.'

Having said this, Parvathy stepped forward and called to the six little boys, her arms wide open. 'Kumara,' she called, in that voice sweeter than birdsong. 'Kumara,' she said, 'come to Mother.' The little boys looked confused; they clutched the Krittikas' hands tighter, looking up into their faces. The six women knelt down and held their little wards. Hugging them to their bosoms, they kissed the boys on both cheeks and on their foreheads, and placed their hands on the six heads, blessing them. They said, 'Go to your mother.' But the boys clung to the women, the only mothers they knew. Parvathy felt her irritation stirring again, and almost as if—actually, exactly as if—he knew, Ganesha stepped forward and called, 'Kumara, come.' Just then, the six Krittika mothers gave them a gentle push. When the boys heard the voice coming out of the elephant-mouth, their faces opened with a wide grin and a laugh that rang out in the forest clearing. Then the six little boys, their curly hair flying, their mouths open and laughing, went charging towards their brother. Ganesha touched each of their heads and said 'Kumara' and smiled, and in unison, the six boys laughed. Ganesha turned towards the Parents of the Universes, his parents and the parents of his little brother, the one who had smiled at him before he was even born, and said, 'That's your mother, and that, your father.'

The six boys smiled, and all six of them went to Parvathy. Tears sprang from her eyes and flowed down her face. The boys were in her embrace—birds began to call, soaring overhead, the sun blazed, the wind slowed, the river leapt, fish stopped, and from far away came the call of peacocks. The sky filled with the sound of clouds clapping against each other and a fine drizzle came down. As the notes of music soared and spread, the six boys disappeared. In their place stood one little boy with six heads, twelve arms and twelve eyes, his tawny body sturdy, his ankles firm, his neck straight, his waist taut. On his shoulders, the stem of his slender neck held six smiling faces, which looked like six flowers from a single stalk. Each of these faces spoke, one at a time, to each of the six Krittika women. They thanked them and bid them farewell. And then five of those heads disappeared, as did all but two eyes and two arms. Parvathy picked him up and put him on her hip and said, 'Because the six of you have been made one, you will be called "Skanda", that which is collected; you are gathered from Shambu's and my strength, and thus too you are "Skanda".'

Shambhu—beaming, his heart melting like butter, as always—blessed the Krittika sisters. He promised that they would always be remembered as the women who had nursed the six boys, and the only ones stable enough to take his hand and walk him down the paths to wisdom. He said to them, 'Kumara will be known as Karthikeya, acknowledging that you are the foundation where his roots are held firm. When he goes to fight the fight he was born to, the second name he will be hailed by will be "Karthikeya".'

Then the six women took their leave of the gods, and of the forest, and ascended to the skies to resume their old positions. In their heads was the same thought: Kumara would remember all his lessons, he *had* practised and perfected them all, except one—how to control his impatience. Before he had been joined into one boy, if something caught their attention, the boys would tear off after whatever it was, and then, from somewhere else, other things would catch their attention and each one would go off in a different direction. The Krittikas looked down at the boy, who was looking up at them, his twin eyes following their upward path. They each prayed that he would learn how to instruct himself in what he needed to do.

They began their travel in the sky. Skanda travelled with his brother on Mushika, the tiny mouse who had grown as big as a cloud when the boy said, 'You're so small, how can I sit on you?'

Ganesha held his brother around the little one's belly, having seen the look of alarm on the boy's face as Mushika dug his four-toed back feet into the earth and lunged into the air. Their parents were soon left behind as Mushika raced on. This was no accident: Ganesha preferred to keep a little distance. In each other's company, Mother and Father often forgot to keep pace with the rest of the world—they talked, held hands, and laughed at jokes they did not even voice out loud; they looked and behaved as if they had just set eyes on each other. Ganesha tried not to be embarrassed but failed, and made sure to stray away on such occasions. Now he and his brother could leave their parents to themselves, he thought happily. *Kumara,* he thought, *the Youth, ah such a sweet name, for a boy who isn't going to be sweet.*

Mushika had seen Ganesha's face—so pleased with himself that the little one had pointed to him when they asked him who he would like to ride with. This little boy would make Ganesha happy and give him a reason to say no to things he was disinclined to do. It was time he did, thought Mushika, with a snort.

After some time, they came down and travelled on roads that led them past the sea. They went through forests and over hills. They could have transported to Kailasa in a trice, but waving her hands expansively, Mother had said, 'Let's go over land, I want Skanda to see all of this.' She did not need any excuse to be out in the wild, neither did Father: their lion and bull had no complaints either.

It was Ganesha who said, 'Let's stop' after some time.

They stopped at a clearing in the forest. And Skanda felt it again, that stir, like a ripple—in everything. It was like when his parents had appeared in the other forest, *his* forest. Now, here, everything was aquiver. He looked around to see if the buds would burst open and the clouds growl and the waters gurgle, and the animals and birds would come crowding around them. There! The same! Why was everything so happy to see his parents? Or was it his brother who had this effect on them all? Uff! These people were not like his six mothers: he always knew what they meant and their affection was like an embrace, he felt it.

But his new family, they were … what were they? He liked them, especially Brother. When he held his brother's hand, it was like he felt with his mothers—safe. When Brother lifted him up on to his shoulders, Skanda felt like he could tell the sky to stop and it would obey, or the river to curl back and it would listen. When he looked at Father, he felt happiness begin to bubble inside his belly. He had been watching all of them, and he saw that Father smiled at everything—he smiled at the sky, the trees, he looked down when he was walking and smiled at the grass. He noticed baby birds hidden away by their mothers and smiled at them. He smiled at ants, sparrows, dragonflies, everything, and he always smiled at Mother. He made Skanda feel that everything was looking at everything else. Now, Mother—he was a little scared of Mother. She looked like she was always doing something inside her head, and sometimes, as if she'd rather be somewhere else. But when she smiled at him, he felt as if he was back in the laps of his six mothers; he liked her too.

Skanda's thoughts were broken by a flash of white. It swished past the line of his sight, and when he turned his head, he saw that it was a large white owl that was now on the top of Father's head, perched casually, like it was her nest. The little hairs on Skanda's arms stood up as he watched: Father's ruddy matted locks hung around his face and on his shoulders; the white bird was on the crown of his head, its face caught in the faint glow of the moon lurking in that forest of hair. The owl bent her head forward, closer to Father's ear, and her hoo-hooooo-hooos, falling and rising, sounded like a story to the boy. Father listened with his head tilted to one side, a loud laugh ringing out every now and then, sometimes rising up over the tops of trees and into the sky, making the clouds rumble. Father made bird noises in response, and in turn, the owl bent her head to listen. Skanda wanted to ask him what they were talking about, but he felt shy … he would ask Brother later.

Ganesha was watching the three of them. Skanda would take a long time to get used to Father and Mother, how busy they were, how they could get so caught up in each other that they forgot everything else. His eyes turned to his parents: his father was leaning against a tree, opposite the one his mother was resting under. He was looking at her and she seemed to be paying no attention to him, but Ganesha knew she was, because she was blushing. He was proved right when she stretched her legs so that one dark foot, with its sparkling toe rings, became visible. Father's eyes turned to look, his lips arching in a smile. Even as Ganesha was thinking, *how sweet*, his father held out a hand and his mother got up, and they wandered off into the forest, holding hands, laughing and talking. 'What a pair,' he said aloud without intending to, and Skanda turned to look at him.

Ganesha was happy. He liked nothing better than to lie down like this, the grass under him tender, the root under his head softened by a long rain, the breeze cooling his head and belly, his mind filling with the light of the afternoon sun, veiling his all-seeing vision. He stretched and yawned. Skanda dropped down next to him, tugging at his arm, and said, 'Brother, why did we stop here? I'm not hungry, and no one is hungry, because no one is eating.' Ganesha laughed. He had one hand under his head, the other was on his belly. He lifted it and patted the little one's shoulder and said, 'Kumara, wait, lie down here and look at the sky. Look, see there, look at those clouds, do you know what they are doing? They're waiting for something to happen.'

'What?' asked Skanda, his body straightening up, his eyes narrowing in concentration. He didn't want to miss anything.

Ganesha laughed. 'Wait and see, it's a surprise.'

'A surprise? For whom? For me?'

'Yes,' the sleepy older brother said, and closed his eyes.

Skanda pulled his legs in and settled down with his chin in his hands. This forest, flanked by high hills, was different from his forest. Its rustles, the birdcalls, the sounds of the wind were all louder, because they hit against the sides of the hills and came back bigger. He wondered what the surprise was. Whatever it was, he wanted it quickly.

Skanda was restless and not in the least bit sleepy. He pulled at the grass, then stopped. *It was grass, he shouldn't pull it*. He ran his hand over it till the little pieces were whole again. What were his parents doing? Why did they bring him here if they were just going to go off by themselves? His other mothers would never do that. He wanted to go see what else was in the forest; he could see a path. *Clear enough for him to follow.* But Ganesha had told him not to stir. Skanda grew more irritated. He picked up a handful of little pebbles, and aiming for the gap between two branches of the tree in front of him, lifted his arm and threw. *There! Right through the gap.* He checked to see if his brother had woken up, but he seemed to be fast asleep. So he threw another one, then another, and would soon have tired of it, but that was when he heard a familiar sound ... like a cat-call mixed with a cuckoo's. Peacocks! Where were they? Must be close by somewhere, he could hear them so clearly. It sounded like there were many. He stood up, then remembered his brother's instruction: *Stay here, don't go anywhere.* He looked down at Ganesha, stretched on the soft grass, his breathing soft, and smelling of grass and marigolds. Skanda said, 'Anna.' There was no response, so he said it a little louder.

Ganesha could hear his brother calling, but stayed still. This was the first of Skanda's tests, the first of his many lessons. *Would he? Or would he not? Would he weigh the situation and decide what he wanted?*

Skanda's face was gathering into a frown. He called one last time, and then, with a stamp of his little foot and a snort, he headed for the path. His eyes shut, he listened, and then set off at a trot, heartbeat gathering pace. The peacock calls got louder and louder.

When the calls seemed to be pushing up against him, Skanda knew he was close. Running now, sweating and panting, he broke into the clearing. It seemed as if he had stumbled into a sea of peacocks. All he could see were peacock wings, iridescent blue, green and gold rising from an undulating mass of bodies, long necks of brilliant blue. On their heads, flying flag-like, their crests. When the boy appeared, it was as if rain clouds had suddenly manifested in a blue sky. The birds raised their heads and called, their voices grew shriller, they shook their plumage and whirled as they called. Not a bit of ground was visible as they moved, jostling, twisting and turning to keep from stepping on each other's trains.

Parvathy and Shiva heard the ruckus. All the ganas on Kailasa put together could not make this much noise. They jumped up and ran in the direction of the clamour. Ganesha was walking that way too. He knew what was happening, and would not miss it for anything: he wanted to see his brother's face when it happened. And, of course, he wanted to hear the words that would come out of his little brother's mouth. For, after that moment, they would all be changed: Father, Mother and he, all of them would become new. He also had a little wager with himself about who the little one would turn to, when it all happened.

Skanda was happy, happier than he had felt since leaving his six mothers and their home in the forest. He felt as if he was back there, where everything was his and everything revolved around him. As the birds began to circle him, their cries now in unison, he laughed loudly, both his hands outstretched to touch them, his touch light, gentle, as if he were stroking flowers. The peacocks rubbed up against the boy, or put their head on the little boy's face or shoulder. If any of them stood still even for a moment, the boy hugged them, kissed their heads, and spread his arms wide and touched as many as he could. Then he too began to whirl with them, and the birds shifted imperceptibly to make place for him. When he started running, they stepped out of his way, thronging around him like ringside spectators. And what a performance it was! The boy clapped his hands, skipping and running, his steps clearly time-marked to a beat, and it was clear he was clapping to keep time. He was also singing. Skipping, running, singing, his ebony-coloured face shining with sweat, his body drenched, his head haloed by flying curls and by the light that pushed its way through the tangle of trees, as if with the sole intention of crowning this child. The birds had fallen silent, the animals too, and the river and the wind, the clouds, everything had gone absolutely quiet, listening to this little boy's song.

The peacocks suddenly took wing and perched on the trees, turning their green into canopies of blue and gold, and Skanda broke off his dance, to stand still in the middle of a stretch of emptiness. And then, as if it had been waiting, a peacock swooped down from the clouds and landed near the boy. He was bigger than any peacock anyone had ever seen, his train was so long you'd have to crane your neck to see all the way to its tip, his crest reached as high as the low-hanging branches of the tall trees, his two eyes were as large as the giant leaves of a lotus. He was still, looking at the boy whose head reached only up to his flight feathers. The bird stretched his neck and emitted a cry that sprinted into the forest and winged into the sky, rousing forest and sky creatures, who responded with cries of their own, until land and air resounded. Streaks of lightning darted through the sky, and the clouds rumbled. As they watched, the giant peacock started shrinking until he was of boy-height. The boy's dark arms went around the bird's blue neck. He hugged the bird tight and the bird bent his head so that their foreheads were one to one.

Ganesha was holding his breath. *Now*, he thought, *Now!*

Skanda put his arm on the peacock's back, and looking at his parents and brother and their mounts, he said, '*Mayil*'. The clouds opened, and a fine rain, like airborne blades of new grass, came floating down. The hundreds of peacocks rose from their perch on the trees and fluttered down, they spread their wings, their trains opened into fans, and they strutted and turned and called in their cat-like voices.

The boy hugged the peacock again and said, 'Mayil, mayil, mayil.'

His brother turned to his parents, who were both smiling, and said, 'Mayil, peacock.'

'How sweet it is,' his father, the Father of Everything said. 'The old tongue, made new.'

The little boy tilted his head and said, '*Amizhhtam*, ambrosia.' And then added, '*Attan*, Father.'

The boy's mother, who is the Mother of Everything, went up to the little boy, who stood leaning on the peacock. She lifted him up, kissed him on both cheeks, and said, 'My son, *Kandhan*.'

And he kissed her back and said, 'Mother, *Annai*.'

She seated him on the peacock, who let out a volley of calls that gathered volume and undulated in the air, like flags from speeding chariots.

Ganesha smiled and said, '*Thambi*, my little brother.'

Skanda raised both his hands in the air and yelled at the top of his voice, '*Anna*, Anna, Anna, elder brother.' They were from now Attan, Annai, Annan and Thambi in the language of this little boy, whose name had just changed again.

Kumara, Skanda, now begins to be called Kandhan, a name that sits easily on the tongue. Light and round and skipping, it warms the hearts of those who speak it and hear it, and brings to mind the image of the little boy, as happy as a forest mahagani stirring in sunwarm.

The cloudburst did not abate, nor did the dance of the peacocks, their trains speckled with a hundred eyes. The clouds joined the dance, dashing about, and big drops of rain fell on the peacocks, who were moving in unison, like one big bird. Up in the skies, the gods had gathered to watch the miracle boy whom they had not set eyes on since they witnessed his flame-birth from the eyes of Shambhu. They had all been waiting, for it was this boy that the mighty Asura had said he would stand against, when the time came.

Kandhan, sitting where his mother had placed him, on the peacock's back, waited. He did not know what to do. He wanted to fly, but could he tell the bird to? Did he have to ask his parents?

Ganesha watched his brother's face do its tangling up, gathering into a glower. He wondered if the boy would figure out that he could just say he wanted to go for a ride, and decided to wait, knowing that Kandhan's chagrin would rise. But Mother touched the little one's cheek and said, 'Kandha, why don't you go for a ride?' And to the bird, 'Why not take the child up into the sky?' And they rose up, over the treetops, over the clouds, and were soon lost to sight. Kandhan's fear of leaving the ground had already dissipated in the time that he had sat on Mushika's back, his brother's protective arm around him.

As they flew, bird and boy had their first talk, the first of a lifetime of conversations. The peacock said to the boy, 'Give me a name. In your language.' And the boy said, '*Paravani*', as if he had already thought it over and selected the name.

'What does it mean?' asked the bird.

'It means generations,' the boy answered. 'Do you like it?'

Paravani nodded and said, 'I like it,' and flew on. After some time, he said, 'Kandha, bring out your six heads and twelve hands, I want everyone to see who I have been waiting for so long.' And the bird grew bigger and bigger, and on his shiny back, the boy grew enormous, till they spread across the sky and dwarfed the giant rain-bearing clouds that stopped and waited for their cue to pour down on the waiting earth. On the boy's neck, there appeared six heads, thick with curls falling over his dusky shoulders and chest and back; there were twelve eyes in his six faces, like bowls filled with sunlight, and his six mouths were grinning. He hugged the bird's neck with all twelve of his hands and kissed him many times. He said, 'I love you, I love you. And you have to love me too.' Paravani nodded and called in his guttural voice, making the clouds bump into each other. Kandhan's belly was full of glee that floated up into his throat and burst out of his mouth in loud peals. *He too had a vehicle!*

They turned back in a short while. Kandhan said, 'Paravani, let's go fast, faster than Vayu, let's race him.' Holding on tight to the bird's iridescent neck, he raised his head and yelled, 'Vayu, Vayu, can you hear me? Come for a race.' The wind sighed and joined the race, thus flagging off a ritual that the boy would continue even after he was no longer a boy.

In the forest clearing, Kandhan's parents and brother, waiting for their return, knew he was close when they heard shouts of 'Vayu, Vayu, you're behind, I'm winning, come on, come on, Paravani, quick, quick!'

Then the bird and his rider appeared overhead. Ganesha shut off his all-seeing eye. Only when it happened did he want to see it: who Kandhan would look at first, who he would run to. He reclined on the grass, his back against a warm rock, his eyes on the duo. As the bird swooped and made to land, the little boy's face turned to his elder brother and smiled, his grin stretched to his earlobes. Before the bird's talons gripped the earth, Kandhan had leapt off his back. Running to Ganesha, he wrapped his arms tight around his neck and said, 'Anna, this was your surprise?'

Ganesha could feel his heart slowing, filling with warmth: this was his baby brother, his ward, and he would be the boy's guide and the keeper of all his secrets. He knew that a time would come when he would have to do something that hurt the little one, but that was still a long way off.

Kandhan broke into Ganesha's rumination, clapping his hands and saying, 'His name is Paravani, you know, and he can get big and small whenever he wants.' He put his sturdy hands on his waist and throwing out his chest said, his grin widening even more, 'And I can too, you know, grow big and small.' Ganesha looked at his parents and saw that they were holding hands, looking pleased, but he knew that they had each thought Kandha would come to them first, Mother and Father.

Then they resumed the journey, taking to the skies, four flying creatures and four riders: the woman on her lion, the man on his bull, the young man with the elephant-head on the mighty rat and the little boy on the peacock.

4

THE MOUNTAIN HOME

So it was that when they reached Kailasa, the four of them were on their own mounts, and the youngest member of the family was on a peacock as mighty as many armies combined, as wise as all the worlds' scholars and as colourful as a forest in spring.

They had flown a long time, and though Kandhan hadn't really been looking, so excited with sitting on the multi-coloured back of this peacock that had come looking for him, getting him to race and slow, and soar and drop, and talking non-stop about his old home and his brother, he knew that they had crossed several landscapes. He knew they were near his new home, for the cold was now palpable. His brother approached them and handed Kandhan a thick robe. 'Put it on now, Kandha, it's cold, and belt it up, pull the cape over your head. Don't make a face, it's very, very cold.' He waited to make sure that Kandhan put it on and knotted it up tight and covered his head. Paravani chuckled and Kandhan said, 'Uff, you wouldn't be laughing if you had to wear this.'

Kandhan looked down, and his head spun. *How high they were flying! How tall these mountains were … he liked hills, they were friendly, these mountains were scary.* He turned and looked for his elder brother, and of course the elephant-head was smiling at him. *How does he know? He always knows everything.* The elephant-head nodded along with the words in Kandhan's head. The boy smiled back, a warmth spreading in his chest and slowly enveloping him. He sighed—as long as Anna was there, he would be okay.

He stroked Paravani's head, and bent and planted a loud kiss there.

Paravani laughed and said, 'Thank you, what was that for?'

And Kandhan said, 'I love you; do you love me?'

Paravani laughed even louder, and for a moment, Kandhan's face clouded, his brows knitted, his hands tightened their hold, his eyes clouded with the gathering tears, and then Paravani said, 'Kandha, Kumara, of course I love you. I have been waiting for you, watching over you. You didn't see me, but I was there, in the forest, when you were with the Krittika mothers.'

Was it Paravani he had heard, all those rustling sounds, the cat-cuckoo calls that stopped when he got near? What about that time he had fainted in the forest, and woken up as if from a dream of being fanned by iridescent feathers, their breeze like a balm, and of being sprinkled with water off a twig of cooling wild jasmine.

'Paravani, was that you?'

'Was what me, Kandha?'

'When I fell asleep in the forest and—'

'When you fainted, you mean,' the bird retorted, not attempting to hide his amusement.

'No, Paravani, I didn't faint. It was so cool and shady, I slept,' said Kandhan, who could still get annoyed by the thought of how weak he had been, to collapse like that. 'But that was you, wasn't it?'

Paravani said nothing, but Kandhan could feel his back jiggling and knew he was laughing.

'It was you,' he squealed, 'it was you! I knew there were feathers. I told them, but my mothers said I had dreamed it. Oh! They also knew? All of you tricked me!'

Paravani's back shook even more.

'You,' said Kandhan, pummelling the big bird's back with his little fists. 'You tricked me for so long? Why couldn't you just have found me then?'

'The time was not right,' said Paravani. 'That was the time for you to study. And you had to grow a little more.'

'Uff,' said the little boy, clutching the bird's neck and resting his face on it. 'I love you,' he said, 'and you still haven't said you love me.' He held the bird's neck with both hands and said, 'You'd better.'

Paravani's laugh rang out, filling the sky, falling over the peaks of the enormous mountains and echoing from the ravines. 'Of course I do, Kandha, of course I do.'

'More than anyone else?' the little boy asked.

'More than anyone or anything else.' The bird turned his head and his eyes were shining like light. He had slowed down, as if to let Kandhan take in the moment.

Kandhan hugged the bird's neck and said, 'Paravani, you're my best friend, you and Anna.'

They flew on in silence for a bit. Kandhan looked for the others. There was Father on his cloud-large bull, Mother on her golden lion, and Anna's lightning-fast mouse. He looked down at Paravani, then at the others, and a thought struck him. 'Can you,' he whispered, turning to look at where his brother was, 'beat Mushika in a race?'

Ganesha turned his face away, lest Kandhan see his smile.

Paravani said, 'Kandha, I can do everything you want me to.' Taking a deep breath, he shook his wings and said, 'Hold on.' With a slight creak, the two wings bent back a little and Paravani's body stiffened, and then he was off, and soon the boy's parents and brother and their vehicles were left far behind. The little god was screaming with delight. 'Paravani, you are the best bird in all the world. And we've raced them all!'

'All the worlds,' the bird corrected, 'and now can I go back to flying normal again?'

'Yes, yes, thank you, Paravani,' Kandhan said. And then he whispered, 'Did they all see? Do they know that you're the fastest?'

When Paravani only laughed, Kandhan prodded his back with a finger and said, 'Tell me.'

Paravani said, 'Yes, yes, they all saw.'

Kandhan's chest was full, he sat up straight, his head thrown back. He couldn't see himself, but if he could, he would have seen that his nose was up in the air. He looked at his parents, his father, whose matted locks shone like burnished copper, his mother, whose hair fanned out like a flag in the wind. They were looking at him, smiling, and for the first time since he had set out from home, leaving his beloved mothers, he felt only joy, and he wanted to call out to them with names that would show how he was feeling. '*Appa*, *Amma*,' he called. They smiled at their new place names, soft and round and warm: Appa, Amma.

Now that Kandhan had Paravani, they stayed in the skies the entire last lap of the journey, and Kandhan's first sighting of his new home was from the air. When they began to slow and fly lower, he cast his eyes down, and there it was, the golden mountain, the hub of the universe: Kailasa. There was no missing it, it rose up high and luminous, giving off a faint resonance that reached all the way up to the sky. What was that sound, he wondered.

Kailasa was just moments away now. It grew larger and larger as they dropped lower, and the drone became louder and clearer. As they slowed and made ready to descend, Kandhan made out words: Shambu, Parvathy, Ganesha. He suddenly felt as if he was alone. *They didn't want him?* And then his brother's voice sounded, filling the sky in all the sixteen directions. He was holding up his hand and whoever was down there had fallen silent. Pointing to Kandhan, Ganesha announced, 'Kumara, Skanda, Karthikeya,' and the crowd picked up the chant. 'Kumara, Skanda, Karthikeya.' Soon, they were only calling his name, and the boy's face was stretching with his smile, which changed to giggles and guffaws.

He raised both arms in the air and shouted, 'Paravani, Paravani,' and Paravani let out a call that bounced off the mountain's flanks and came back magnified. The birds in the sky called out, the winds hissed, clouds thundered and, down below, the thousands of creatures assembled sent their voices skywards with the chant 'Kumara, Skanda, Karthikeya. Kumara, Skanda, Karthikeya.'

Then, Ganesha was near him and saying, 'We are going to land now. They are all waiting for you. Straighten your clothes and remember to greet everyone. See there,' he said, pointing to a figure who was emitting a bluish light. Beside him stood a woman whose ornaments sparkled so bright, they were like lamps. 'Those are Uncle and Aunt, he's our mother's anna, and there, that one with the ektara, is Narada. He gets miffed easily, so be nice. Come now, let's land.'

As Paravani landed, his talons gripped the snow-covered mud so hard that the mud showed through. Kandhan realised that there were more people here than he had imagined, and began to feel as if there was not enough air for him to breathe. He wanted to be back in the sky, in the wide-open, wind-filled sky, or in his forest, with the trees for an umbrella in the rain. He gripped Paravani's back and took a step closer to the bird, feeling his heart beat harder. Now, the blue man was coming towards him, and he felt like running. Just as he was lifting his leg to climb on to Paravani's back, to say, *let's go*, his brother was beside him, taking him into his warm arms. 'Kandha,' Anna said, 'I'm here, don't worry, you'll get used to them. When this is over, you can go fly in the night sky. Come now, let's greet Uncle and Aunt.'

Ganesha was still carrying his little brother when he neared Vishnu and Lakshmi, his mother's brother and sister-in-law, both of whom were smiling. Ganesha turned to Kandhan and said, 'Kandha, greet Uncle and Aunt.' The little boy looked at the two people in front of him: the man was different from his father, his eyes were like lotus petals, his hair was soft and curly and he smelt of flowers, like Mother. His clothes were bright and soft, he had a flute stuck into the knot of his waist cloth. Kandhan thought, *Ooh, I'd like to smell like that*, and his brother nodded and whispered in his ear, *You can, you will.*

Vishnu, looking at his sister's son, felt his heart leap in his chest. *What a face! Those eyes, it was like looking in a mirror, he could see his own face in them.* He held out his hands and said, 'Kandha, come,' and reaching forward, took the boy from Ganesha and kissed him on both cheeks, his forehead, and the top of his little head. 'I'm your mother's brother, your uncle, and this,' he said, turning to the woman, whose nose now drew Kandhan's attention because it was decorated with a nose-pin that seemed to be alive, blood red, sparkling, its light reflected on her cheek. She too smelt nice, but it wasn't of flowers. His aunt was wearing fine clothes with golden threads, not like Mother's, bare, white and rough. Uncle said, 'This is your aunt,' and she took him into her arms and kissed him on both cheeks and on the top of his head, saying, 'You have all my blessings.'

The little boy did not know, but his brother did, that she was the Goddess of Good Fortune, and without her blessings, nothing and no one could succeed. Lakshmi and Vishnu looked at each other. Ganesha knew that they were thinking of the two children, the two baby girls who had been theirs for a very short time, before they gave them away to honour a promise made to a very taciturn sage. As he thought of this, Ganesha smiled and a little laugh broke from his lips. *Ah, those two girls!*

Hundreds and hundreds had lined up to meet Kandhan, who at first refused to sit down, so excited was he by the gifts they brought him. He set aside the irritation he had felt because all these people were here to look at him, and so he must smile at them. His hands tore open the cloth or bark coverings, and then he got so busy looking at the gift that he forgot the person who'd given it to him. Though Ganesha counselled him and Mother scolded him, Kandhan kept forgetting. When he was done looking at one gift, his eyes had already gone to the next person in the long line. Mother Parvathy shook her head, sighed, and asked Nandi to make sure that some adult was at Kandhan's side to prod him to smile and thank the gift-giver. When he was prodded, the boy, eager to get on with it, turned the full beam of his grin onto the person who'd given him the gift, and all thoughts of *what a rude boy* disappeared. Kandhan's smile made them feel like they had received, rather than given, a gift.

Besides, everybody wanted to be in the good books of this boy who had the power of the Parents of the Universes. It would take a book to list all the gifts he was given, and another to describe what they could do, but there were some that merit a description.

His aunt and uncle gave Kandhan anklets that sounded the seven svaras in ascent and descent every time he moved, armbands that called out the minutest fractions of the four directions, and a little finger-ring with a big, blue stone in which he could see and speak with anyone he wanted to. Ganesha knew they had more gifts for him, but those they would give only much later, when Kandhan was ready to go into battle and meet the Asura king, Surapadman.

Mighty Garuda, the enormous eagle on whose back his uncle and aunt rode, held Kandhan's hands in his talons and said, 'Little one, I hope I never have to stand against you, for I see your might.' That made Kandhan giggle. Garuda also gave him a box of sweets so delicious that Kandhan, and Ganesha who loved sweets, wished would never finish, and it didn't, for when they took one out, another appeared in its place.

Tumburu, the divine musician whose voice could melt the hardest rock and the stoniest of hearts, gave Kandhan a small lute and told him that, soon, the boy would have to start music lessons with him because 'warriors, musicians, poets, lovers and kings, all of which you will be one day, must have perfect rhythm'.

Kandhan was partial to some of the gifts—the stylus gifted by the gurus of the Asuras and Suras, Shukracharya and Brihaspati. The two men, privy to all the secrets in the many worlds, knew what this little boy was, and they had greeted him with folded hands and bent heads. Kandhan held out both hands, took the stylus, and as if to affirm that he knew they were exceptional, he bent down and touched their feet, one at a time, and said, 'Thank you.' The stylus they gave him was made of three metals welded together, an impossible task unless you knew how to coax each one to re-arrange their insides to make space for a little of the other to move in there. Later, Kandhan asked his brother for a pouch for this stylus. Ganesha gave him one that was made from the soft skin of an animal whose life mrtyu had claimed. It came with a long drawstring, so he wrapped the stylus in fine cloth, slipped it into the pouch and pulled the knots tight. He held the little pouch by the length of its three strands and slipped it around his neck, and adjusted it so that it passed over his heart and lay under his ribs, on the right side.

The royal couple of Lanka, scholar-queen Mandodari and her musician-husband, King Dashagriva Ravana, arrived after the initial frenzy was spent, to see and bless the child of Shiva and Parvathy. They brought with them many gifts for Kandhan: the queen gave him an illustrated compendium on bird habitats and calls that she had got copied just for him. She also gave him a lexicon that magically opened to the meanings of words in languages spoken by any of the millions of creatures in the universe, and a bracelet made of the blood-red rubies that were found on their famed island. The king gave him two gifts, one of which was a thing, while the other had neither shape nor substance but made Kandhan drop whatever he was doing and come running whenever he heard the sound of the Pushpaka, the flying chariot, that brought the royal couple from Lanka to Kailasa.

It happened thus: Kandhan's mother sent for him to come and meet the visitors, and he came into the room dragging his feet, but his reluctance disappeared very soon. When his mother introduced him, saying, 'Kandha, this is Queen Mandodari, and this is King Dashagriva Ravana,' she was surprised to see Kandhan fold his hands without being prompted. The queen was as shiny as his aunt, her face shone, her clothes shone and her ornaments shone; she was wearing a jasmine perfume. The king's skin was tawny. On his face was a thick moustache curled upwards at the ends, and his eyes were like Uncle's—lotus buds. Kandhan's eyes moved on to the instrument that reposed next to the king, the magnificent Rudra veena, named after Father. The veena's two large gourds were joined by a long fingerboard, with brass-overlaid frets of wood, ending in a yali, a dragon's head at the top end.

Kandhan's wide eyes, his smile, the way he clenched his hands made the Rakshasa king smile. He held out his arms and said, 'Skanda, come,' and Kandhan, who rarely approached strangers, ran into them, laughing, his anklets ringing with the notes of the sargam. The king put him on his lap and asked, 'Do you sing?' Everybody was surprised to hear Kandhan say 'Yes' and nod emphatically. No one had got him to sing before, though he was always humming to himself in the made-up language that people were calling 'Kandhan's language'. If anyone asked him to sing loudly, and they did, Kandhan shook his head and said 'No'. And here he was now, clearing his throat, straightening his back and taking a deep breath, readying to sing!

King Dashagriva sat Kandhan down opposite him and put his own hands together, palm to palm, rubbing them. He flexed his fingers and then, from a little silken pouch, took two conical metal plectrums that fit over the halves of his right index and middle fingers. He picked up the massive veena and rested the top gourd on his left shoulder and the right one on his right thigh. The sunlight flowing in through the windows hit the jewelled rings on his fingers, then splintered and ran all over the gathering. The king said, 'Skanda, check your shruti,' and Kandhan sang the three marking notes repeatedly as the king adjusted the instrument's strings. When that was done, with a very Kandhan-grin, his eyes on the king's face, he sang a single line and stopped, his eyes unwavering. The line went like this: *jataata-veegala-jjala-pravaaha-paavita-sthale.*

Ravana's head shot up, his eyes widened and his lips quivered. He looked over at his wife, who smiled and nodded. The boy had just sung the first line of the fifteen-verse hymn the king was composing. Addressed to the Dancing Lord, Shiva, it was almost complete. Of the fifteen verses, the first thirteen and the last, the fifteenth, were written, edited and tuned. It had taken him long hours of work to find the words and metre for his song, in which he evoked the god's moods: the playfulness, the reclusive, meditative stillness, the blazing anger, the intense longing for his spouse, the love of all things and the overflowing kindness. The verses began with a description of the waters of the river in the Lord's matted locks, it went over his appearance, and then spoke of his generosity, his might, his artistry and his generous grace, and the boons of unchanging happiness and energy he bestowed upon those devoted to him.

Ravana had written lines that resounded like the damaru, others that had the clap and thud of a dancer's feet striking the floor, some that slowed and lingered, like the conversation between lovers, and in this way, thirteen stanzas were done, as was the fifteenth, the customary signature verse. But the fourteenth—he was stuck with this one; whenever he tried to work on it, his head closed itself and neither thoughts nor words or music could enter. He took it up every day, for days and weeks, and nothing he put down would fit. The vision he had created in his own words encompassed everything he knew of the glory of the god he was describing, and each time he wanted to complete the song, he found himself overwhelmed. How could he conclude? How could he tie it up? What words were big enough to be an 'ending' for a song that sang of the One Without End and Beginning?

So it stayed incomplete, the fourteenth verse. When Kandhan began singing, Ravana also joined in, and they ran through the lines, each stanza and its refrain. As the stanzas ran on and they came to thirteen, the king felt his breath begin to swirl in his belly. It rose up, thick and hot, making his throat burn. As the king's eyes turned to the boy's, he saw Skanda shut and open his eyes, once, then again, as if prompting him. Ravana shut his eyes and felt his belly and breath cooling, his throat grew cool, and he knew that She had come to his aid: the Goddess he worshipped, the guardian of his beloved island, She who nourished his body and mind, his words and music. His voice swelled, the words floated out, perfect in their sound and perfect in their sense and rhythm: a perfect conclusion for all that had come before.

'This is,' said the fourteenth stanza, 'the best of the best praise songs, and whoever sings it will be blessed by the great Guru, Shiva.'

'Just the thought of the Lord,' promised its last line, 'removes all delusion.' Just as it had removed from him the delusion that his words and music could not sum up the glory of the Lord of Song and Dance.

Ravana's eyes were shut, but he could hear the boy, this son of Shiva and Parvathy, singing along, without faltering—*he knew the words!* When the last resonance of the song stilled, the king opened his eyes and turned to his wife. Her face shone, the light reflecting off the jewel of her nose-pin adding to its sheen. She was smiling at him, her hands open-palmed on her thigh, as if the song rested in them.

That was an evening no one would forget in a long while, especially not the king, for his guardian Goddess had come to his rescue, her grace had filled his song, given it wings to soar triumphantly into the evening sky, rather than collapse like a wounded creature with missing limbs. The boy would also remember the evening for many reasons, but mostly for the other gifts the king gave him.

When the song was done, Ravana patted Kandhan on his shoulder, and touching the top of his head asked, 'Kumara, do you want to learn to play the Rudra veena?'

Kandhan, who had wanted nothing more from the moment he set eyes on it, said, 'Yes, yes, yes.'

The king sat him down, cross-legged, and placed the veena horizontally, resting both ends on piled-up cushions to keep the weight off the boy's legs. He took Kandhan's hands and held them in his own, gently warming them. Then he stuck a hand into the silk pouch with the brass plectrums and pulled out two. Ravana held these over Kandhan's tiny fingers—the boy's whole hand could fit in one, they were so big—and with a rustle, the shining metal shrunk and slipped on, as if made to measure. The king held Kandhan's fingers and demonstrated how to pluck the notes with one hand, and hold down and slide along the strings with the other. After a couple of rounds, Kandhan ran through one set without faltering and played on for a while.

When he was done, Ravana clapped, as did Ganesha and his mother and father, and everyone else. Ganesha called Kandhan to him, handed him a tray and said something to him. The boy returned and stood in front of Ravana, who stood up, held both hands over his chest and shut his eyes for a moment. He then held out his hands for the tray, in which there were bilva leaves, flowers, a golden stylus, a vial of ink, and a bundle of palm leaves threaded through with red silk. The king took it with both hands, held it up to his eyes and set it aside. Kandhan knelt and prostrated at the master-musician's feet; the king put both his hands on Kandhan's head, blessed him and picked him up. The boy put one arm around the Rakshasa king's neck and asked, 'When will you teach me some more?' He received the promise of another lesson soon.

As for the other gift, Kandhan pulled off the silken wrapping as soon as King Ravana handed it to him, and there it was: a small, stringed instrument, a coconut-shell cup with a bamboo stem and a little bow.

'This,' said the king, 'is a Ravana hatha, and it's for you to carry along wherever you go, so that you can have music for your songs.'

Kandhan giggled. 'Ravana?' he asked, 'isn't that you? Is this your hand?' And the king joined in his laughter.

Kandhan ran the bow over the strings, and in accompaniment to its plaintive sound, under his breath, he hummed words in his secret language.

Kandhan's father also gave him two gifts, though well after he had got all his other gifts. The son was sitting with his mother, practising the rules of a poetic metre, when Father came and sat down with them. He said, 'Uma, can you guess what I've brought,' and she said, 'Do you have two?'

It was a joke in their home now: Kandhan sulked if someone got a gift and he didn't. And everyone bringing gifts knew to bring two. Shiva's burst of laughter made the trees send a drizzle of flowers over them. He said, 'Yes, I have two. Three, actually.' Kandhan's eyes were wide now, and he was grinning. Three? Two for him and one for Mother? Or would it be two for her and one for him?

Kandhan's father opened his fist. In his palm nestled five or six buds of the dark blue vajranaga that bloomed in spring. He tucked them into the knot of Parvathy's hair. Then, crushing a saffron flower, he pressed the mush of its red on her forehead, and looking at her said, *Ah!* She smiled and touched the hand that lingered on her face.

Kandhan, of course, grew restless. *Where was his gift? What would Father give him? This would be his first real gift from Father, brought just for him.*

'Kandha, come here,' said the father, and the little boy got up and went up to him, his saucer-eyes full, his smile stretching to his ears and almost falling off his face. As he stood there, waiting, the smell of wild tulasi wafted into his nostrils. His father drew him close and kissed him on the forehead. Kandhan waited; his father made no move. *Where was his gift?* Kandhan looked at his father's hands. *What,* he thought, *a kiss? That's all he was getting?* He started when a warmth suffused his face. His forehead was throbbing. He shivered and felt a bit dizzy. His father laughed and steadied him, his hands cool on Kandhan's shoulders. His mother said, 'Oh! Kandha, what's on your forehead?' And she too laughed.

The boy felt his forehead. It was burning. *Was there a bump?* By then, his brother had come up to them, smiling. Kandhan turned to him with a what's-happening gesture of his chin. Ganesha looked for Galabajja, the One With Mirror Hands, and the gana came and stood in front of Kandhan and held out his hands—they shone and rippled, their surfaces two spotless planes of crystal, mirroring whatever was in front of them. Ganesha turned his brother to the mirror. Kandhan's eyes flew to his reflection: the tawny skin of his face was lit up by a tiny sliver of golden light issuing from his forehead; his eyes widened, and so did the slit. *Ooh, what was this? He couldn't believe what he was seeing. Was that an eye on his forehead?* 'Eeee,' he screamed, jumping up and down and running circles around his brother, father and mother.

'I have a third eye, I have a third eye, I have a third eye.' He shut his eyes and the warmth went away. He looked in the mirror and saw that it was gone, the eye. He widened his two eyes and thought of the third one, and there it was! Back again.

Then his father was saying, 'Kandha, I have another gift for you, here, take this.' And Kandhan saw a staff of hardy agaru, its knobs and bumps roughed out. 'Take this. For now, this is to be your weapon, and you must always carry it with you. And because you are armed with a dandam in your hands, you will be known as Dandayudhapani: the one who is weaponed with a staff.'

The agaru, or, as Kandhan said in his language, *akil*, was not entirely smooth, though it wasn't rough. As his fingers curled around it, the wood grew warm, and he remembered what the Krittika mothers had taught him about the rasa that ran in all things. He bent his head in reverence that was partly for his six mothers, partly for his father, and partly for this dandam, inside which the same thing that was inside everything in the universes now rippled and crackled: its sap, its rasa. To the boy, this was a sign that he had done well in his lessons.

As always, when he was happy, he went looking for Paravani, calling his name in a steadily more sing-song voice, and they were soon off, across the skies, though careful not to stray where Mother had said they must not go. The boy spoke to the bird only in his language, the language that he was re-building, and Paravani stored the sounds and vestments of Kandhan's language, its decorations and its ways, in the storeroom of his memory. He often repeated the boy's first utterance in his language, *mayil, mayil*, and felt like he did when clouds gathered overhead, waiting to fall in a rhythm that would cause everything to join, in step to its beat.

It took Kandhan a long time to become acclimatised to living on the highest mountain in the world. He missed the warmth of the forest and of the bodies of his six mothers. It wasn't easy: the first two years of his life, he had lived in a forest in the far south of a land on Bhu, where the sun's heat was close. The only clothing he had worn through the day, if any at all, was a piece of cloth looped over his loins and tucked into the back and front of his silver waistband. In the evenings, after a bath, during which he swam and cavorted in the river till it began to get dark, his mothers put him into long robes, all six of him, because nights in the forest could be chill. The winds came laden with the day's-end sighs of the trees, the hills and the sky, but that was nothing like the cold on Kailasa.

On Kailasa, the wind was heavy, a hissing creature, its sides sharp needles of cold that sought you out and pierced through to your bones. Over time, and with patient instruction from Ganesha, Kandhan learnt to make his body suck itself inwards and bolt up like a hardy gate that the chill could not shoulder open. He learnt to keep his eyes half open, half shut, the lids like visors, repelling the snow that fell often and without warning. He had learnt that, though he hated wearing them, clothes seemed to say something to the dread winds that made their attack less sure. But even then, the cold caught him unawares.

Sometimes, when Ganesha stepped out, he found Kandhan sitting in a patch of dim sunlight, shivering and huddling under Paravani's wings. Ganesha would call, *Kandha*, and the boy would spring up, his features relaxing in relief. He would run to his older brother, arms outstretched, to be enveloped in a big hug and carried against Ganesha's chest, which was always warm. They would sit like that, Kandhan's cold bones warming, and soon he would fall asleep, and Ganesha would carry him to his bed in the room that had been specially made up for him before he came home. But as soon as he was in bed, Kandhan would open his eyes and say, 'Take me outside.' Ganesha would tell him that it was very cold, and that he would fall ill, and then sing him a lullaby till he fell asleep. But when the elder brother retired to his own room, Kandhan often jumped up in his sleep, sweating and calling for his mothers. He would get out of bed, pull a blanket over himself, grab another, and go outside to the wooden seat by the side of the half-wall. Spreading one of the blankets over the seat, he would lie down, wrapped in the other. He would shiver, his teeth would chatter, but he would lie there, curled into a ball, the blanket over his head.

One night, Paravani came upon Kandhan shivering on the bench, and it was he who found a solution: he promised Kandhan that, after everyone was asleep, he would sneak up and open the window of his room, so that the boy could look out and see the skies, and see his six mothers there, sparkling. Paravani also promised Kandhan that he would be there, just outside the open windows, and that he would shut them again before Mother Parvathy woke up.

Kandhan explored Kailasa, he knew the rooms, corridors and likely hiding places of its buildings, he found every tucked-away cave, he made note of the treacherous turns that plummeted down into ravines, he returned often to the fabulous viewpoints from where you could see sky and valley and, way below, the golden snaking of rivers lit by the sun. He knew what flowers grew here, and when they blossomed, and the names of the bushes, animals, bugs, the many different kinds of beings that lived and visited. Kandhan knew his home so well that he could find his way around with his eyes closed. And even if his eyes were closed, Paravani was with him.

The days passed and he began to enjoy the stillness on the mountain. In his other home, he had been so used to the sweat and the heat that always hung low in the air, and the constant rustle of the wind in the lush trees, the scamper of forest animals and the dropping of ripe fruit.

His guardians and mentors, the twelve Matris, allowed Kandhan to roam free, to go further, for longer hours. When Mother Parvathy handed him over to their mentoring, she had told him about how they had been born from lightning during a fight that became so ferocious, she had needed help. As Kandhan became more familiar with Kailasa, he met the many beings that had their home there, and developed friendships with many of them. Of these, he grew especially close to the Gandharva brother and sister, Ragaparimukta and Subahu, who, like all the Gandharvas, were gifted musicians. They were the guardians of Father Shambhu's hidden cave, which could be accessed only through a gruelling climb and invisible paths.

No one was allowed to enter Father's cave unless he invited them in. Even Mother informed Father if she was going there. And Anna, too, asked his permission. Kandhan followed his father there once on tiptoe, his anklets removed and tucked tightly into his waistcloth. He stood far away and watched as his father stopped to greet the Gandharva siblings and then went inside alone. Kandhan waited to see if something would happen, but nothing did, and so of course he made up his mind to go into the cave. He asked his brother what was in there and was told that it was a place where there was nothing to get in the way. He warned Kandhan not to try any of his little tricks there, because it was guarded by fierce beings who would catch him and make him practise all the lessons he had been neglecting. The younger brother nodded his head, inside which plans were already hatching on how to get in there. But if he was caught, those lessons—tch! All he had to do was not get caught.

And so, one day, he sneaked up to the cave, the akil staff in his hand bristling, reflecting his own excitement. He headed up the slope, sure-footed from practise. He stood on a ledge overlooking the cave. *Were they there*? He couldn't see anyone. How to find out? He hid behind a boulder and flung a handful of pebbles at the cave. No stirring, nothing. Were they not there? Maybe they were trying to trick him. He took his dandam and whispered, go, and raising his arms high above his head, sent it flying. The staff flew and landed at the mouth of the cave. It spun round and round, emitting an ear-piercing sound. There was a flash and the twins were standing right next to Kandhan.

'Ah,' he said, 'so here you are. Trying to trick me, are you?' He made a sign with his hand and the staff rushed into his palm. He smiled at the twins, who had by now materialised fully, their golden bodies covered with fine cloth, their hair strung with jewels, perfumed and decorated. They were armed with swords, as thin as a line etched by the nib of a stylus, and as fine as light.

'Kumara, salutations,' they said, their left hands stretching to touch the boy's hand in greeting.

'Salutations,' he replied, bowing his head. 'I'm just going inside now, I'll be out soon. Wait here for me.'

The twins smiled. Ragaparimukta said, 'Kumara, we have not been told to let you in. Father Shambhu hasn't sent word.'

Kandhan said, 'Oh, that's alright, he told me to tell you. See, he sent this for you.' He opened his hand, and on his palm lay two leaves of the bilva, so dear to his father. Their eyes shone and they held out their hands for the leaves. While they were absorbed in taking a leaf each and holding it to their hearts, Kandhan was slinking off to the side. But before he took two steps, they were there, blocking his view.

'Oh no, Kumara, you cannot go in there, you know that, be a good boy,' Subahu said.

'No,' said Kandhan, 'I'm going in there.' He pointed with his staff to the cave, which, of course, had become even more attractive. He stood, feet apart, hips out, back straight, one hand on his waist, the other holding the staff. 'Please move, I don't want to hurt you.' He made as if to push past them.

They smiled and said, 'Kumara, we cannot be hurt by you, or anyone else. Your father's boon protects us.'

'Oh no!' said the boy. 'Nothing can protect you against me because, you see, I'm Father and Mother's combined strength, that's what Nandi said. So, if you won't move, come and fight.'

'We cannot fight you. You're a child and our Master's son,' said Ragaparimukta.

'But I'm going to fight you,' Kandhan replied, striking out with the staff, 'because I want to get in there today.'

The two Gandharvas disappeared with a snap and Kandhan stood there waving at thin air.

'Argh,' he said, 'you can't do that, that's a trick.'

He walked ahead, and nothing stopped him, but when he neared the mouth of the cave, he could go no further. An invisible wall blocked his way. He hit out, he kicked, but to no avail. His free hand closed into a fist, he grit his teeth, he strode up and down, he screamed, he shouted, 'You can't stop me.' His eyes were burning, his jaw set, there were drums thundering in his head: he was furious. He would not return without having entered the cave. Oh no, he wasn't going to give up, he couldn't be defeated by two people who refused to even fight. What would everyone say? That he was too weak to beat two puny musicians? That was when it hit him: he *could* defeat them. He knew exactly what to do.

He felt in the fold at his waist for the anklets he had taken off earlier, and put them on. Holding his staff aloft, Kandhan began to circle, slowly at first, with an unhurried beat, allowing the anklets to sound the scale, one note after another, then speeding up, his steps swifter, the circling accelerated, creating an energetic, tantalising rhythm. Then he began to sing, his voice as sweet as that of the black bulbul who flies on the lower slopes of the mountain.

The words were nimble, the tune enchanting, and the rhythm of the dance artful, but more than all that, the words that came out of his mouth were like drops of water from the first snow-melt: cool, pure, still bearing the memories of its overwintering. Kandhan was singing in *his* language. He continued to dance and sing, his body swaying, his hands gesturing, the staff of akil glowing. His eyes were shut, and he looked like he had forgotten everything else. The tempo slowed, the beats grew longer, the steps extended over beats, and then he stopped. And there they were, Subahu and Ragaparimukta, their eyes shining, their faces glowing with smiles.

Ragaparimukta said, 'Kumara, your father said you would show a sign that we would not mistake, and we should let you in.' They led Kandhan in, and he walked around before sitting down on the skin that was spread on the floor as if waiting for him. *Escaped the lessons*, he thought.

When he was leaving, they wanted to know what Kandhan had said, and what language it was, for the Gandharvas are great linguists and they knew this was not the old tongue, even though it reminded them of it. They wanted to learn it, but he said, 'Not now, there is a man that I must teach it to first. After that, I will teach you.'

And that's the story of this great friendship, which continued even after Kandhan departed from Kailasa.

When Kandhan first arrived on Kailasa, his body would not stop shivering, and his skin stretched and cracked. His mother, seeing this, rubbed him down with oils, sat him on an old grass mat on the veranda, and after what seemed to him a very long time, took him down to Gauri Kund, the lake, for a bath. At home, he had run into the river whenever he felt hot. It was cold here, but he still wanted a bath, and when he saw the water, a lake of golden ripples, he did a little skip and clapped his oily hands. As they got closer, it seemed to him that the water was smoking. But how can water smoke, he wondered. When they got to it, he saw that it was steam rising from the water's placid surface. His mother said, 'Kandha, see, the water is warm, you'll feel nice in this cold.'

Kandhan took another look at the steam and tried to run away, but his mother's hold was firm. He grumbled and made such a fuss that finally she just picked him up and jumped in, holding the wriggling, shrieking boy against her body. When they hit the water and dipped, he screamed, 'burning, burning, burning', but slowly stopped, because here, for the first time since he had left his forest home, he could feel the earth's warmth, rising up from an underground volcano.

The hot evening bath, after a thorough oiling, become a daily ritual that he looked forward to. They would come down here, he'd be oiled, and then allowed to swim around and wash himself with the powders that his mother packed into a little pouch. Parvathy brought him here herself usually. She oiled him and tried to make him wait so the oil could work its way into his skin, but she would often lose her patience when confronted with his litany of 'Now? Now? Now? Now can I go in?' Shambhu and Ganesha sometimes took turns with Kandhan's bath, and occasionally one of the Matris.

When his father brought him, everything was different, and Kandhan waited for this, because Father always surprised him. For one thing, he always sat him up on his shoulders, sometimes making Kandhan wonder what he would have done if he was still six boys. The boy would observe everything his father did: Shambhu's eyes sweeping over the land as he walked, humming, stopping to look up at the sky or down at some shrub that had flowered, or at the prints of animal feet. Kandhan was full of questions, and no one was as happy as Father to answer them and to show him things. He saw his first coral kasturi flowers springing out from under small outcrops of stone, the tracks of leopards, and the dark arc of winter birds surging in the sharp aquamarine of the sky, on these trips.

Sometimes the father left the path and climbed up towards something he had spotted, and the son would say, 'What is it, Father? What is it?' while remembering to hold on tight, knowing from experience that, in his excitement, he might wiggle too much and fall off. When they came to whatever it was, it would be worth the wait and excitement: fruit just ripened that would drop into Father's hands as soon as he was standing underneath, and which they would eat, one at a time, or a nest with the eggs hatching, or hawks who seemed to have been waiting for them and flew up close. The thing that the child liked the most, though, was how his father looked at everything and was interested in everything. Kandhan saw that everything welcomed his father wherever he went—birds wheeled in the sky and swooped down, the strange frogs that could stand this cold leapt so high that they landed on his shoulders and chest and head and sat there going trr-ritarr-ritarr-trr-ritarr, and ants climbed all the way to his face to sip of the traces of toddy in his beard. To Kandhan, it seemed as if his father was a huge pot of food, open to all, and everything and everybody came and ate from it, while his mother was like … like … *like a mother: she measured out food for everybody.*

His mother rarely took him on walks or to go looking for flowers, but when they went walking, her footsteps made little creatures come darting out of burrows and birds out of their nests; flower buds burst open when her feet or hands or her trailing hair grazed them. It came to Kandhan one day, as his mother was oiling him and humming to herself: *Mother's busy and she just lets Father do the fussing.*

When Ganesha brought him, Kandhan mostly didn't notice the flowers or birds or trees. With his brother, it was words: as they walked, the elder would suddenly say things like 'Red, blooms in winter, how many syllables?' or 'What should you not do if you're writing a manjari?' or 'Find a perfect rhyme for this or that.' And then, he always told a story, and though it would be told on the condition that, till it was over, Kandhan would sit with the oil on his body, he didn't mind, because he didn't notice how long it took, and he didn't mind that each of the stories was a lesson. It was on these days that Kandhan heard about Bhringi's antics and why he had three legs, about why the tantras named their mother Aruna, about how their uncle could charm the worlds with his flute.

It was here that Ganesha told his younger brother the story of creation. He knew that the little one would get impatient. Kandhan liked stories with people, especially if they were measuring themselves against each other in competitions. He liked to hear about people who went in search of things and met with dangers that they had to physically push against or use tricks to get past. But this one was abstract, and nobody was doing anything other than talk. It was going to be difficult anyway, best to get on with it.

The story of the beginning would have to be told before he could get to a story that he did want to tell: the story of Surapadman. He could not tell the whole story just yet, he would set the stage, giving Kandhan hints of the Asura's genius, which would, he hoped, remain in his head and make him do what he was supposed to.

Ganesha oiled Kandhan and sat him down. He began to speak about things he thought were a good introduction to the topic. Kandhan got fidgety, he looked off into the distance, then back at his brother: *this was no story!* Eventually, Kandhan screwed his eyes up, looked at the sky and said, 'Anna, I think it's going to rain. I'd better finish my bath, you can complete this lesson later.'

The elder brother, who'd noticed every little gesture that Kandhan made, looked at the sky, his face impassive, and replied, 'Yes, Kandha, it's going to rain, but not now, next week. Sit still and listen, this story is really interesting.'

Kandhan snorted. 'Story? That's a lesson, not a story; you can't make me sit here. Unless you tell a story, I'm going.'

Ganesha decided to take the plunge. 'Kandha, I was going to tell you about Surapadman, but for that, I need you to understand other things.'

At the mention of that name, Kandhan's breath tripped. 'Surapadman, the hero?'

Ganesha nodded. 'Yes, Surapadman, the hero.'

'He's really waiting for me to grow up and fight him?' Kandhan asked, his eyes now fixed on his brother's face. When his brother said this was so, Kandhan said, 'Okay, okay, tell me, I'll sit still, tell me.'

'But it's a lesson, Kandha, you have to get a story for the oiling. It's okay, I'll tell you a story about the monkey and the crocodile, and then you can go bathe. We can keep this for another day.'

'No, no, it's okay, Mother said I have to do what you say because you're older,' the younger one said, his face so suffused with pretend sweetness that the elder laughed.

'Listen, then,' he said, and began the story of creation.

'In the beginning, Kandha, there was nothing. And it was dark and still. But in that nothing, there was something.'

'What?' Kandhan's interest was piqued. 'What was it? Was it a mother?'

Ganesha smiled and continued, '... something that knew it was there, and that it was full.'

'Full of what?' Kandhan asked.

'Hmm, no, just full of itself.'

'But isn't that a bad thing, Anna? Didn't Nandi say that Narada is too full of himself and needs to get lighter?'

Ganesha leant back against the rock and sighed. This was going to take longer than he had thought.

'Kandha, there are many kinds of full,' he said, taking up the telling again. 'Some fulls are better avoided, other fulls are good. Look at the lake, it's full of water, and look at the sky, so full of stars. The lake wants to be full, and so does the sky. If they didn't want to be full, then where would the fish and lotuses and crocodiles and tortoises and all go? And the—'

'But that's not people, what's a good full for people?' Kandhan asked.

'Mother, Kandha, she's full: full of everything—she's clever, kind, happy, loving—'

'And strict,' Kandhan added, 'she's full of strict, too.'

'Yes,' said Ganesha, 'and she needs to be full of all those things for her to be her, and if she lets some of them go, then she won't be able to do her work.'

'But Narada's fullness is not necessary for him, no? He only has to float through the worlds singing.' Kandhan did not want to let it go.

'Yes, maybe that's what Nandi meant,' Ganesha said, getting that out of the way before continuing. 'In the beginning there was just something without form or shape, it couldn't be seen or heard or touched—'

'Or tasted?' Kandhan broke in, sticking his tongue out and wiggling it.

'No, Kandha, it couldn't be tasted either. But it was there, it spread everywhere, a spreading field that wanted to become things with form and shape and smell and—'

'And taste, Anna, taste also.'

'Yes, that too; so, it brooded and gathered itself.'

Kandhan grabbed his brother's hand 'What's "brooded"?'

Ganesha, whose eyes were staring into the distance, turned his face towards his brother, which was what Kandhan wanted. He knew what 'brooding' meant, he had studied it, he knew that it was to think about something, to sit and wait, like a hen.

'It's like a mother hen sitting on her eggs, Kandha,' his brother said. 'So, the vast field of nothing, it brooded and brooded and gathered and heaved itself until it rose up into thin waves that became heavier and flowed like water. The waves that arose of these waters blazed and resounded, and some of them rose up and took the shape of a giant egg. Inside the sparkling egg, which had the blue of Mahendraneela, light swirled and sound radiated in all directions. Outside, the whole Vast was swirling, too. And as waves rose and lifted and slapped against each other, the waters began to hum, a low steady drone. Then, the egg slowed down, lay still and split, without separating, like a giant door, and out of that opening, Mother emerged, but only an outline of her, a shining outline. When she stepped out, the Vast, which has never been called anything else, rushed up to her and filled her and gave her a body the colour of mahagani bark. Her eyes emitted beams of light. She held a parrot in one hand, in another a stylus, and in the third and fourth, a pouch of seeds and an inkwell—'

'Ooh! So many hands? I've only seen two.'

'She had six, Kandha, when she first appeared. In the other two hands were a plough and a pail of mud. Then, there came from the egg an outline of Father, lightning streaked through his hair. His third eye was flaming, and from the reddish-golden shape of his body there came the same hum as from the outside. He looked at Mother, and raising his head, emitted a loud roar. Because he had roared, she addressed him as "Rudra". He smiled at her, and they held hands and waited, for there was another there, lying still, as if to ensure that everything was going well before himself standing up and coming out of the egg-home. When he rose and came out, he looked exactly like Mother, their bark-brown skin tinged with the hue of early-night blue-black, their eyes like lotus petals, their smiles like slivers of white moon. In his hands he held a shoot of sprouting bamboo. He smiled at Mother and said, "Narayani", and she called him "Narayana". Father set up a beat with his hands, the first beats of all time, and Uncle Vishnu, for that was who it was—'

'Where was Aunt? Where was Aunt Lakshmi?'

'She will come later,' Ganesha assured him. 'Uncle raised the hand with the bamboo shoot and swung it this way and that, and the air bristled, the Vast sprung and surged in dancing waves that smashed against each other and emitted the seven notes of music. There was great joy, because the Vast was happy and it laughed. From the laughter appeared many suns, moons, stars and other things, all of which were only outlines till the Vast ran into them and their outlines got bodied. Afterwards, the wise ones saw that, inside the Vast, there was a power that made everything, and they called it Shakti. They said Shakti makes everything, Shakti fills everything and everything lives in Shakti. And because Mother was the first to emerge out of the Vast, the first one to be made by Shakti, she came to be called Shakti too, and it came to be the name for the strength that Mother has.' Ganesha knew that the little one listening to the story would also be associated with that name. But that was for him to discover. It was one of the conditions that the astute Surapadman had specified.

'Mother, Father and Uncle then set about creating everything. Their minds were filled with images, they saw creatures that walked and ran on two legs, and on four or six or twelve. They saw small creatures that scuttled along and bored, and worlds filled with beings that looked and acted different from one another, and things that flowed, others that were frozen, and yet others that had no form. Mother said, "This is a lot of work, and it has to go on continuously. We should make someone to take care of it," and Father and Uncle agreed. So, she clapped her hands and, with a smile, pulled out a flower from Uncle's navel and said, "Here, find our Creator here." And Uncle shut his eyes and snapped his fingers, and the outline of an old man appeared there. He had white hair and a white beard, and he carried a little pot in one hand and a string of beads in the other—'

'Brahma, I know,' Kandhan said with a grimace. 'Go on.'

'So Brahma was made, and when they looked at all that he had to do, it was clear that there was too much for one person, and the thing about Brahma is, you see, he was a little dazed as he stood up in the Vast. He stumbled and shook like a ripe leaf, so he didn't get filled all that well. It was decided that Brahma would need assistants.'

Ganesha looked at Kandhan, whose round eyes and the way he sat, the akil dandam flat on his lap, showed that he was rapt. 'They considered whether the worlds that they wanted to create would be better as bubbles floating, held apart by the force of the Vast, or woven together, like a mat, or like lines running parallel to each other. Eventually, it was decided to create fourteen worlds, stacked one over the other, with Patala at the bottom, Satyaloka, Brahma's world, at the top, and Bhuloka, where you lived for two years, somewhere in the middle. Bhuloka is also the home of the brave Surapadman. And of your favourite, King Dashagriva. Bhu is the world inhabited by Manavas.'

Kandhan nodded vigorously and Ganesha continued with a smile, 'To keep the worlds from floating away, Mother and Father created a mountain that began as wide as the widest of the worlds and tapered up to a peak. It was to be their home. They called it "Kailasa", and Kailasa impaled the fourteen worlds, beginning before and extending beyond, and so Kailasa is at the core of every world but is separate too.'

'Impaled?' Kandhan asked. 'Like a skewer? Like meat when we hunt?' He giggled.

'Now, let me tell you how we divide things into before, after and now—' Ganesha began.

Kandhan protested, 'Anna, I'm not a baby: that is past, present and future.'

His brother continued in a crisper tone, 'Well, Time began when The Three came out of the blue egg, and that first moment was the first matra—the first step of Time. After a lot of back and forth, they arrived at a plan for how Time would work in each world, and in the beings that would inhabit these worlds.

'Once Time began to work, Brahma brought to life from his imagination twelve assistants, and he called them prajapatis, and these prajapatis created their own offspring. One of these was the venerable Kashyapa, born to Prajapati Maricha, and it was to him that Brahma gave the task of producing all the creatures for these fourteen worlds. Seventeen of the daughters of Prajapati Daksha agreed to marry him and to give birth to all the creatures, and to each of them was born—'

'Wait, wait, Anna, wait,' Kandhan said, waving both hands in Ganesha's face. 'Kashyapa married seventeen wives? But he was only one, he needed only one, why seventeen?'

Ganesh's laugh rang out across the lake as he answered, 'Kandha, that's because they had to give birth to all the living things that were going to live on all the worlds. One person would not want to spend so much time doing that. Besides, they would all be together if they married one person. They sat together and talked about the kinds of creatures they would like to birth, and in the course of time, from them were born single-hooved and double-hooved animals, eagles and parrots and the chakravaka, dogs and tigers and all the fierce animals—'

'What about fish?' Kandhan asked.

'Yes, fish, snakes, scorpions, Aruna, Garuda, Adisesha, Vasuki, the Sura and Asura, the Gandharvas and all other beings were born to Kashyapa and his wives.'

Kandhan's face had grown round as Ganesha was speaking. He asked, 'Appa won't marry any more wives, will he? One mother is so tough to hide from. If there were seventeen, I wouldn't be able to move.'

That made Ganesha laugh, and they sat like that for a moment, the brothers, the list forgotten. The elder was thinking of how his life had changed, and the younger that Brahma was deaf to music and that's why he had stumbled and rocked on his feet when he stood up.

The most important part had not yet been told, so Ganesha picked up the story again. 'When all that work was over, they sat in silence, pleased with what they had done. As they sat, they saw that, in the rippling expanse of waves that was the Vast, there were spots of agitated surge, with the waves leaping and fountaining upwards, then splintering and splashing in very wide circles. They also saw that there were spots of complete calm, neither lunging nor flowing with the rest of the waves, but only expanding or shrinking or shifting where they were, as if to stay contained. Mother looked at the way the tumult rose and stilled, and she said, "It picks its own shape and way: the Vast is one but wants to do varied things and take different forms." Father and Uncle Vishnu heard her words and saw what she was seeing.'

Their mother, Ganesha explained, said that 'just as the nature of the exuberant part was fierce and unmindful of its own form and place, the beings that rose from there to enter into the wombs of their mothers-to-be would be known as "Asura". 'The word "asu" would mean "breath", and the beings that chose this form would be filled with untiring breath as they rushed towards knowledge.'

Kandhan was still, attentive.

'Thus the Asura are those parts of the Vast that choose to be born with an undying desire to seek, make and break and try again, learn and explore and experiment without boundaries and limitations.'

'What about the other part, Anna?' Kandhan asked.

Ganesha told him what Parvathy had said. 'Of the other part which is still, and which holds, protects and keeps bounded, the beings that it chooses to be born as will be, like it, still. They will want to look around and create boundaries, put order in place, and plan, strategise and work to contain and to keep order. Let them be called "deva" and let "div" mean "to shine", let them remember to be lights for themselves.'

Ganesha put his arms around Kandhan. 'It is only the Asura and Sura who can choose the form they want to take: one or the other. And because the Asura are eager for everything, it is only natural they would choose the time and manner of their return to the Vast.' The story was over, and Kandhan sighed. He waited, because he knew that Anna was going to give him something to take away from it.

Sure enough, Ganesha continued, 'Many were the Asuras born in this way, and then there came a time when, its hum escalating, the Vast rushed into a gigantic wave, swirling and leaping like no other wave before or after it. The wave spoke to Brahma: "You know that I will be born an Asura; know this too, when the time comes that I want to return, let me stand against the son of the parents of Creation.' Ganesha stopped and looked at Kandhan.

'I know that's me. And that big wave was Surapadman. Go on with the story, Anna.'

Ganesha watched Kandhan's face as the tale came to an end. 'That's how creation began, Kandha, and of the many great Asuras, there is none as learned and practised, no one who can invent the way the bold Surapadman does. And he will not combat with you unless you are worthy of him. You understand that, don't you, Kandha?'

Kandhan, whose undivided attention Ganesha's tale had got, now looked at him and said, 'I don't want to fight him—I want to be friends with him.'

That, thought Ganesha, picking up his little brother and running with him into the warm water, was exactly the problem. Of course Kandhan would want to be friends with him, they were *... ah, but he cannot know that.*

Every day, something reminded Kandhan of his six mothers, but slowly he also began to feel at home with this other family, and started thinking of them as *his*. The Mother of the Universes was *his* mother, and the Father of All Things was *his* father. With Anna, the bond had been formed even before Kandhan was born.

With him, Ganesha was never in a hurry, nor too busy or too lost in his work, like their parents sometimes tended to be. It wasn't because he didn't have as much work or that he was lazy, it was just that his manner was like that, he made everything slow down, ease up. His good humour and patience made even the most nervous person relax. He, like Paravani, could scold Kandhan without having the boy go off in a huff.

Still, Kandhan missed his six mothers. Especially since, with Mother Parvathy, he felt he had to be on good behaviour. He told himself that he must not go running to her and leap into her lap, or sneak up from behind and cover her eyes with his palms, or ask her to carry him, because she was always in the middle of something. Kandhan did not know that his mother wondered the same thing: why did he not come running to her, climb on to her lap, demand that she carry him? Was she so different from the six Krittikas that the boy had clung to? What should she do to make him treat her with the same insistent affection? It bothered her even more when she saw the way his eyes lit up around his father.

Kandhan slowly began to understand how things worked in Kailasa, and it was not so difficult: everything revolved around his mother, just like Father, whose eyes followed her when she was nearby and looked for her when she wasn't. They asked each other what they were working on, she asked him to read every change she made in her *Rasaragavairagyamanjari*. He asked her to watch as he worked to smoothen out a mis-fitting step in a new dance. They gave each other things. And they were always looking at each other when they were working, talking, eating, or when someone came to visit them with gifts, complaints, requests, or when they were all just sitting, doing nothing. Kandhan understood why they were often referred to as Shiva-Shakti: they seemed to move together, even when they weren't close by, they seemed always tuned to the other. They seemed, as everybody said, a single person, rather than two people. But they were not like each other. In fact, they were very different, and Kandhan noticed these differences.

Mother and Father both taught, they always had students around them: all the varied ganas, old and young, came to Kailasa asking for knowledge. Sometimes, if Kandhan was nearby while he was teaching the old rishis, who were constantly with him, his father called the boy and put him on his lap. Kandhan sat there, his head on his father's chest, his little hands resting on his own belly. And sometimes, in the course of the lessons, his father leant down, so that his chin touched his son's head. Sometimes, he would be explaining something, using his hands, and then he would wrap them around the little boy and kiss the top of his head. At these moments, it seemed as if everybody sitting there had got that kiss too, for Kandhan's face glowed like the moon in a clear sky, the rays of which fell on them all. Sometimes, when his father said something Kandhan liked, his little hand grabbed his father's arm and his little head bobbed. But he never spoke. He just listened. Kandhan was like a baby animal when he was with his father, lolling and happy.

When he was with his mother, the happiness was different. It was a *serious* happiness. He learnt things from her that were different from what he learnt with his father. It was she who taught him how to hold his stylus properly, so that his finger and the metal supported each other. If you didn't get the angle just right, the finger would resist and the lettering would be heavy. She taught him how to pluck leaves and flowers from plants, the names of which she only had to tell him once, and showed him how to squeeze the sap out of them. She strained and poured the sap into little jars, tied up their mouths, and buried them in the snow. Mother also taught him what to use it for: cuts and wounds, eyes dry with the cold, little plants that were in danger of wilting. From her, he learnt the thrill of working: she could turn even the smallest, dullest chore into an exciting adventure—like cleaning a stylus after use. She had a set of porcupine quills with their ends sharpened, instead of the slit and dried end of a twig that most people used. She looked at the stylus and selected the right quill, and then proceeded to run it along the nib, then through the little decorative cut in its squat middle, so that every last trace of ink came off; it was fun for Kandhan to do. When she made inks, it was always in many shades, light blue to crimson. 'To suit the occasion,' she replied, when he asked why he couldn't just use any ink to write. He remembered his Krittika mothers when he was with Mother Parvathy. They too had been particular in their tasks.

There were other ways in which his parents were not alike: Father's heart was like butter; it would melt when someone said his name with devotion. Kandhan learnt that his father was called Bhola, the innocent one, the naïve one. His mother was sharp. She loved all beings in creation and would defend them without thought, but she was not one to grant foolish boons. Sometimes, when someone had worked so hard that she could not refuse them what they were asking for, she gave it, with an addendum: something that would undo the power of the foolish boon.

This difference was evident in the way their anger was expressed: his father's anger was dramatic, almost like a dance, and dance he did when he was angry. His body quivered, his eyes grew red, he grabbed his damaru and proceeded to leap and swirl until he'd danced himself back to calm.

Kandhan liked to draw his father dancing like that. He had found rock faces along the mountain slopes on which thick charcoal spread easily, and he often clambered up looking for surfaces he could draw on. He was never short of subjects. The tone of the drawings changed depending on who was in it—his picture of the inhabitants of heaven, their faces and limbs mirroring their natures, made Paravani and the Matris roar with laughter. Who else but Kandhan would imagine Indra as a mountain, towering, unknowing that a tiny mouse had gnawed away all but two fingers' width of its base?

But Kandhan always drew his mother calm and smiling, for he had not seen her anger. It was something he could not imagine. But finally, it was Parvathy's anger that brought them closer.

Kandhan loved his mother, there was no doubt about that, and she loved him. About that too, there was no doubt. But right from the time he had hesitated when she held out her arms to the six of him, and clung instead to his six Krittika mothers, there had been a reticence between them. He knew he liked being a single boy with a single mother, but he had also liked being six little boys, each with his own mother.

On the day that things changed between them, mother and son were outdoors, under the clear night sky. The stars twinkled harder, hoping they would look up, especially the little boy, who had once been six little boys nursing at the breasts of six of their sisters. The family of four was seated around their favourite granite table, almost on the edge of the towering mountain, as if on the edge of the worlds, an arm's length away from the canopy of stars. Kandhan and his anna were on one side. He was thinking, *the stars would make a nice rangavalli; if he got up way before Mother did, he could make it in the sky and she would look up and, hmm, what would she do? She might be angry, you never know.* His appa and amma were sitting close together, discussing something; they were talking and laughing. And so, when it happened, it was so unexpected that Kandhan's body shot up and his hand reached automatically for his dandam. Ganesha leaned over and picked him up and hugged him close, his own calm heartbeat in contrast to the racing of the little one's heart. He kissed the top of his brother's head and said, 'Kandha, look, it's only Amma.'

And indeed it was: her eyes were like the setting sun in the twilight sky of her face, and from the lair of her mouth the red serpent of her tongue lunged forward, emitting terrible cries. Her hair stood up like pennants. In her right hand, instead of her trishula, was a cutlass. Kandhan was shaking now, his body rocking; it took Ganesha a moment to realise that the little one was laughing!

Their mother turned and looked at them. Kandhan jumped off his brother's lap, staff in hand. He jumped and leapt, rapping the staff on the ground, and said in his sing-song reciting voice, 'Amma you look like night, your eyes are stars, and your tongue is like the red sun, your teeth are like the tusks of elephants, shining under the moon.'

The mother looked at the little boy, who was now looking at her like he looked at his father. She laughed, a loud, rough laugh, and bent down to pick him up. She kissed him on his forehead and was about to put him down when he held on to her shoulder and said, 'Amma, take me with you.' Her smile grew wider, her eyes moist, her chest was full. She sat him on her hip, and with a roar, leapt onto Simha and proceeded to Bhu. In this form, she would be called 'Skandamata', the mother of Skanda. Every time she roared, the little boy roared along. After a while, he no longer waited for her, emitting loud, piercing roars and raising his staff to the skies.

So, that was how Parvathy and Kandhan crossed the distance between them, and how he finally felt completely at home in Kailasa. After this, on nights when he was cold, he went to his parents' room, clambered into their bed, and called to his mother to sing him to sleep. Kandhan was now the child she had wanted: loving, needy, but capricious enough to not want her all the time.

Afterwards, Kandhan would recall with a giggle that, when his mother had leapt up roaring, in the split second before he shut his eyes, he had seen his father's hair standing on end!

One slow morning, Kandhan was lounging in a corner of his father's workroom, surrounded by an assortment of students, visitors, and the ganas who lived on Kailasa. They sat exchanging news and gossip, and passing around little mud pots of the toddy made from mountain-tubers that hunters from the valleys sent up regularly. Kandhan had his eye on those pots: if he was quick, without anyone noticing, he might be able to get a taste. He had seen ants crawl up Father's face when he lay down after a drink, running around his lips and combing through his beard. He knew it must be tasty.

Suddenly, Father jumped up and, grabbing his trishula, went running up the mountain. Snow was falling thick and fast. Kandhan jumped up and ran after his father. It was so cold that he shivered, and was glad he hadn't shrugged off the skin wrap his mother had knotted him into. The matris Dhumi and Megharava called out to him, 'Kandha, stop, come back.' Matri Meshavahini said, 'We will tell Mother Parvathy.' He didn't listen, of course. What was everyone so afraid of? Wasn't he going with his father? Then he heard Anna say, 'Let him be, he knows what he's doing.'

The paths were all gone, blanketed over with snow. His father's trishula sounded measured beats, its three prongs striking the hard ground and gripping as he raced along. Kandhan's little feet fit nicely into the quickly closing hollows of his father's tread. He hurried to keep pace as his father climbed, his snow-whitened locks swinging wildly, his shoulders hunching as he climbed, his bare legs and the wrapping of skin at his waist all white, the air from his nostrils leaving a trail of shimmering breath. Kandhan did not call out, he was sure-footed enough, having climbed here a hundred times. And he knew now what had got his father up and racing. He could hear it, a slow, heavy grunting interspersed with ragged breathing. They were at the mouth of the cave now. Father was going in.

Kandhan followed, and there she was: white as the snow that was falling fast. She lay on her side, heaving and moaning, her belly distended, and he could see it jumping. *So,* this *was the leopard Nandi had talked about. What was wrong with her*? Then Father was kneeling at her side. She looked up at him, her eyes fiery, and growled: sharp, short scolds. Father stroked her belly and felt her neck. He called out, 'Kandha, come here,' and held out his trishula. 'Hold this.' Kandhan held out his hands, but his father said, 'Brace yourself now, make sure your feet are firm.' Kandhan readied himself, feet apart, back bent slightly. His father's hands lowered the trident slowly into his. Kandhan felt as if he was holding his brother's weight. He staggered, and Father steadied him, saying, 'Okay, okay, hold still, make yourself heavier.' Kandhan remembered the lessons his six mothers had taught him. His body told itself to become weighty. He felt the heaviness leaving his hands and filling his whole body. He could swing the trishula now, but no, this was no time for that.

His father was bending down towards the animal. 'Chitra, I'm going to lift you up now, just be calm.' He lifted the leopard into his arms, cradling her like a baby, and said, 'Go, Kandha, use that to get a grip.' Kandhan walked ahead, striking the trishula into the snowy ground as he negotiated their way down. This time, the father followed the son, his big feet touching the little hollows, deep and sure, as if the little feet had little fires burning in them. All the while, the leopard was growling and Kandhan's father crooned to her.

Then they were down, and Father was shouting, 'Uma, Uma, medicines.' He called out to the crowd to make place, to lay out a mat, to go tell Ganesha, who arrived and unrolled a mat of kusha grass. Someone lit lamps and placed them around the mat. Father washed his hands in the warm water that Nandi was holding out to him. Later, when Kandhan asked what was in the water, Nandi showed him all the things that had gone in: devadaru, abr, kusha grass, tulasi, turmeric, and the clot-inducing wool of kasturikamalam.

Kandhan stood back. His father was kneeling by the great beast which lay grunting and whimpering, talking to her, one hand on her belly, while the other, dripping with the medicated oil that Mother had poured on it, slid inside. 'Come on, Chitra, push now, ah, like that,' he said, his hand following the rhythm of her contractions, gently turning and guiding the head of the first cub till it emerged, a little version of the mother, white-furred and black-eyed. Two more cubs slid out, head first, as the leopard heaved more easily. When the first white head came out, Kandhan shouted and ran towards it, but his brother held him back and said, 'Wait.'

They all stood there, Father smiling and stroking the leopard's head, Mother smiling but a little distant—Kandhan would see this every time a birthing was done. She was a little distant, though always kind and helpful. In time, he understood that it was because she herself had never given birth.

The leopard licked her cubs and they suckled from her teats, then they were dried off and tender meat was brought in for the mother, who ate heartily, occasionally licking Father Shambhu's hands as he sat rubbing her belly and hind parts. Eventually, Ganesha cleaned Kandhan's hands and told him he could touch them. 'First the mother, then her cubs.' Kandhan's delight was evident, laughter rushing out of his mouth in great big bursts, and soon everyone was smiling. The first cub was the one he liked best. He said, 'I'm calling this one *Chirutai*.' It was a girl, and the name he gave her was in his language.

5

EXTRAORDINARY EVENTS

If Kandhan liked someone, his affection was effusive, and the warmth of it flew into the hearts of those receiving it. But if he didn't, it was another story: he would ignore them if he could, or if Mother was around and giving him a warning look, he would make a polite gesture and then find some excuse to leave. His parents and brother tried to get him to be more decorous, but gave up eventually. Anyway, the people Kandhan didn't like were so few, you could count them on the fingers of a single hand.

One of these was Sage Narada, a mind-born son of the creator, Brahma. Whenever he came visiting, Kandhan made a quick exit—this was easy, since the sage's arrival was always preceded by the strains of the ektara slung over one shoulder, which he plucked as he walked, chanting the name of his god, Narayana. It was never clear why Kandhan took such a marked dislike to Narada, who was a great musician. The humble, single-stringed instrument came to life in his hands and, joined with his voice, it could draw anyone in. But not Kandhan. When he heard the sage's voice, he quickly stopped whatever he was doing, picked up his things and left. Narada had also brought Kandhan a gift on the day he arrived in Kailasa—a beautiful wishing-box in which would materialise any physical thing he wished for. They found it a few days after, lying in the snow, frozen beyond use, and when his mother asked Kandhan how it came to be there, he said, 'Isn't it supposed to be magical? Must have grown legs and walked.' He didn't look up from his lettering, and since she would rather have him write than offer an explanation, she let it be. Afterwards, by unspoken agreement, Kandhan was allowed to deal with his dislike for the sage in his own way.

But there was another that he took a dislike to—a dislike that created a furore and also became a turning point in Kandhan's life.

One morning, Ganesha was sunning himself in the cool light of the winter sun. Kandhan leaned against a rocky outcrop near the stone bench on which his brother sat, looking off into the distance. There was a general bustle around them, as important visitors were expected for a meeting.

Ganesha's eyes were on Kandhan. *What was he doing? He looked more pugnacious than usual.* For all his brother's playfulness, Ganesha knew just how tough he was. There was not a tree, not a cliff, not a target, not a race, that he could not best; if he failed at the first attempt, he would not rest till he did it. His little frame always seemed ready for combat, ready to spring into a chase or to leap on his peacock and be off.

Kandhan. That was the name he liked best for his baby brother. Ganesha was both brother as well as parent to Kandhan, and this morning, he knew something was up. The furrowed brow, the glowering face, the muttering … he had looked like that since he returned abruptly from his morning ritual of flying around the worlds, looking at 'what everyone was up to'. When Ganesha asked him why he had come back so soon, he said, 'Nothing, just saw something; I'll fix it.' Ganesha was certain there would be trouble. The boy was clutching his dandam like he wanted to strike. *I'd better stay around, who knows what he's going to do now.*

Kandhan smiled through gritted teeth. Anna was beginning to get anxious, he could see the frown on his brow, and the way he was sitting up straight. Kandhan knew he was going to be chastised, maybe Mother would punish him, but nothing was going to stop him. He felt the anger course through him again as he remembered what he had seen, and heard, that morning.

The sound of wings overhead signalled the arrival of Brahma on his swan, and then he was coming up the steps. In his hands were a little pot of water and prayer beads, emblems of his office as the Creator. Kandhan was watching Brahma. And Ganesha was watching Kandhan. When he saw the boy lean back as if he had not a thing on his mind, Ganesha knew the trouble was going to be big and dramatic. Ah, there! His grip on the dandam was tightening. What had Brahma done?

'Greetings, Brahma,' Kandhan's voice rang out loud and clear, but Brahma was muttering to himself, his head down, as he scurried towards the meeting place. Ganesha saw Kandhan's hands tighten, his body lift itself up to assume the familiar striking pose.

Again Kandhan said, 'Greetings, Brahma.'

And still no answer.

Kandhan moved with swift steps to stand in front of Brahma.

Now, the four heads looked up, they saw Kandhan and said, 'Kandha, son, move, I'm in a hurry.'

'Why didn't you greet me?' asked Kandhan. 'I wished you twice.'

'I didn't hear you, son, I was thinking about something,' replied the Creator.

'So, when the mind is working, do the ears stop?' asked the little boy.

'No, no, Kandha, it's not like that. You're a child, you won't understand these things. Now, be a good boy and let me pass.'

'No, Brahma, I'm a child and I need to understand. So, tell me, how is hearing affected by thought? What is the connection between sound and the mind?'

'Kandha, I will come back and—'

'No, Brahma, that won't do, you have to answer me. As an older person, a wise person, it's your duty to clear the doubts of eager learners, and I am one. Come now, tell me.'

'I was preoccupied. We have trouble in Svarloka and I was worrying about whether we are capable of dealing with it, that's why I didn't hear you. That's all, Kandha, nothing more. Let me make up for my lapse and greet you now. Come, let me embrace you, dear child, and then let me pass.'

Ganesha took a few steps closer to them. He sensed a rise in the tempo of his brother's drama. Something had got to Kandhan on his morning ride.

Kandhan was not having any of Brahma's pacifying. He asked, 'How can you be so lost in thought? Are you not the one responsible for creating? For the making of all things? What will happen to the things you are making if you get so caught up in your thoughts?'

Brahma was getting impatient, and, of course, his vanity, which had been known to blind him to the importance of others, and to his own insignificance, blinded him now. Instead of realising the import of what was happening, he let his irritation get the better of him. It was clear that he was rattled, and that he was grasping for a hold on the turn of events, when he addressed Kandhan by the formal name that had been given to him in the heavenly assembly. It was a name that Guru Brihaspati had said 'underlined the boy's intelligence, and his status as one who could resolve problems'. 'Subrahmanya,' he said sternly, as adult to child, forgetting that, when the gods gave the child that name, they were acknowledging the truth that he could plan and execute what was beyond them: they were acknowledging a reversal of the equation of immature child and mature adult.

'Subrahmanya,' said Brahma, 'please move out of the way. I have an important meeting to go to. Your parents will be angry with me if I'm late, for the meeting can't start without me.'

'Answer my question then.' The little boy was now so angry, his ears were glowing. 'Tell me, how important is sound? What is its work?'

'What silliness is this,' Brahma said, and tried to move the boy aside with his hands, but Kandhan was like a rock, unmoveable, literally. That is when Ganesha finally understood what it was all about. Kandhan had heard Brahma at his morning intonations. He was known to be a little inattentive, dropping syllables, sometimes whole words, as he sat in the space over the universes, waking up everything with his incantation. And everyone knew that sometimes the source of this inattentiveness was his glad eye. He simply could not stop his eyes, and thus his mind, from roving when an apsara, a gandharva or a naga woman, a yakshi or a goddess passed. And Kandhan knew this, he knew about Ushas, too. He had overheard someone referring to the time when Brahma, blinded by lust, chased his daughter across the skies. When Kandhan went to Nandi to find out what they were talking about, and Nandi told him the tale, Kandhan had struck the ground with his staff and said, 'Couldn't Brahma hear? Didn't her voice remind him that she was his daughter? How can the Creator be tone deaf?'

Yes, that must be it, thought Ganesha, he must have heard Brahma's careless chanting. He went up to his brother, who was now trembling with rage, and said, 'Kandha, let him go, he has work to do.'

Kandhan said, 'How can he work when he doesn't know what he's saying? But let him just answer this one simple question and he can go.'

Ganesha agreed because Kandhan was right, and also because he knew that the little one's rage could be terrible. He nodded and said to Brahma, 'Sir, that's a simple enough thing, isn't it? Just answer his question. It should take you no more than a moment to do so. All he's asking is, what is the role of sound in the functioning of things?'

Brahma said, 'You too, Gananatha? You should know better. You're supposed to be a leader to us all. Of course I know what it means, but I can't say it now, like this … it's too undignified.'

Kandhan stamped his foot. 'Undignified? Undignified is what you were this morning, chanting with your eyes open but not seeing what you were making because they were following the steps of Neelakamalini. And twice you forgot the beat, the rhythm, the punctuation. So, whatever took birth then would be a half-creature, a half-person! What kind of creating is that?'

'Subrahmanya!' Brahma's voice was shrill now, and trembling. 'How *dare* you! Even your parents would not speak to me like that.'

'That's because they're adults and polite. I'm a child, see, and I don't know how to be. Now, tell me, what is the importance of sound? Why do we need to pay attention to it in everything we do?'

Brahma was sputtering, but began to speak an answer.

It clearly wasn't what Kandhan wanted. He just said, 'Yes? And then what?'

Brahma was panting with humiliation. Several ganas had gathered, as well as Nandi, and the twelve Matris. They were silent, all of them. Brahma looked at Ganesha, but he was looking away. *How could this be happening? He was the Creator and this little boy had the temerity to—* He put his hand out to move Kandhan aside again. In a jiffy, Kandhan had grabbed Brahma's hands and was holding them. He called to Nandi and said, 'Please take him and lock him up.'

Nandi said, 'Kandha, I cannot do it as I'm bound by rules, but we can ask Galabajja here to do it.'

And that was that. Galabajja locked him up, and Kandhan went up to Ganesha and stood beside him, leaning against a boulder. Ganesha put his hand on Kandhan's shoulder and said, 'It was time someone did that, and no one wanted to be that someone.' *Because no one else hears and comprehends sound like you do.*

Then arrived their father, uncle, mother, aunt, Indra and Brihaspati. They asked the little boy to release the prisoner. Kandhan repeated his original ask: let Brahma explain to him the role of sound in creation. They reasoned and cajoled, but Kandhan stood his ground. Finally, his father said, 'Enough, Subrahmanya. Brahma has paid for his negligence, let him go. I will answer your question.'

And Kandhan let Brahma go on the condition that he would do the work of creation now, not Brahma. He turned to his father to say, 'Okay, let's go.'

'Go where?'

Kandhan, his body still tight with anger, said, 'Somewhere private, where no one can hear us, for you are going to ask me what I know, and I cannot tell you in other people's hearing.'

His father laughed, and the two of them climbed up to the rock seat under the great banyan, from where you could see all the peaks around Kailasa and the blue-and-white clouds were only a hand's reach away. They saw the boy take the seat and the father kneel. The father folded his hands, bowed his head and waited, and the boy spoke at length, and the father listened. When they came down, the father was carrying the son on his hip, one arm around his back, the other holding his trishula; the boy had one arm around his father's neck, in the other he held his akil dandam. They were both smiling. The son was silent, but the father, it is said, was humming what sounded to bystanders like words in the boy's language.

'Kandha.' Someone was calling him, but he couldn't see anyone. 'Kandha, Kandha.'

He looked everywhere, turning his head from the trees to the benches, the bushes, the swings where sometimes people lay down to catch a quick nap. But he still couldn't see anyone.

Kandhan grit his teeth. His face was getting warm, his hands curled into fists. He called out, 'Where are you? Who are you?' But there was no sound other than the garden sounds, and then, when the little boy began to stalk off, his back straight and his jaw clenched, there it came again, the booming voice, 'Kandha, Ka-n-dha.'

The boy stopped; he stomped his foot so hard that a cloud of powdery snow flew up. He threw his hands in the air and said, 'Coward, come out, or else I'll catch you and thrash you so hard, you'll never arrrgggg!' He was so angry that the words crashed into each other.

'Oh, but you have to catch me to do that, and you can't, because you can't find me,' called the voice, now so close, the person was speaking into his ear.

'Arrrgh!' Kandhan screamed again, and swung his dandam around his head and rubbed his ear vigorously.

He turned a full circle without the staff connecting anywhere, and the voice laughed, loud and out of reach. Kandhan began to run up and down, striking out with the dandam, swinging it in front of him; with each step, he shouted, 'Here, here, here, here, take this, and this and this.' And the voice said, 'Ouch, ouch.'

But before the smile was fully formed on Kandhan's face, the voice started laughing. It said, 'Oh, you thought you could actually hit me? Think again, little one.'

'Don't *little one* me, you sneaky coward, hiding and fighting and then calling me "little one".'

Just then, he saw a movement from the corner of his eyes. It was Ganesha, tapping his own chest and then pointing at Kandhan. *What was he saying, breathe slowly*? *Spread my chest?* He raised his eyebrows and mouthed *What*, but his elder sibling continued to point to his own chest. Miming the chest-tapping, Kandhan yelled, 'What? What? Just tell me. Don't do this!'

Ganesha spread his hands, palms up: *See, this is what I was saying*. And then, it came to him: anger! It was the anger Anna was pointing to. His six mothers had taught him spells for every occasion, and all of these required that his heart be empty of anger. He stopped and felt a wave of shame washing over him: he had tripped himself up. Again. With his irritability and anger.

Kandhan stopped, held the dandam to his chest and stood still. He shut his eyes, but his thoughts were rushing round and round, and it seemed as if each thought had its own dramatic stage voice, and they were all speaking at the same time. His hands began to clench, but he uncurled them, and grunting, pressed down on his heart, making it slow. As it slowed, he heard Ganesha laugh. This made him smile and laugh, the laughter filling his head, silencing the other voices. Kandhan felt as if his brother had held him upside down, like a full goblet, and his anger had poured out of him. He felt light.

The voice came again, calling, 'Kandha, I'm still here, admit you can't find me. Admit I've won.'

Kandhan stopped himself from running blindly at it. He was surprised to hear himself say, 'Oh, don't fool yourself, I'm going to find you. I'll do it in my own time. Meanwhile, you hang around there, hiding like the coward trickster you are.'

He sat down, laid the dandam next to him, within easy reach, and shut his eyes, trying to recall the spell. *How had it gone? This anger really takes up a lot of room*, he thought, shaking his head to dislodge the last remnants of it, and then he waited. He had had no occasion to use any of these spells ever since he had stopped practising them with his Krittika mothers. Into the emptied space in his head, slowly the words came pouring in: *One shape, two fillings, nine pathways, breath fill the heart and let the hidden eye see past all veils.*

A loud gasp rang out, and Kandhan heard a sound as if something heavy had hit the ground. His opened his eyes, and there lay a man such as he had not seen: there was simply a lot of him. His legs were *so* long, his head was *so* big, his two eyes were large, his ears like two big sea shells. His hair was knotted on top of his head, held in place with wooden pins, although several strands had come loose. And his heart was beating so loud, it sounded like a drum.

'Abba! You're a naughty one, little brother, come here and help me up,' he said.

Kandhan glared at him. *Little brother! Who was this man, calling him that?*

'Come and help me up now, Kandha, I've taken a hard fall.'

Kandhan looked at him and took a step back. *He wouldn't trust this one, even if he was smiling.*

'Kandha, are you deaf? Help me up.' The man was holding out a hand.

'No!' said Kandhan. 'You'll trick me again. Get up by yourself, and don't call me your little brother. Ganesha is my anna. No one else.'

The man laughed, loud and rumbling. 'I am also your anna, now be a good boy, help me up.'

'No.'

Then Ganesha was there, helping the fallen man up and bending to touch his feet, saying, 'Anna.' The man placed his large hands on Ganesha's head and blessed him. The two of them turned to Kandha and began to laugh.

Kandhan's anger raised its head, but he stopped it and breathed slowly. Smiling, he said, 'I beat you.'

The two men laughed, and the stranger said, 'Yes, indeed, you did, and you passed my test.'

'Test? What test? Test for what?' asked Kandhan, the irritation returning.

Ganesha said, 'Come here, Kandha, this is our elder brother, Veerabahu, come and take his blessings.'

He had another brother? No one had told him. Kandhan went reluctantly and folded his hands to the big man, saying, 'Greetings.'

Ganesha looked at his little brother. Veerabahu would have to earn his respect before Kandhan allowed himself to be blessed.

'Greetings,' Veerabahu said, not attempting to touch Kandhan's head, instead leaning down to touch his shoulder. 'I'm going to teach you, that's why I am here. So, I had to test you, to see if you have the mettle to go through with my training.'

'Teach me, teach me what?' Kandhan didn't try to quell his annoyance. His voice was sharp and a little high as he said, 'My six mothers taught me before, and now Amma and Appa and Anna and Nandi, and Brihaspati and Tumburu, and Uncle and Aunt and King Dashagriva are all teaching me. And the Matris. What's left to learn anyway?'

'I am going to be your teacher, Kandha, and I'll teach you something that no one else has taught you yet ,' said the man. 'I'm going to teach you diplomacy.'

Diplomacy! That was a topic nobody had brought up till now. Kandhan's interest was piqued. 'What's that,' he asked, 'and how long will it take for me to learn it and try it out?'

'How long it will take depends on how attentive you are,' said the man.

This was how Kandhan first met Veerabahu.

However, when Veerabahu explained what the topic of his instruction was, things changed. Kandhan refused to learn 'diplunacy'. 'It's a waste of time, it's for cowards. If someone comes to attack me and I stand there talking, I'll be dead and everyone will call me a coward.'

No matter what Veerabahu said, or anyone else, Kandhan refused to learn. Veerabahu had not expected it to be like this. To him, diplomacy was a blend of valour, etiquette, sophistication, articulation, quick-wittedness and foresight, and it could prevent waste, loss of honour and death. He was no coward, and if there was a fight, he would be at the head of it. He did not fear a fair fight, but he did fear unfortunate fights ignited by misguided pride, helplessness or words spoken under duress. He was a practised diplomat who knew the value of the work that people like him could do—not only could it avert destruction, it could spark friendship, inspire sharing and bring peace.

Veerabahu did not let it go. He would not be allowed to, of course, but also, he knew that Kandhan would need this skill to deal with the demands of the worlds. He pretended to give up on his lesson plans and stopped mentioning them altogether. Instead, he turned up during Kandhan's weapons training and cheered him on. He also began interrupting the lessons to add subtle nuances to the exercises that the boy was learning. When Kandhan sprang in the air, sword in hand, and came down, Veerabahu said, 'Mid-way down, if you twist, then the opponent, expecting to be hit from one side, will be taken by surprise when the attack comes from the opposite side'. Kandhan did not realise that he was going through one of the primary lessons of diplomacy: how to get the ear of a person by winning his admiration in a completely different context.

It took many days, and tricks with stick-fighting, running, sword fighting, wrestling, and many stories of successful diplomatic missions before Kandhan finally agreed to learn the lessons that Veerabahu had to teach. As the lessons progressed, he understood that a diplomat required not only patience but also a degree of slyness to constantly run ahead of his opponents. Unlike weapons or combat, which came to him as naturally as breathing, Kandhan could not easily be trained to weigh circumstances, to think how his head, rather than his body, could better tackle sticky situations and angry opponents. Veerabahu persisted, though. And there could be no better proof of his success than when, years later, though it was clear that battle with the mighty Surapadman was unavoidable, Kandhan himself opposed popular opinion and insisted on a diplomatic mission to the Asura court before settling on war.

6

KANDHAN'S LANGUAGE

On Bhu and Kailasa, those who heard the words that he muttered or sang were intrigued by its sounds and how much it absorbed his attention. Some may have thought it childish babble but most sensed that it was more than babble. However, those who knew that this was indeed a language, were few. Some of them may have wished to learn it, there were those who questioned Kandhan about it, and a few who asked him to teach it to them. Kandhan's reply was always the same: he had first to teach it to someone else.

That person was a Manava from Bhuloka. No one remembers his real name; we know him by the name the northerners gave him, the name of the brilliant star that mapped his way from the southern tip of the land of Himavan and of Ganga, to Kailasa and back. But let's start at the beginning.

He was a sage whose fame as a teacher, a physician and a grower of plants and flowers was no less than his fame as one revered for his knowledge across the fourteen worlds. The sage was a little man: his arms and legs, his face, his nose, his ears and eyes were all little. He was like the last clay figure made by children, who, falling short of clay, reduced the scale of everything for that last one.

By the time he enters the tale here, the sage had become taciturn. His eyes darted around, looking past everything as if to push aside what he was seeing, certain there was something hidden behind it all.

The sage knew not what he was seeking, only that he must find it—the thing that would be a treasure for his homeland, the lands that he loved, the South. He loved its rivers, landscapes and people, the grains that grew there and the food that was made there. Dearest of all to him was the red rice, with round grains and a husk so soft, it didn't need to be roughed off. There were few things that pleased him more than to walk in fields of ripening rice, the golden stalks bending. He even dreamt of it—the shape of its grains, its texture, the fragrance of it cooking, the feel of it in the mouth and in the belly. Everywhere he went, he took with him this rice to cook and eat piping hot, with spoonsful of fresh butter or old ghee poured over it, mixed with salt and accompanied by the cooked leaves and flowers of a little tree.

It all started with a dream. The sage was resting under the shade of a tree when the Goddess of the South, short and brown-skinned, visited him in his dream and said to him, 'My son, you have dues to pay to me. In all these years, I have given you good health, knowledge and fame, and you have done your duties to students, and living and non-living things, and to the gods, but you have not done the work you were born to do. You have to bring to this land that is your home something that will forever distinguish it. Go now, climb up to the hub of the universes and wait on the Mother and Father of Creation till you win it from them.'

The sage woke up shivering and gasping for breath. He shook his head to clear the dream from his eyes, washed his face and bathed, ate a meal and taught a class. He tried climbing a hill, sleeping, talking, meditating. But the face of the goddess remained—her eyes, two long bowls in which flames danced, enflaming her face; on her chest was armour, and in her hands, a begging bowl. He tried to tuck the memory of the dream out of his conscious thoughts, but it pushed through into his chest. It became impossible to sleep, speak or eat. Wherever he went, he heard her voice saying, *give*, and saw her hand, bare of bangles, the wrist thin, stretching towards him with an empty begging bowl.

He sent his students to other teachers and began to walk through the regions of the South. One day, as he was passing through a crowded marketplace, a woman bearing a basket of bangles on her head stopped him and said, 'Sage, aren't you on the wrong road? This doesn't go to Kailasa.'

He realised then that the dream had been no dream, but an order. He pulled up a sapling of his favourite greens and covered its roots, stems, leaves and buds with a mixture of clay and ash, and begged the elements to keep it from wilting and decaying. He placed it in a cloth pouch, which he wound around his waist.

Barefoot, the sage walked, stopping only at midday to sit down and rest his legs, and to eat his only meal of the day: two or three leaves from the plant. Every day, he laid the plant out on the ground, and as the sun and the wind touched it, the plant put out fresh leaves.

He often thought about what he wanted for his beloved home, and what he was willing to give up for it. Sometimes, it brought tears running down his face; sometimes, his heart felt so heavy, he feared it would drop out of his body. At other times, his body became so heavy that he dropped to the ground and lay there, unable to move or cry. He feared he was going mad, but the memory of the goddess' fire-eyes and bare hands would drive him on. No matter how long it took, he would go to Kailasa, and he would not return till he had a prize that would please her. A prize worthy of this great land. He marched on with renewed energy, not talking to anyone or accepting food from anyone, so that nothing would slow him down. He ate only the leaves of his plant, and said not a word on his entire journey up to the highest mountain in creation.

Many asked him his name and where he was from, and where he was going. Did the heat not tire him, wearing as he was only a white cloth around his waist? Then, as he went further up north, didn't he feel cold, wearing only a cloth? They offered him food, all kinds of rice and lentils and vegetables and fruits, but he refused everything. He walked at day and at night, and he covered the distance to the Great Mountain in a fraction of the time it would have taken anyone else. It was as if his goddess held both his feet at every step and gave them a gentle heave, for she was eager for him to reach his destination.

In this way, he arrived at a little town at the foothills of Kailasa, and there, finally allowed himself a day's rest. He walked down its streets, past the little shops and homes, till he came to its edge, where he found what he was looking for—a group of yogis and sanyasis readying to make the trek up. They recognised the look in his eyes and their hearts went out to him. They offered him food, which he turned down, they handed him a mat to sit on and a blanket to cover himself with. He accepted nothing, folding his hands and shaking his head. Then he looked at them and, pointing to the white cloth around his waist, now ochre with stains that would not wash off, made a gesture of open palms. They understood that he wanted a clean waist cloth. One of them reached inside a bundle by her side and drew out a stretch of fabric, given to her by a householder as an offering. It was fine ivory-coloured cotton, fragrant with neem and dried lemon rind, a delight to both eyes and nose, and no doubt to skin as well. But our sage was insensible to any of it. He went to a bathhouse and washed and changed.

When he returned, the group offered him food and a steaming hot beverage, and again he refused. Instead, as was his wont, he took out his plant and ate of its leaves. The woman who had given him the cloth asked him his name and where he was from. He pointed to the skies, to the bright star that he had followed like a beacon on his journey. They looked at the star, now barely visible on the horizon, and understood that it had led him, and that he had discarded his given name on his journey. They saw what his eyes held, and one of them said, in one of the 'unrefined' old languages of the northern lands, 'Let that be your name from now on: Akaththi.' Another one smiled, and in another language said to have been 'refined' out of speech and prayer, added, 'Agastya'. The women pointed to the plant he was carrying and said, 'Let this be known by the same name too: Akaththi.'

From there, he and the others made their way up Kailasa mountain, and arrived at the home of Shiva and Parvathy, whose welcome was like the whole world embracing them. They stayed the length of two full moons' passing, then made their way down, to return to their own homelands. But Akaththi did not leave. He turned his face to Shiva and Parvathy. They knew he would not leave till he got what he had come for, so they smiled and said to him, 'Stay.'

Akaththi was no longer being shaken awake from his sleep by dreams of the goddess. He took this as a sign of her saying to him, 'You have reached Kailasa; now it is only a matter of time.' Each day, he opened his eyes hoping this would be the day it happened. He bathed and went to his plant, now potted and placed over an underground hot-water stream. The leaves and flowers were growing in profusion, but he still fed on a leaf or two, and sometimes, one white flower.

That was the way things were when Kandhan ran into the sage one day. He was on his father's shoulders, trying to copy his whistling, while his eyes followed a flock of mountain pheasants. His father stopped suddenly and Kandhan clutched at the jata piled high on his head. 'Ow, Appa, don't stop like that.'

He heard his father say, 'Ah! There's the poor man.' Kandhan turned to look at the short, tubby man who stood looking out over the valley, facing south. 'Isn't that the sage from the South?' he asked. His father hailed the man, calling him 'Akaththi, Agastya'.

The little man started, and his face lit up when he saw who it was. He came towards them with excitement in his tread but none on his face, for he had on many occasions thought he was about to receive his long-awaited prize, only to be disappointed.

'Akaththi, don't look so sad,' Shiva said. 'I don't have a prize for you just now, but the time is near, and you will get what you left your home and land for. Why don't you visit Parvathy? She's ready to start editing her *Rasaragavairagyamanjari*. Perhaps you can help with that. You know she values your opinion.'

The sage brightened up and started to walk away even before Shiva had finished, causing the god to laugh and call out, 'And good day to you too!' That set Kandhan off giggling and repeating, 'And good day to you too.'

When his father put him down, Kandhan said, 'Do you have a prize for me?' and Shiva said, 'Yes, I do!' He pulled out the vial of oil, and holding the wriggling boy firmly, began oiling him. The father looked at the back of the sage and smiled at the son, who returned his smile.

After that day, Kandhan started to look out for Akaththi and discovered that nothing seemed to shake him out of his misery. When the divine couple were dancing and everyone else was awed and ecstatic, Akaththi stayed impassive. Even when the Father and Mother of the Universes sat with him, talking, laughing, reading to him, his expression of sorrow remained. It did not change even when Mother rolled a mouthful of hot rice from her plate, fragrant, cooked to perfection, and held it out to him. Other eyes grew damp, other hearts thought, *lucky man*. The sage simply put out his hand, took the ball of rice, cupped it in his palm and gestured to say, 'later'.

One morning, Kandhan was pottering around, re-arranging his mother's writing tools on the stone bench and muttering in a sing-song voice words that only he could make out. Parvathy had just come back from her bath and was sitting in the sun, drying her hair and humming to herself; Shiva was smiling and humming along. Just then, a glint caught her eyes, and she remembered the pair of anklets someone had brought for her that she had been meaning to wear when she was less busy. Parvathy walked towards the little bowl in which they lay, uncoiled them with a quick flick, and sat down to clasp them on to her ankles. But before you could say 'Kandha', the boy had leapt up, grabbed the anklets and begun to run around in a frenzy that was surprising even for this little whirlwind of a child. As he ran, he recited loudly in his language, his voice giving the words a vigorous emphasis and his running feet underlined their rhythm.

This was when Akaththi walked up, carrying Parvathy's manuscript. Kandhan circled his mother, and as he ran, his voice grew more and more melodious, the rhythms softened, the recitation became a song, and all who heard it felt as if the air had been shaken out and collected again. They did not want him to stop, it seemed as if they could understand what he was saying. It seemed as if he was singing to Time, which in response seemed to slow, then stopped to watch. He whirled, his hands gesturing, holding the anklets aloft. His parents watched, as did his aunt and uncle, who had arrived earlier, and Ganesha, who had come out of his room; Paravani was there, of course, and scores of others. The boy was absorbed, unaware of them. When he slowed and stopped, no one spoke or moved.

Kandhan went up to his mother and said, 'Here, Amma, now you can wear them. Whoever made them didn't do it right. There should be one male sound, then one female, but one bead was not sounding properly. If you had worn them, Mother …' He trailed off, looking serious.

His father stepped forward and asked, 'And what did you do, Kandha?'

'I just spoke them right,' the boy replied, now smiling.

'And what language,' asked his father, also smiling, 'did you just speak?'

'*Tamizh*, of course,' replied Kandhan, '*which knows the measure of Time*.'

Ganesha turned to Akaththi: his face was glowing; he was finally smiling. He had found his prize.

Kandhan was wearing a half-smile, his eyes now trained on the sage. Akaththi's eyes flowed over, the hair on his body stood on end, and sweat flowed down his face. His body shook with sobs, and through all that, he was also smiling and laughing. The words that came out of Kandhan's mouth seemed to have snapped him out of a trance. The stubborn man who had not eaten a single morsel or shed a single tear since he left his home in the southern lands, now wept; he finally allowed himself to mourn his own exile.

Stretching out one hand, Kandhan said to him, '*Akattiyan*'. The sage looked at the boy who stood there, his face shining under the sun's rays, which snagged on his unruly locks and gave his head a tangled halo. Paravani came up behind him and spread his opulent wings like a royal parasol.

When Kandhan called to the sage, his voice rang, as if he were six boys, not one: 'Akattiya, come.' The old man approached the little boy, his body trembling uncontrollably, tears flowing, as if their will was different from his.

Kandhan held the old man's shoulders and said, 'Kuru Muni, I have been waiting for someone to teach my language to, and here you are, waiting for a prize.'

The sage heard the words *Kuru Muni*, and he knew that the boy-god had just addressed him as the little muni—he could understand! There was a voice in his head, as if someone was there, speaking to him. His lips parted, his mouth opened, and his tongue uttered a word he did not know: *Muruga*. And just as Agni, when he sang in tune for the first time in his life, knew who had made that happen, so too did Akattiyan. He said 'Muruga, Beautiful One, give me this prize if you will. Teach me, so that I may go back to my home with this treasure.'

'I will teach you,' Kandhan said, 'and you will teach others, and what they learn, they will speak and sing, and the Mother who protects your land will be gladdened, and she will dance in its soil and rivers, in its air and sky, and in the hearts of its people.'

Akattiyan stood speechless, as the gods and ganas watched. He did not ask about the terms of his apprenticeship or the length of the study—he could not speak even if he wanted to, because his belly, so long kept under control, now rebelled; the juices began to flow, and they rose up through his guts, mixed with his breath, went through the tunnel of his throat, and sat under his tongue. And so, he just stood there, with his lips shut, his eyes wide open, his hands holding his belly.

Kandhan leaned towards the sage and said, 'Akattiya, for your untiring wait, and for your love of your land, from which you exiled yourself for so long, I now give you a reward; I give you ழ.' He raised the akil dandam and tapped the sage's chest.

In Akattiyan's mouth, the taste of the red rice of his home stirred, it flowed over his tongue, which lifted off the floor of his mouth, and he repeated, ழ, zha. Volleys of thunder erupted in the sky and lightning flashed; the ganas lifted their hands upwards and raised cries of Muruga, Muruga, Muruga, Muruga. The little boy held aloft his staff of akil, and waving it, began to dance, his steps following the tempo of the chant. Akattiyan, the kuru muni, folded hands clasped to his chest, repeated over and over a single word, in the same cadence as the boy's movements: Tamizh, Tamizh, Tamizh, Tamizh.

Thus was born this language, which would in time be called 'sweet', 'cool', 'divine', 'musical', 'the language that Murugan hearkens to, with passion'. This is how Tamizh came home with Akattiyan, and he began a new life as if the old one, like his old name, had never been. He carried with him bags of palm leaves from the stock on Kailasa, with thousands of words and meanings, their roots and the rules for their transformation and combination, notes on their mechanics. When Akattiyan reached the foothills of the majestic Vindhya, the mountain that had once allowed Sarasvati and a baby passage through him, bent his head in reverence at the treasure that baby had sent for the lands he guarded. The sage crossed over and headed for his old home in the vast spread of lands that were known by the name of Dravida, now *Thiravitam* in Tamizh.

He sought out the ancient mountain, Pothigai, and there, cared for and looked after by the gentle Kani people, he wrote the *Akattiyam*, Tamizh's foundational grammar. Then he returned to the towns and cities of his land, and accepted the invitations of its kings, assemblies, schools and patrons to stay and teach the language of the Beautiful God, Murugan. Disciples and apprentices came seeking him. He tested them, accepted and imparted learning to them, and tasked the disciples with writing and teaching. Of these, the quick-witted and humble Tolkappiyan chose to continue his master's work with an accompanying grammar, *Tolkappiyam*. The years passed and the lands of the South, where this new language spread and thrived, came to be known as *Tamizhakam*: the home of Tamizh.

after

a prelude

TAMIZH

If the fourteen worlds are chunks of meat skewered through by Kailasa, then the fire over which they cook is Time, and like a fire roasts the meat but merely heats the skewer, the effect of Time on Shambhu and Parvathy's home is momentary. The measure to which Time journeys through the worlds is based on the nature of each world and its inhabitants. Every created thing carries within it a precise beat to which it grows, changes, slows, stops, and passes back into the Vast. This beat is held within Time's measure, and the ensuing rhythm is called 'gati'. Thus it is that gati came to mean pace and tempo, but also 'fate' and 'destiny', leading to the benediction that you would 'find your true gati', and the curse, 'may you never be able to catch your gati'.

On Bhu, Akattiyan, touched by Kailasa's Time, still lived, though several thousand years have passed. In this time, Tamizh has grown, evolved and spread. Many generations of sovereigns who considered it their duty to nurture and protect the language, in the same way they did their people and land, have come and gone. To those drawn to Tamizh, and there was no woman, nor man or child who was not, the language seemed filled with the sounds of their lives, work, love, war and death. When they learnt it, they saw how the God of Tamizh had made its alphabets like their own bodies, some soft, others muscled, some short, others tall, some fleshly, others lean, and also the middling, neither one nor the other, and filled them all with the same breath. They understood how, just as people who wish to live together have to leave room for each other to grow, if their union is not to be futile, so too it was with letters and words. They noticed that, just as plants, when transported from one soil to another, become like that new soil, gritty or loamy or heavier, the language also changed as it travelled from one place to another. By the seaside, it had the lilt of rising and falling waves and the music of seashells; on the hills, it soared with bird wings and drifted like mist. And they rejoiced in the language's pliant good nature, its hardy will to belong wherever it went. They also saw how, when they spoke from their hearts, the words rejoiced as did the elements, rewarding the speaker with signs that guided them or answered their questions, or like shadows that took on substance, they became whatever was needed in the moment.

When poets and musicians observed how the landscape transformed over the duration of each day and over the seasons, and how these changes affected their bodies and hearts and their mood, in turn affecting their words and music, they recorded these connections. In the course of time, every part of the landscape—the high mountains where the kurinji blossomed, the valleys where crops were cultivated, the forests, the seaside and the arid wastelands—was attributed with a corresponding scape of emotions. When a poem described the elements of a landscape, it was possible to understand the human emotion that was inherent there, because everyone knew what each element signified. They knew that the purple kurinji that flowered every twelve years stood for first love's richness, in the same way that the tired elephant in barren tracts indicated separation and loss.

Just as the stringers of words represented the beauty and endless variation of nature in words, the musicians whose hearts surged with the thunder in the skies, or danced with the fall of rain on mud, made instruments to replicate these sounds and the effects they had on listeners. It was too large a task for a single person to compose the words, set music to them, then perform the songs to musical accompaniment, so these tasks were divided among them. It became common to see groups of performers vending their way towards towns and assemblies, and to the dwellings of patrons and kings, singing and beating on the tudi.

Women and men also sang songs to the god who had made this language; they danced wildly and imagined him in their lands, as the redness of the soil, the red on the tips of their javelins and swords, as the red in the eyes of lovers and the red of kadamba flowers. They made him the owner of the best of their lands: the high hilltops where the sun shone at its fieriest and the clouds first burst, where the fruits and flowers were sweeter, these lands where the purple flowers, warmed by the sun and wetted by rains for twelve years burst open, all together, turning the mountain sides purple. The flowers gave the landscape its name: kurinji nilam, kurinji lands. They sang of their god's love for the purple flowers and called him Kurinji Kizhavan, the Hero of the Kurinji. They celebrated his love for Tamizh, they called him Tamizh Theivam, the God of Tamizh. They also called him Seyyon, the Child, and the Red One, for they imagined him with blood rushing to his heart and his face, passionate. They also imagined his skin to be the colour of the bark of mature mahagani, or young ebony, or the newly sprouted leaves on the peepal: reddish brown and black.

They imagined him with long arms that reached down to his knees and they imagined themselves in the safe embrace of those arms. They imagined him as armed with a staff of sturdy akil and with a wit that outwitted every trick of language and logic; they imagined him as waiting for the oracles to break out of the bounds of their senses and invoke him, so that he could appear before them.

Time passed, and generations of poets, scholars and bards of Tamizh lived, worked and passed on. Their fame remained, spurring those who came after to strike out further, dive deeper. In their words, Tamizh grew surer and more adventurous, it sank roots, and like a giant tree, rose firm out of the soil, and on its branches perched the mighty-winged birds of poetry, grammar and music.

In this time, Akattiyan had become quiet, having spent his words over these many long years, teaching but also grammaring, analysing and repairing Tamizh for generation after generation of learners. He had walked all over the South, looking for those who worked Tamizh, and with the help of kings and gods, he had brought together grammarians, bards and poets of the land and presided over them at the Great Assembly, not once but twice. He was helped in this task by Lord Shambhu, who had promised to do so, since Murugan could not leave Kailasa till he had crossed five—that being Parvathy's condition, for agreeing to let him spend his first two years away from her.

The Assembly thrived, its halls and rooms filled with the sounds of the language, of correction, praise and censure, and of the bustling of feet rushing excited to a performance, or dragging when they had not been allotted one, or worse, had failed at one. Poets continued to produce exceptional works, and on two occasions, when it became impossible for the Assembly to resolve issues that cropped up in writing and editing, Akattiyan appealed to Lord Shambhu, who came to the Assembly's aid.

Many long years passed, and the Assembly changed locations; when the first was destroyed by the sea rushing in and swallowing everything in its path, the second was started further inland. That one was destroyed when the Earth opened her jaws wide and gulped. It was decided to build the third Assembly in Madurai, inside the temple of the Goddess Meenakshi, but this time, to the request to once again lead, Akattiyan said, 'No more.' The poet Nakkeeran was then chosen to fill this role. Akattiyan said that he believed a woman should lead, and nominated two that he considered most capable of the work required. But neither of them wanted the bother of dealing with the egos of poets or the tedium of administration and, most of all, neither wanted to give up her nomadic life.

Akattiyan left Madurai and returned to Pothigai. There he grew silent, having had his fill of the sound of languages and grammars, and his tongue grew lighter, his ears quicker. He was content and happy, as he waited for the god who had taught him this beloved language—the treasure that he brought home, the alms that he reverentially placed in the empty bowl in the bare hands of the Goddess of the South, making her smile and put on bangles and dance.

In the years that followed, Nakkeeran proved to be an efficient leader, and though rule-bound, his loyalty to the language was never in doubt. But then, a new kind of problem beset the Assembly. Nakkeran prayed to Lord Shambhu, as Akattiyan had before him. The Lord appeared in Nakkeeran's dream and said that he would not go to the Assembly this time. He said that the boy god, who had made the language that was the life-breath of the Assembly, was himself on Bhu, and he must be asked to solve the problem. He appeared again, in the poet's dream later the same night, to warn him, 'Murugan loves tricks, he will play games with you, be alert.'

1

PAZHANI

It was Narada, of course—he was the one that always brought the props for these divine plot turns. Whoever allotted him that task knew what they were doing. If someone asked him how it felt to be the sutradhara of numberless little and big calamities, Narada simply said, *Narayana, Narayana*, and moved off with an air of detachment.

He felt nothing for those whose lives were turned inside out by these upheavals he initiated because he was a great believer in Fate—nor did he feel any anxiety about it, because he saw himself as beyond its grasp. One day, Fate would take hold of him and dunk him in Time's swirl, which gathered and dispersed past, present and future in endless ripples. And when he sputtered and gasped his way back to the surface, he would not be Narada, the divine sage; he would be a woman, someone's wife and the mother of many children, and he would live like that till Narayana, his god, snapped him out of this event that Fate had kept readied, just for him. After that, Narada would feel sorry for the lives his props had dissolved in the way that navasara dissolves metal, in the beaker of a rasavadi, attempting to transform it into gold. But when he brought the prop to upturn Murugan's life, none of this had yet come to pass.

They all knew what needed to happen: the boy had to be tossed out of the pouch of love that held him back from himself, to enable his transformation into what he must be if the Asura king's condition was to be fulfilled. The list of those who knew this is long, but what is important is not who knew, but the fact that the little boy did not. He was not yet six, he was happy, cocooned in the indulgence of everyone and everything that lived in and around Kailasa.

Murugan was at play when it happened. He was squatting in a patch of sunlight, absorbed in building a chariot: four big, round seeds for wheels, pressed into twigs planed down by Mother Dhumra, a large slit-open seed pod for a body. He was trying to balance a twig with a tiny leaf that he said was a flag. When Murugan was doing something, he became quiet and happy: he would simply redo whatever wasn't working, calmly, over and over, without asking for help or advice.

On the day it happened, Murugan's chariot was doing alright—all the parts were to scale and holding together, except the flag. He had tried everything, but the twig stuck into the space between the seed-pod body and the wheels would not stand, not even when he tied it to the reins or stuck it into the wooden horse's ears. He looked around, and then he had an idea. He covered his mouth with one hand to muffle his giggles and began to walk around, stopping to pick up things, then putting them down with loud exclamations of 'This won't do'. Every now and then, out of the corner of his eyes, he looked towards Paravani, who was slumbering in the sun. In the sunlight, his feathers rippled gold, silver, blue, green. He took a deep breath, pulled his lips down in a show of sadness, made his shoulders slouch, and began walking towards Paravani, his feet dragging, his face long. He plonked down next to the peacock and let out a huge sigh. Paravani felt the laughter stir in his belly, but asked in a serious voice, 'Muruga, what is it? What happened?'

Murugan's voice was barely audible. 'I'm building a chariot, and it's all done, but I don't have a flag. I put a twig, but it won't stand, then I tried a flower, but nothing's working. I think I'll just forget it; I don't think I can get a flag. Where else can I look now?'

Paravani asked with a straight face, 'Have you asked your mother for a hair pin? Or your father for one of those needles he uses to clean his chillum? Or—'

Murugan interrupted, 'No, no, those are too dull, I need something shiny, something that will catch the light and shine bright. And it can't be heavy, like metal.'

'Oh,' replied Paravani, 'where can we go for something like that? Maybe they have something in heaven, but we're not allowed to go there.'

'No, no,' Murugan said. He stroked the bird's back. 'I'm sure there's something somewhere nearby.'

'Okay,' said Paravani, 'you go look, I'm going back to sleep.'

'No, no, Paravani, you have to help me, no one else will. Everyone is busy today, and Anna is not here either. If he was here, I wouldn't have troubled you.'

'Ha ha ha,' Paravani finally burst out. 'As if I don't know what you want. You're a wicked little boy. How could you even think of plucking my feathers?'

Murugan's face darkened, his eyes narrowed, and in a moment, he would have burst into tears. But, at that moment, Paravani stood up and shook himself, and a small iridescent feather fell into the child's hands. He stood up and danced around Paravani. He kissed the bird's face and ran off.

As all of this was unfolding, Narada was with the boy's parents, telling them that it was time. 'Don't look like that, you know it has to be done.'

The little boy, unaware, had built his chariot and was now drawing a boundary around it. He was smiling and humming to himself. When he heard the sound of Mushika's snort, and the patter of his feet and hands, his face lit up. Clapping, he called out, 'Anna, Anna, come see my chariot!' Ganesha knew what would soon happen, and had left at dawn to meet their uncle and aunt. They had comforted him, and eventually the elephant-headed god had calmed down, but he had not eaten. *No food in the days to come, not for forty days.*

Ganesha turned to his brother as Murugan came running and grabbed his hand. 'See, see, my chariot.' Ganesha knelt down and looked at the construction, with its sparkling feather-flag, and his sadness left him, like water rushing out of a just-unclogged canal. Kandhan was inventive, he would invent a way to get over what was going to happen to him. He said, 'Kandha, this is a strong chariot, and this flag is such a good idea. Did you have to persuade Paravani to part with it?' He knew Murugan thought he had tricked Paravani and the great peacock had tricked Murugan into thinking that he did not know. *What a pair!*

Murugan giggled and said, 'I tricked him!'

Ganesha said, 'Come let's go in, I think we're wanted inside.'

'My chariot!' Murugan cried.

Ganesha gestured to the others around them and said, 'They're here, your chariot's safe.'

He took Murugan's hand and walked into the hall used for meetings. The boy hesitated when he saw the crowd of people, but in these situations, he had a way of sweeping the room in a half-circle through half-closed eyelids, so he knew who was where. The sage Narada was there, and that was enough to make Murugan want to leave, but his brother had him by the hand and in any case Mother would talk his ear off if he was rude.

Narada greeted them. 'Children of the parents of all creation, greetings from this humble wandering singer.'

Ganesha returned the salutation. 'Greetings, sage who can read time, devotee of the Lord Who Sleeps on Time.' He heard Murugan snort and squeezed his hand.

Murugan wore his polite face—a vapid expression, wide-open eyes—and made a movement with his head that looked less like a salute and more like he was shaking off a pesky fly. Without looking at Narada's face, he mumbled, 'Greetings, Sage.'

Narada had brought a fruit that, when eaten, would make the eater wise beyond measure. It could not be shared, he said; only one person could eat it. He added that their parents and aunt and uncle had turned it down because there was only one, so now, one of the two, Ganesha or Murugan, should take it, since no one else could contain that much wisdom.

Murugan fully expected that he would get it, because everyone always gave him special things, and the fruit seemed like part of the pampering he was used to. He thought Ganesha would say, 'Give it to Kandhan, he's the little one.' And his father and his mother would say, 'Give it to Kandhan.' But no one did.

Narada asked, 'Ganesha, what shall we do?'

The elephant-god replied, 'I don't know.' Ganesha's heart was racing, he felt faint. All he wanted was for this to be over.

By now, the hall was full. Narada turned to Shiva and Shakti and said, 'We could give it to Murugan, since he is the younger, but that would not be fair. Ganesha's fondness for food makes me think maybe we should give it to him.'

Murugan grit his teeth. *How dare he!* He stepped forward and said, 'Give it to me, I'll share it with Anna.'

'But, my child, it cannot be shared, only one person can eat it. This is the fruit of wisdom, it will blend with the nature of whoever eats it.'

Murugan grunted and turned, as if to leave the room, but Ganesha held him back with a hand on his shoulder. The boy slouched against him, leaning on his brother's thigh, his head reaching the other's waist. Their parents fidgeted, reaching for each other's hands. The father's face was still, though his heart was bursting. The mother's sadness spun in her belly, a typhoon snatching into it everything that she loved: her love for the world, for words, for Shambhu and for their other son, Ganesha—nothing else mattered now, except the sadness and the anger that Skanda, the six children she had embraced into one, would feel. This child who copied her ways, and in whose eyes she was the one who held everything together, he would soon be homeless, orphaned. With effort, she held back her anger, for her son was the only one who could stand against the mighty Surapadman, and everything he did reflected on her, for he was Kumara, son of the Mother. She had to contain her grief and her anger for now. It could destroy everything.

'I have a solution,' Narada was saying, 'let there be a competition!' A ripple of excitement went through the assembly. *A competition!* Between these two brothers who loved each other so much? What sort of competition would that be? Would Lord Shambhu and Mother Parvathy agree? It must have been evident that this was no game, for the very air was different.

Narada's suggestion was accepted. Murugan, of course, agreed. He delighted in competitions and had never lost one, not even the one against Veerabahu, the warrior that warriors feared.

The terms of the competition were very simple: whoever went around all the worlds thrice and returned first would win the prize.

Murugan looked at Paravani and the bird nodded back: *Ready!* They were always ready: if you woke Murugan from his sleep and said, 'race', he would be on Paravani's back before you finished. Every day, Murugan and Paravani went around the worlds, and every day they raced with Vayu, who rarely won. Not because he didn't want to, but because he could not summon up the kind of focus and stamina that the bird and boy could.

So, Murugan leapt on to Paravani's back, the peacock drew in his breath, shook out his mighty peacock feathers and soared into the blue sky above the golden mountain. The clouds moved out of their way; the wind lightened to let them gather speed. Paravani flew even faster than usual, urged on by Murugan—'Faster, faster'. This was his first real competition, he had to win. It wasn't about the fruit anyway, he was sure they would give it to him, he was the baby, after all. But he would not take it unless he won it. That would be wrong. Only, he *was* going to win. Every now and then, he craned to look back, but there was no sign of his Anna or Mushika. Murugan giggled, so slow they were.

They finished one circumlocution and a second, and as they went on their way, they could hear the Guardians of the Directions call loudly, 'Bravo, bravo, no one can beat this', 'The younger son is the winner', and so on. Murugan's chest swelled, and he felt warm, he laughed happily, Paravani joining in.

Then, they were done, all three rounds, and flew down towards Kailasa and the fruit. Murugan leapt off Paravani's back and ran into the hall, calling out, 'I'm back, I'm back! I won, where's my fruit', only to find his brother standing there with the fruit in his hand. How? How had he arrived before them? They had been nowhere in sight. Did they know routes that were hidden to everyone else? Had Anna used a trick, had he cheated? No, Anna would not cheat.

When Narada told him that his brother had made the worlds come to where he was, and had thus won, Murugan ignored him. What was he blabbering? He looked at Ganesha, but his brother remained silent. The sage continued, 'The Leader of the Ganas, the Elder, said that his parents are the Parents of Creation, and thus, to go around them was to go around all creation.'

Murugan felt as if someone had won a duel with him with their first strike; he heard jeers, though no one was so much as smiling. His breath rushed into his head, making it spin. He clenched his fists, and to Ganesha, whose eyes were on the little boy that he was raising like a real child, it seemed as if his own heart was in that clenched fist. Was this what you did to a child? Why had he done it? He shook his head to clear it. Kandhan had to transform, and this humiliation was the utprerakam, the catalyst, for his transformation—it would burn and dissolve his sense of self, and the dross would slough off.

It is difficult to describe what Murugan felt at that moment: he knew that his brother was right, but he knew that he was right too. He was ashamed that he had not had a single thought in his head, and had rushed off. And he was ashamed of what he was feeling: *Why had Anna done this to him? How could he? Didn't Anna know how bad he felt about losing? Didn't he know that he* never *lost? How could he bear to win with a trick?*

'Ganesha has won because he took only a tiny fraction of the time that Skanda took.' Narada smiled and looked at the fruit in Ganesha's hand, and continued, 'He needed only that much time, not because Mushika was swifter than Paravani, but because his mind is quicker than Skanda's.'

The crowd grew still. The eagerness with which they had reacted to the competition was now gone, and in its place a nameless dread filled the air. Murugan stood there for a while, unspeaking, then walked towards Paravani, his feet dragging, his stick in one hand, while the other clenched and hung loose at his side. His lips were set, his chest had caved in, and his waist had collapsed. But his eyes were dry.

Paravani's eyes stung. He wept to see Murugan looking defeated, it was like seeing the sun get speckled with grime, or a forest dry up all at once. He looked at Ganesha and caught him wiping his eyes. This could not be, this should not be, this little boy was the breath of the universes—the only one that the great Asura warrior considered worthy of combat. Kandhan could not, must not, slink out of his home. This was an important turn of events and it required fanfare. Paravani stood up, called out in his deafening voice, shook his feathers and spread them into a full fan of shimmering gold, silver, blue, green and grey.

Murugan's head shot up and his body transformed, his collapsed chest rising as the breath surged into it. He turned back, his face averted from his brother's, raised his dandam, like a hand, and pointed it towards his parents. With that, he walked away, unheeding as they called out to him. He stopped, put down the staff of akil and pulled off all his jewellery, the kundalam hanging from each ear, his armbands, bangles, bracelets, waistband, anklets, rings, the jewelled pins in his hair and, finally, the silken cloth that covered his lower body. He stood there naked, except for the thread across his chest, from which hung the pouch with the stylus. He removed that gently, and as the crowd watched, aghast, he held it upwards and it disappeared with a loud snap. His body was not even registering the cold, which on other days would have had him squealing, 'Cold, cold, cold, cold'. He went towards the chariot, built over long hours, and with one hard kick, broke it. Then he climbed on to Paravani's back and they rose into the sky, accompanied by loud wails and voices saying, 'Stop, come back, don't go.'

Narada stood watching the bird and boy disappear around the top of the great mountain. Then he turned and walked away, his long hair billowing behind him. The sun bowed to the sage from the sky, but he was blind and deaf to everything. Narada was tired. Something about the way the child had stripped himself had pierced through his ribs and struck his heart. His lips pressed shut, he continued to walk away from Kailasa, away from the competition. He had thought this would leave him unaffected, because what had to happen, had to happen. But it hadn't.

Though it had been explained before the competition, Murugan had believed in his heart that, no matter who won the contest, he would be given the fruit. He was *the child*. When that didn't happen, it was as if he had been unseated. He didn't know what to do with himself. Who was he? Kailasa was his home because he was Kumara, the child born to its householders, Shambhu and Parvathy. But now, it seemed that his parents had stopped parenting him in order to parent Creation, and he had no home. Walking away, Murugan did not look at his brother—he did not want to cry, he was angry. He wanted to stay angry.

Murugan's rage rose from him and lifted into the sky, like the mist hanging over a placid lake rises at the day's end and drifts over land. It ploughed up and upturned everything in its path, it raged on to the accompaniment of thunder and lightning.

All living things shivered in fright and cried out. The Guardians of the Directions sent their messengers on swift mounts to Vishnu, the One Who Keeps Order. He smiled and said to them, 'Go back to your places, no harm will come to you. This child has come to rearrange everything. What Skanda overturns in his anger, he will set right; he has his parents' rage but also their combined kindness. Remember how his anger with Indra dissipated as quickly as it grew? Skandagiri stands as witness to that day. You have my word, no harm will come to anything in any of the directions that you stand guard over. Now go in peace.' And they went away, holding on to those words, even as the worlds shook and trembled, for they remembered the incident with Indra and were calmed.

It was a long time ago. Kandhan had only just arrived on Kailasa. One day, he snuck out and told Paravani, 'Let's just go near the gods' home.' Paravani rolled his eyes and said, 'Kandha, you have been forbidden to go there.' Since that was Mother's instruction, Kandhan would not usually disobey, for he knew he would be punished. But today, she and Appa were both away. So, Paravani flew close to Svarloka and circled it, and though Kandhan was dying to investigate the shimmery glow, the soft tinkle and the fragrance that filled the air, he decided not to risk it. Yet.

As they flew on, below them, there rose up the peaks of Mount Meru. On the wind came a jumble of voices. Kandhan said to Paravani, 'Let's go down, don't let them see us.'

Paravani turned his feathers from their shiny gold and green and blue to the stark white-grey of the snow-tinged mountain. When they got close enough, Kandhan recognised Indra, king of the gods, and Vayu, Agni and Yama among the group. Their voices were clearer now. He said, 'Oh, they are talking about me!'

'What if,' Indra was asking, 'this child of Shiva and Parvathy is not strong enough to stand against the Asura?'

'Or, what if,' someone else said, 'he grows up to become a terror? As it is, he's locked up Brahma once and taken creation into his hands.'

'And I must say,' piped up Vayu, 'he did a better job of it than Brahma ever did. Everything was happy because the boy attended to everything.'

'That's not the point—' Indra began.

Someone else broke in, 'Of course, you're afraid you'll lose your throne to him, Indra, that's your constant fear, but not this boy, your throne is nothing to him.'

How could Kandhan resist intruding? How could he not be part of the scene in which he was being discussed?

'Paravani, they're talking about me,' he said. 'Let's go closer, and can you turn me into a fair, pale-faced, Sura-type child?'

Paravani laughed, and in an instant, Kandhan's glowing ebony had turned pale; his brown eyes paled too and took on a slight greenish tint. He was now clothed in brocade and adorned with jewels: chains around his neck, golden pins in his hair, rings, bangles, bracelets, anklets, waistband. On his feet were sandals, and on his forehead a long line of vermilion. He asked Paravani to set him down and to stay invisible, while he went and 'participated in the conversation', because that was the 'polite thing to do, as Mother said'.

He walked towards the gods, the sturdiness of his body disguised: his waist loose, his belly rolling. His left hand, however, still held the dandam of akil, the sap leaping. The boy looked at the gods and they looked at him; he neither hailed them nor introduced himself, but stopping a little distance away, asked loudly, 'So, which boy are you talking about?'

Indra and the other gods saw the dressed-up child and laughed. One of them said, 'No one.' They continued their conversation.

Kandhan called to them again. 'Look at me,' he said, 'when I talk to you. Do you know who I am?'

'Go home, little boy, you shouldn't be out here.' Indra's voice was high, impatient and snappy. He was turning back when Kandhan tapped his staff on the ground. The sound that ensued was deafening—a high-pitched hum that wound down and started, over and over again. The gods covered their ears. Indra stepped forward and said, 'Stop that! Who are you, you ill-mannered little boy? What do you want?'

Kandhan said, 'I can tell you who I am not; I am not you.' He started to guffaw at this, as if taken by the cleverness of what he had just said. He raised his staff and waved at them.

'Who are you,' another god called out, and Kandhan echoed him. 'Who are you? Who are you?' He took a step forward and Indra, whose ire was rising by the moment, cried, 'Stop where you are, don't come any further.'

Kandhan grinned. Paravani, still invisible, knew that grin. Thank god the boy's mother was away. Kandhan held his staff aloft and cackled with laughter. He began to whirl where he stood, calling out, 'Who are you? Who am I? Who are you?' Beating his thigh with his free hand, he opened his mouth and roared—not the roar of a child. He reached down and ripped up a part of the mountain's side and flung it in the air. It crashed back down with a thud as loud as the footfalls of a thousand charging elephants. The gods were caught in a rain of boulders, mud, pebbles, rocks, and struggled to call to their lips the words with which to invoke a protective shield overhead. Indra was trembling with rage. He clenched both hands, stamped his foot and was instantly transformed into a white ram, as tall as a battle horse, with massive curling horns and hooves that thundered towards the boy.

Paravani could hear Kandhan giggling, 'Come on, come on, just a little closer.' As Indra, on ram hooves, in his ram body, ran at Kandhan, his ram horns aiming to scoop up the annoying boy and fling him into the air, Kandhan stepped aside, and pressing his dandam into the ground, vaulted onto the back of the charging animal. He held it by the horns and ordered, 'Stop!'

Indra's head was reeling, his hooves dragged, and he felt as if he would go careening into the abyss. He shut his eyes and called for his guru. Brihaspati appeared instantly between the ram and the precipice. In that instant, Kandhan snapped out of the disguise and sat smiling, his skin brown, his eyes black, his waist taut, his shoulders squared, his chest rising and falling with his exertions. He leapt off the back of the king of the gods and saluted the Sura guru. 'Greetings, wise Brihaspati, who sees what is, as it should be.'

Brihaspati saw the boy's hand go to the thread running from his shoulder to his waist, on which was strung the stylus of silver and copper and gold that he and Shukracharya had given him. He felt as if Kandhan had wrapped him in a warm shawl. He folded his hands and said, 'Greetings, Skanda, wise beyond your years, forgive the gods who unknowingly became part of your little game today.'

The old man gestured to the debris and Kandhan waved his dandam of akil. Instead of returning to their original positions on the mountain, the large sheets of ripped mountain flank, the huge boulders, the scattered debris and rock dust, all rose into the air and settled next to Meru, as another mountain. Brihaspati folded his hands and said, 'This peak will henceforth be known as Skandagiri.'

Paravani became visible again and spread his feathers, and Kandhan climbed on and raced off back home, while the gods stood, thanking their guru for his timely intervention.

It was this that Vishnu wanted the gods and the Guardians of the Directions to remember, so that they would be reassured.

The enormous span of Paravani's wings took them far away from what had been their home for three years.

Bile filled Murugan's chest and throat and spewed from his mouth. As they flew, banners of green and black vomit streamed behind them. Paravani was worried but did not speak—*this is as it should be, the boy has to empty himself.*

Eventually, Murugan asked Paravani to stop somewhere. The peacock found a hilltop, its sides soft with spring grass, its trees leafed, flowered and fruited, streams running down its sides. Murugan had to hold on to Paravani's back to dismount. As soon as his little feet touched the ground, the hill exploded, boulders rocketed skywards, the streams began to boil, the green grass charred, and the ground reverberated with the sound of its own spasms. Murugan stood impassively. He raised his dandam and let out a roar that made the feathers on Paravani's body retract. The clouds shot off in fright, leaving the sun uncovered and shivering. The agitated strands of wind became tangled. Then, Murugan shook himself, as if waking from sleep or a dream. His eyes settled back in their sockets, he arched his body like a cat and stretched like a dog, and saying, 'Let's go,' he climbed on to Paravani's back. As they rose into the sky, he looked down and waved his staff. The hill gathered itself: boulders rolled into the depressions of their old homes, the dead things came back to life, the streams returned to their banks and the wind blew smoothly again.

They flew on, not stopping to rest or to refresh themselves till they had covered the distance between the head and tail of the land. Murugan remembered the time he had flown in the opposite direction and began to cry, a long wail that made those who heard it clutch their bellies and shiver. On Pothigai mountain, far south of where Murugan was, Ganesha too clutched his belly, empty since the time he had walked out of Kailasa, following Murugan's departure, and wailed.

Murugan and Paravani passed the forests where he had grown up, where he had spent two happy years, and the forests recognised the little boy whose proximity had made them flower and fruit and grow, as if he was running not on the forest floor but inside them, saying grow, grow, grow, and they rustled and called, and he waved his staff in acknowledgement.

His anger swelled and billowed again. This had been his home, he had been happy here, all six of him, and they had come and taken him away to the highest place in the land, and he had half frozen to death, and then, just when he was getting used to it, they had chased him out of there. What were these people? What was *he*? Like a lifeless thing, he had let himself be transported here and there. This was the last time, he decided. After this, he would make a home that was his alone, to which no one would dare lay claim.

Soon, they came out over habitats in the valleys, where streams and rivers flowed. Murugan's heart slowed, he felt warm, as if he were standing over the steam rising up from boiling water. His eyes, nose and belly stung, saliva formed in his dry mouth. His body shook and he felt like vomiting again. 'Paravani,' he said, 'stop, stop, let's go down; there's something here, it's … it's calling, Paravani. Let's see.'

The bird began to descend. As they flew lower, they saw the hill: squat, stony, shimmering in the sun, waves of heat soaring up and colouring the invisible air a rippling, silvery grey. The heat hit Murugan, and he recoiled. It was the opposite of what his body had done when he first reached Kailasa—there, it had wanted to curl up and grow warm, and here, it wanted to shed everything, all its layers of skin and fat and blood and marrow, because everything burnt. A whimper escaped his lips and Paravani hesitated, but Murugan said, 'Go down, land there. This is going to be my home.' As they went lower, Paravani felt Murugan's hands tremble violently on his neck. *Poor boy*, he thought, *poor little boy*, but he neither slowed nor spoke.

The hill steamed, and there was nothing to lessen or to take the mind off the heat: no trees and no shade, no birds, no fruit-bearing creepers, no hill stream, nor any hill creatures. It was as if this hill had repelled everything—there was nothing on it, except Murugan and Paravani.

With every step he took on the burning stone, his feet hurt less; he stood for a long time, leaning on the dandam, the sun overhead scorched him, but he did not move. When he suddenly crumpled in a heap, Paravani did not cover him with the cool shade of his wings. The boy lay in a swoon for long hours. When he came out of his faint, the image of the competition came rushing into his head, and he jumped up and began to race up and down the hill. When his lungs hurt, he slowed to a walk, and then he began to run again. He walked, ran, clambered, sat down, got up again, and went on and on. He wished his mind would cloud up so the pain might decrease, but the hill would not let him: it was as if it had known the day would come when this boy would need its burn, and it had stood accumulating this heat.

At the end of forty days, Murugan finally stopped and sat down and heaved a sigh: *it was done*. He had tasted the fruit of his defeat, bitten into it, chewed, swallowed and digested it. In this time, he had relived the scenes of his life up until his defeat and had sloughed off each day, another layer of that former life. Now, here he was, no longer the same. He rose and went up to a little cave hidden by rocks, slid inside it and fell asleep.

He slept for a long time. When he woke, Murugan saw that hundreds of worms had burrowed out from the earth and formed a mattress under him. He smiled and clapped his hands—his first laugh after leaving Kailasa. His laughter seeped into the fiery hill, and when the coolness reached its heart, the hill changed: grass and bushes sprouted, flowers budded and opened, birds flew down to perch on the bushes, bees and flies buzzed towards the honey of those flowers, clouds gathered overhead and drizzled rain on the hill. Up in the sky, the sliver of moon lingered, while the sun appeared over the horizon.

Murugan spun in the shower of rainwater. He scooped up a little mud and rubbed the grime off his body, until the faint reddish-black of his skin shone through. The rain stopped, and the little naked boy sat under the sun drying himself. He closed his eyes and breathed in deep, then knelt down and pressed his lips to the stone of the hill. He sat down on a cool rock and said, 'You are the fruit, you are wisdom, the fruit of wisdom, *pazham nee*,' he said. '*Pazhani,* my hill, my home.'

2

KUZHANTHAI THEIVAM

When Murugan's anger had run itself out and he stopped running, his legs trembled, not knowing why they had stopped, his chest protested at the vacuum left behind when the rage vacated. He sighed at the helplessness he was feeling. *What now? What should he do? What was he waiting for?* What was this feeling that something else needed to be done? Something to mark what had gone before from what was about to start. He wanted someone to announce the change of scene, to give him the appropriate costume, props and dialogue. Although, really, he was not going to speak, *enough of talk*.

He shut his eyes, and all the images that had been churning in his head slowed and gathered and, like butter in a churn, his brother's face appeared. He wanted to see his Anna. Murugan turned to tell Paravani to go look for him when they heard a familiar scuttling sound, a scrape and rustle, and then Ganesha was standing there, looking down at him.

When Ganesha put his foot down on the rock, it burnt his feet and turned them red, and he smiled: this was the hill punishing him for betraying his brother's trust. He picked up Murugan and held him against his chest. Murugan sighed. His brother's body was cool, so cool, and he smelt of vetiver. He wrapped his arms around his brother's neck and kissed him. 'Anna,' he said.

Still holding Murugan, Ganesha sat down on an outcrop. He rocked his little brother in his arms and said, 'It's over, Kandha, it's over.' He felt the thin child body shudder, the bones poking into his own flesh, now thinned by forty days of fasting.

Murugan fell asleep and Ganesha sat unmoving with the child in his arms. The hours passed, and it was only when the sun rose up high and stood over their heads that Murugan stirred and woke. He stood up and said, 'I am hungry.'

Ganesha said, 'I am too.'

He took a pouch tucked into the fold of his veshti, at his waist, drew from it the fruit of the competition, still luscious, and handed it to the little one, who took it, looked long at it, and flung it into the undergrowth. The older brother said, 'You are wise, Kandha, you will be the fruit of wisdom in the bellies of those who seek you. That fruit will drip its nectar into the hearts of those who climb, asking for nothing but to know you, and they will say, "Pazham nee". You are the fruit, and to them, this hill and you will not be separate.'

Murugan wanted food to eat, for himself and his Anna. Paravani was about to fly down to the village to bring something for them when Ganesha instructed him to also acquire a strong length of soft cord, a strip of white cloth and a sharp knife, *to mark out what had gone before from what was about to happen, a change of costume and role.*

The brothers ate their meal and rested. They were expecting a visitor, a little man of enormous intelligence, who had left his home in Pothigai several days ago, to walk towards this squat, rocky hill.

Akattiyan had said to Ganesha, *I will walk there. Everybody else has deliberately done something to ease their minds about Murugan's suffering; let my feet feel some of it too.* When he appeared, the siblings were waiting for him, refreshed after their first meal in forty days, and for Murugan, his first bath too. Akattiyan huffed his way up to the top, along the paths that snaked between rocks, and arrived at the wide-mouthed cave outside which Paravani waited.

He was panting a little. When he stopped to catch his breath, Paravani laughed and said, 'The rice has been good to you.'

Akattiyan glared at him and quickly stepped inside the cave. Light streamed in through cracks in the rock, and Akattiyan saw the two brothers seated, one next to the other. He stumbled and stopped; his breath caught in his throat. The little boy who had apprenticed him on Kailasa and patiently taught him the language he had made up, had been like lightning—quick and unpredictable, full of laughter, his thick, wild curls tumbling down his shoulders and back. But now there was not a lock of hair on his head. His shaven scalp was rubbed over with sandal paste, and he wore nothing but a stretch of white cloth around his loins, looped through a thread knotted around his waist—a komanam.

As Akattiyan took in the sight of his Master, he saw that Murugan's eyes, which in Kailasa had always been wide with laughter, mischief or wonder, were half shut, as if that wonder was inside and the lids were trying to keep it from spilling out. The old man's breath tangled in his throat and his eyes filled up. *This little boy, this god who had given him the prize for his beloved land, look at him, he was like a bag of light.*

The old man sensed that the transformation of Murugan meant a change in his status too. As he half walked, half ran towards the boy, he expected a laugh, a child's tinkling, giggly laugh to ring out, and from the child mouth, the boisterous sound of Murugan's Tamizh to hail him, saying, 'Akattiya, Kuru Muni.' But Murugan was still, he neither spoke nor smiled.

The sage slowed. His heart stilled, as if the silence inside the cave had shamed its clamour. As he got closer, he felt like he was being embraced by the warmth of morning sunlight. He started, his hands went to his chest, and he said, '*Kuzhanthai theivame*.' His feet took him towards the boy, once his teacher, who had made him feel that he must make the most of every last matra of time spent with him, and filled him with eagerness to read, write and perfect the learning of sweet Tamizh. Now, the eyes of the child-god made him glad, as if they were assuring him that he had done well what had been asked of him. He just wanted to stand here, like this, looking at the bald-headed child, his staff of akil the only thing that remained from Kailasa. He heard the words, 'Akattiyare, *summa iru*.' *Be still, do nothing*, his god was saying, the child-god, the God of Tamizh, the God of Akattiyan.

A bird flew across the sage's vision, its wings turned to light by a ray of the passing sun, and disappeared before he could fully see it. He laid his head on the god's feet. Murugan bent down and laid his left hand on the sage's head, the thick, knotted, untidy hair fragrant with the smell of the vetiver that clung to everything that lived on Pothigai. He said, 'Go now, be still and wait. I have lessons to learn and another student to ready. When the time comes, I will meet you in Madurai on the Great Hill, and I will need your help once more.'

In the cave, the two brothers were quiet and still too. Eventually, Ganesha said, 'Kandha, you have become like this cave, retreating into itself. You have become alone, surrounded by a cave of nothing that will always stand between you and everything else. May you be known as Guha, the Great Cave.'

Murugan looked at his brother and smiled. He sensed that a lesson was coming, and he was glad that his brother was not making him talk. He knew this story would be about Surapadman. Such a major change could only have been necessary if it had to do with the reason why he had taken birth. Murugan was glad to be talking about the Asura king, he had thought about him often, on Kailasa.

'Kandha, Guha,' began Ganesha, 'you are different now, changed in these forty days. And now that your rage has calmed, do you see why you were so angry? Was it only that you felt we had let you down?'

Murugan cast his mind back to the day of the competition, the blinding disorientation. *What had he felt?* He had felt orphaned; he had felt as if he had been turned inside out, and the side that was exposed had nothing, no skills, no thought. He had felt shamed and humiliated by how his Anna's cleverness had left him looking like a simpleton given to thoughtless action. Yes! That was it. He had wondered why he had not been able to invent a way, as his brother had, for the situation that arose, instead following an oft-repeated reflex to take to the skies and speed away. That was what he was most ashamed of. He looked at Ganesha, who nodded and said, 'Yes. And henceforth, your mind will always look for the best way, before your body leaps into action.'

Murugan heard the words as if from a distance. He had thought this in those forty days, he had thought many things, and they had all settled inside the cave of his heart. Now he wanted to hear more about Surapadman.

Ganesha began, 'Let me tell you about the Great Asura, who is waiting for you to grow up. Let me tell you about his inventiveness, about how his mind leaps towards possibilities.

'You know that the Asura are women and men of keen vision whose minds are always seeking the elusive. Others, especially the Sura, might easily say that this or that is the best, or this or that is the truth, but the Asura always wonder about the possibility of something more or better. They build laboratories and observatories, they study and test, they calculate and tabulate their findings, and wait to see if their predictions are proved correct. To the Asura, searching is like breathing. And Surapadman, who, as you know, rose up out of the deepest part of the Vast, has a mind that leaps like the swirling waves from which he arose. His mind delights in inventing ways to search, as much as in formulating answers. Which is why, when King Dashagriva built his first Rudra veena and found that despite many trials and corrections, the sound was short of perfection, he requested Surapadman to help him out.

'Dashagriva's Rudra veena was built over many long months, its parts assembled with utmost precision and care. He was pleased with this magnificent instrument he had made in the name of the Lord of the Dance. One day, it was all done, and he sat down to play it. Gathered around were his scholarly wife, his dear brother, his golden-voiced son and his court, all eager to hear the sound of the instrument the king had been working on for so long. King Dashagriva raised his eyes to his audience, folded his hands in salutation, and then, evoking the Goddess who guarded his life and kingdom, he placed his hands on the veena and plucked out the notes. There was utter silence as the notes glided out, sweet, sonorous, gladdening to ear and heart. There were smiles on every face.'

Murugan smiled. He recalled the first time he had heard the Rakshasa king play, and he recalled the Ravana hatha, now left behind in Kailasa. He said, 'Anna, I want my things from Kailasa, especially my musical instruments, and the shoulder cloth that my Krittika mothers gave me. And my scrolls and styluses.'

Ganesha nodded. 'The story is not over, Kandha, let me finish. Because it is in the ending,' he said with a smile, 'that the lesson of this story lies.'

Murugan smiled and leaned back to hear him out. This is the story that Ganesha told him.

Everyone who heard the music that day was pleased, but not Dashagriva—his ears had heard something that shouldn't have been there: he sat with his brother, the inventor Kumbhakarna, and then with his wife and son, and the court musicians, but no one could hear what he thought he was hearing. They said that perhaps he had spent so much time on it, he was just imagining he heard a flaw, or maybe he just wanted an excuse to continue working on it. But the king would not let it go, and then it occurred to him that there was someone on Bhu whose hearing, like his sight and his speech, was perfect: the great Asura king. He sent his son, Indrajith, to the Asura court to request Surapadman to come and take a look.

The fabled pushpaka vimana carried Surapadman over the waters from his own island kingdom, Veeramahendrapuram, to Lanka. He brought with him a toolbox of copper, wrapped in soft brown leather and fitted into a bag that he wore belted on to his chest. The invisible lock of the toolbox opened only to a command in Surapadman's voice, and inside it were instruments of unimaginable finesse. As the flying chariot descended, fireworks rose up into the skies, garlanding it in many-coloured lights. Across the waters of the sea, in the slumbering town of Chendur, people looked up and marvelled.

The king's brother, Kumbhakarna, whose underground laboratory and work were the stuff of legends, was there to welcome Suran. His subterranean workplace was where he hid away from small talk, diplomatic missions, spies and warriors, all of which kept the kingdom going, surfacing only on select occasions, such as this.

When Suran later went down to Kumbhakarna's laboratory, his eyes widened, and he sat down on one of the stone benches to survey the fabulous workshop. A laugh escaped his lips: this was beyond anything he had imagined. Kumbhakarna's chest swelled with pride—he recognised that laugh, it was the delight of someone who looked at a well-stocked workshop and wanted to build something. 'What are you thinking?' he asked the visitor.

Suran, the wonder still in his eyes, said, 'Your brother has a vehicle that takes to the skies, why not give him one to plumb the depths of the ocean?'

'Come, see,' said Kumbhakarna, guffawing and unrolling a parchment.

Suran's eyes quickly went over the lines, curves and numbers. His hands shook with the strength of the delight he was feeling, the delight of meeting one with a mind that searches for ways to make real the things of dream.

They spread the parchment on the floor, went over the numbers and deliberations, and made fresh drawings in the fine sands spread out on the polished red floors of the laboratory. This they wiped and wrote over, again and again, until they were finally satisfied. A draughtsman was called in to copy the drawing on to parchment with a stylus dipped in ink made of the purple gorkai fruit. Then workers arrived and work began, and they worked without stop for three days and three nights, and then, it was ready: a vehicle for the depths of oceans and seas. It was shaped like a fish, its belly round and built of metals melted and infused with mixtures to keep it cool and light. It could hold four people, seated two-a-side, face-to-face, and as soon as it was placed in the water, its motors would turn and its engines fill with water, like a fish belly fills with sea foods. Once the door was closed, all a person had to do was to put in the heavy key, embossed with the name of the Lord of Lanka, and the metal underwater boat would descend, to float midway between surface and seabed.

King Ravana had no idea what was happening, but he understood that his brother and his friend shared a love for making things. This would be special, he knew.

Meanwhile, the thing that Suran had come there for, the Rudra veena—that was a story in itself. The day after he arrived, King Ravana led him to the music room, where the magnificent veena reclined. Suran looked at it and stood a moment, eyes shut, head tilted, as if listening to what the instrument was saying. Then he sat down and ran his hand over the long stem of the veena, pressed his ears to the two pots. He lifted the instrument onto his lap and ran a finger over the strings. The sound that came from them was the same sound that had seemed perfect to everyone but King Dashagriva. To his ears, the twang from the second string rose, but instead of rising and floating into the air, it stopped and looked back for the fraction of a matra before ascending again.

Suran heard it too. He did not waste time adjusting the frets or tightening the knobs, nor did he try changing the metal strings. Of course King Ravana would have tried all that. He looked at the king, who shrugged to say, *I don't know*. Suran asked the king to play, and there it was: the sound from the second string was a tiny part of a matra short of perfect timing. Again and again he played, and they heard from that one string a strange inflection, as if of regret. 'What is it,' Suran wondered aloud. 'Why is the sound reluctant to leave?' It was no flaw, for both the instrument and the musician were accomplished. And then, it came to him! He knew what was missing, and in that instant, his heart leapt and sank, then rose again, as if it had been lightened and given wings. He had sensed something: the time was drawing near for both himself and the glorious Dashagriva.

Surapadman turned to Queen Mandodari and said, 'Perhaps, if you played?' She sat down and took the veena on her lap, plucked the strings one by one, then played a snatch. Both Suran and Ravana sighed aloud: the sound from the second string rose, and raising its head and eyes to the skies, it flew on, free.

Ganesha waited for a while and then said, 'That, Kandha, is the man who has specified that he wants you to stand against him, and only when you are able to match him—attack for attack, answer for answer and seeing for seeing.' He stopped and looked at his brother, the bald-headed, komanam-wearing boy whose eyes were still, his admiration for the hero of the story clear in them. 'Kandha,' he asked, 'do you know what it is that Surapadman understood? And what was it he saw that made him sad and happy?'

Murugan continued to look away into the distance, the stick of akil held to his chest. 'Yes. Of the four strings on the veena, the second represents will and action, which are like parents. This was the first time the notes were going into the world from that veena, and it was only meet that they had the blessings of both Queen Mandodari and King Ravana.' Ganesha smiled, relieved that Murugan had spoken. He had not doubted that the boy knew.

'And what of the realisation that made the Asura both sad and happy?'

Murugan turned to his elder brother, and looking him in the eye said, 'He was not sure whether my will was firmed enough to make me persist in learning what I needed to. He was uncertain whether my actions made me capable of being a worthy opponent to him.'

Though Ganesha said nothing aloud, Murugan said, 'It is, Anna, and I will be; there is none I would rather prove myself to than King Surapadman.'

The two brothers sat in silence. Again, as if he had heard the question in Ganesha's head, Murugan said, 'I know I wished he could be my friend. But I no longer wish that.'

Afterwards, Murugan allowed his parents and the rest of his family and friends to visit him. *Let them set foot on Pazhani*, he said. That was his condition: that they trek up the hill on foot, not on their mounts. And climb they did, in the heat of the burning sun, past bushes of inhospitable thorns, snakes and peacocks. Pazhani was not big—in comparison to Kailasa, it was less than a sesame seed to a pumpkin—but never had these gods struggled so much.

Murugan stood where he could see the group. His hands clenched and tears sprang to his eyes when his mother, striding ahead of everyone, gasped. A thorn had pierced her foot and blood gushed out. But she walked on, with the thorn wedging in deeper and the blood leaving a trail, a miniature rivulet of red. Ganesha, Simha, Vishnu, Lakshmi, they all saw, and said and did nothing. But Shambhu! He could not bear it. He said, 'Uma, stop, let me take that out.' Vishnu laid a hand on his brother-in-law's arm. That was when they heard a scuttling sound and a porcupine appeared just ahead of them on the hill face. It stopped and glared at them. Body pulled back, ready to pounce, it waited, and Nandi said to the group, 'Stop!'

The little creature then made its way to the Mother of All Beings and placed one paw on her unharmed foot. She had to stop. The creature turned sideways and pressed against her foot, its quills out. It made a rubbing gesture, and the blood spurted from Parvathy's foot in an arch. The thorn fell out. On the spot where the blood had fallen, there sprang up bushes of bright green leaves and flowers the shade of blood. The porcupine made a porcupine-sound and Mother Parvathy reached down and touched its head. It scampered off. The wound closed.

It was the evening of the forty-first day since Murugan had left home, and for the first time, his mother smiled. On the top of the hill, the little boy who owned that hill smiled too. Soon, the hill and everything around it was ringing with his laughter. Ganesha sighed as he watched his family climb. The squat little hill was tricky, like the god who had come to live there: it hid its steepness, its slipperiness. When, panting and sweating, the group reached the top, everything that happens in a reconciliation happened and everyone heaved a sigh of relief.

The next day, the family was down in the foothills, in a grove. The townsfolk had cooked a feast for them, which they partook of, and then people came up to give them gifts, to be blessed, to make requests. One of them was a poet who wanted to recite a poem he had composed about Mother Parvathy just days ago. When the recitation was over, there was a collective sigh, for the poem had moved every heart. The poet looked at the goddess's face, he waited for praise from the lips he had described as the twin wings of the Bird of Wisdom. But before anyone could speak, they heard a shrill voice saying, 'Ah ha! What a poem! You should set a tune and sing it.'

They turned to see a little girl, sturdy like a young tree, walk out from behind some bushes of orange kanakambaram. Her hair was tangled around her face and back, and she wore a white kora cloth fastened around her waist. When she saw the motely gathering, her eyes widened, and like a swift sunbird, raced over them to settle on the little boy who sat between the two awe-inspiring adults. Her eyes went to the poet and returned to Murugan, who was now sitting up, smiling the smile of a child among adults at the appearance of another child. He tried to get up, but his mother's hand restrained him, and so he bit down his impatience. Perhaps this was some adult thing of etiquette because the girl was human? *Oh no! Was his mother going to conduct one of those tests of worthiness?* His eyes stayed on the little girl. Something told him that this girl, as little as he was, and with all the seriousness of an adult, would be equal to whatever his mother came up with.

He grinned; she frowned. Then, folding her hands, she greeted all the adults, her eyes returning to the poet once again. 'Sir,' she said, 'that was wonderful.' The poet, taken aback, opened his mouth to make what might have been a sarcastic comment, when Shiva asked gently, 'And what's your name, my dear?'

'Aambal,' she said, quickly adding, 'the dark one, not the pale one, the dark blue.'

Shiva laughed. 'Who named you?' He had that look of utter affection that Murugan recognised. If the girl asked for a boon now, she'd get it.

But she was not interested in asking for anything, it seemed. 'My father.'

'Is that because you're as pretty as a blue lily?'

Even before he could finish, she straightened up and said, 'No, it's because I am as strong as an aambal, which can grow anywhere, and which fights disease.'

Murugan liked Aambal. He wanted to jump down and go look at what she had been doing before she appeared here. But his mother was still holding him and her face didn't have his father's look of indulgence.

'Aambal, why did you say the poem is good?' Parvathy asked. 'And why do you think it should be a song rather than a poem?'

The girl stepped closer and said, 'Mother, the poem is good because its meaning is strong and its sound beautiful. This poet describes you as the Most Beautiful Woman because you make everything, not because of how you look. My mother also looks just as the poet describes you: face like the reflection of the moon in the water, rippling with concentration, arms like corded rope, taut with the strain of pulling and knotting.'

Murugan felt his mother's hand relaxing its hold on him. He could feel her whole body doing that smiling thing—it was the thing he liked best. When she smiled, her whole body smiled, and it skipped and jumped and leapt into whoever was nearby. Right now, the smile was calm, and it flowed like the slow warm of dawn's rays into Murugan's belly and his head, his face and the hand that gripped the stout staff of akil.

Mother gestured for the girl to come closer. 'Aambal, I like that, and I like the sound of your mother. You're a clever little girl, come now—tell everybody why this should be sung rather than recited.'

Aambal was nodding, her face serious. Standing still straighter, she said, 'The metre is more suited to a song, it has a song's gait, and the words seem made for upper and lower octaves. That's why.'

Ah! Murugan thought with glee, there's no getting the better of this one. He wanted to be friends with her. Then he stopped, and perhaps for the first time in his life, asked himself, *but will she be my friend*?

Meanwhile, because everybody was impressed with Aambal's answers and her manner, they asked who had taught her, and learnt that she was in a kalari, a school not only for learning the reading and writing of languages, but also preparing for life.

Nandi turned to them and said, 'You know the man who is her teacher, her aasaan—it is Bogar.'

And Shiva said, 'Ah! If it is he who teaches, no student will miss the questions inherent in the answers. No wonder Aambal speaks like this.'

'I want to go too! That's what I want to do. I want to join the kalari and study with Aambal's aasaan,' Murugan burst out.

Ganesha smiled. He had known, of course, that this would happen, but hadn't said a word when his family and friends were pondering how to find out if Murugan would go back to Kailasa with them. *Let them suffer a little*, he had thought, *it won't be even a thousandth of what I went through to play that trick on Murugan.*

His mother's arms were still holding Murugan. He tugged at the one that was around his waist and said, 'Mother, let me go, I want to go down.'

Murugan jumped off and hopped across to Aambal, stopping only to pick up his dandam. He slowed as he came to her. Ganesha, watching, saw how difficult it was for his brother to actually make a friend—that was what Murugan was about to do now. He stood on one leg, then the other. Aambal looked back at him, her face serious. He touched his belly and said, 'I'm Kandhan, Aambal. Will you be my friend?' He looked so uncertain that Ganesha laughed.

Aambal looked at him and said, 'I like you, Kandha, I'll be your friend. We can be friends. Do you want to see more peacocks? I can take you inside the forest if you want, there are so many.'

Murugan looked at his mother, who was smiling. 'Okay,' she said, 'but come back soon, there's work to do.'

Aambal took Murugan's hand and led him towards the forest. As they walked, she pointed out many things, but Murugan registered very little. He had never walked with another child, no one his size had held his hand before.

'Kandha, Kandha, dreaming or what?' Aambal was shaking his hand. 'Did you hear what I asked you?'

'What, what? What did you ask? I was listening to the birds.'

'Don't lie, Kandha, I saw your eyes, they were dreaming. I asked you if that stick is heavy. Why do you have to carry it?'

'My father gave it to me and said it's my weapon, and that I have to keep it with me always.'

'You're a god, no?' she asked frankly. She didn't bend and bow and speak in that small voice that people put on when they came face-to-face with Mother, Father and Anna.

'I'm a boy,' he replied.

'But that's Mother Parvathy, Father Shiva and the Most Holy Leader of the Ganas. They're gods, so you have to be a god, too. How can you not be?'

'Do you like gods?' Murugan asked, his voice just a tiny bit shaky.

Aambal, for the first time, smiled. 'Yes, I like gods, especially those three there. I go to the lake every morning to swim and to pluck the red lotuses to offer to your mother in the temple.'

Then she stopped and said, 'I like you also, Kandha.'

The boy tapped his staff on the forest floor and said, 'Really? Really? More than them? Or less?' She put her hand through his and said, 'Most of all.'

The two of them walked on, hand-in-hand, their stout ebony-dark bodies glowing with sweat. The little swaddle of rough cloth around their waists was the colour of elephant tusks.

Murugan said, 'I like the blue aambal best.'

And she giggled and said, 'You'd better!'

They walked a while. Suddenly, Aambal stopped and looked at Murugan. Raising her eyebrows, she held out her palms, face up, in a gesture of *what?* He realised that she was asking him if he knew where they were. When he shook his head to say, *no*, Aambal giggled and gave his arm a pinch. It felt like an ant bite.

'Silly,' she said, 'guess, guess.'

He felt warm in his face and chest. She confused him, this new friend. What could it be? Was this her home? No, they were in the forest. She was excited, her eyes were jumping, what could it be? Ah! Of course, that's what it was! 'Blue aambal!' he said loudly. She clapped and said, 'Yes!'

She darted around the corner and there it was, the lake. She kept running, shouting, 'Kandha, run, run, don't stop!' Then she was tugging the cloth from her waist, flinging it to the ground, folding her legs under her, and with a *splash!* she was in the water.

Murugan had stopped by the edge. When she came back up for air and saw him standing on the bank, she asked anxiously, 'Kandha, why didn't you jump? Come on, haven't you swum in a lake before?' He had, of course, he was born in water, and his Krittika mothers had taken him swimming in lakes, rivers, streams, waterfalls. He recalled the Gauri Kund, the steam rising, and for a moment, all the sadness he had set aside came back.

'Kandha, what happened?' Aambal was asking, and then she was next to him, holding his hand and shaking it. 'What happened? Are you scared, don't you know how to swim?'

'No, Aambal, it's nothing. I know how to swim, I'll jump in.' But he couldn't stop the tears from rolling down.

Aambal looked at him. 'Oh, Kandha, you're crying. Don't cry. Are you sad they're going back?' She wiped his tears, pulled off his waist cloth, flung it to the ground, and pulled him towards the lake. Still holding hands, they jumped in. The water was so cold that Murugan screamed and shivered, but then Aambal said, 'Look.' There they were, the blue lilies stretching on and on—that part of the lake was blue. 'Come, let's go and pluck some for your mother, and for all of them.'

They swam towards the flowers and she showed him how to dive right underneath and come up close to the stem, then pluck the lily at the notch of the joint of flower and stem. They went back with their arms full of blue aambal.

On the way, Aambal said, 'When Aasaan lets me go back home, do you want to come with me? Will you be allowed to? You will have to go to Kailasa, no?'

Murugan said, 'No.' With a striking movement of his staff, he added, 'I can go wherever I want. Take me home with you.'

That was how Aambal met Murugan and Murugan joined the kalari. On Pazhani, he had sloughed off his old life, like a snake does its old skin. In the kalari, under the kindly guidance of Aasaan, he underwent more moulting, and things became clearer. He felt settled, as if this was not an in-between place—that the kalari at the foothills of Pazhani was a place of stop, not pause. The kalari gave him the chance to be like others, and to be a part of others' lives. He was not the centre of everybody's attention. And that made him feel light and happy.

By the time Murugan reached Aasaan's kalari, word had got around that the divine visitors were headed there, and all the townsfolk had gathered to welcome them. They stood in front of the school, waiting, and hailed the gods that had come to their little town at the base of the hill, now called Pazhani, seeking out their aasaan. Reed mats were laid out for the visitors, who sat down and smiled at the people come to make their offerings, one by one, and stood with expectant eyes. Murugan was fidgeting as usual, but smiled at everybody, less because he was being polite and more because he was just so happy, with Aambal next to him. His mother was calm and smiling, as was his brother, but it was Father Shambhu who made everybody's hearts full. He laughed and downed each bowl of palm toddy handed to him, the liquid dribbling down his chin and onto his chest, till one of the elderly women sat next to him to occasionally wipe his lips and chin and chest, making Mother Parvathy smile. Murugan quietened down after a while, but his hand did not let go of Aambal's, and she half sat, half crouched next to him, her eyes looking away from anyone who looked in her direction.

A sudden commotion made everybody turn toward the forest path. An apparition rushed towards them, tall, taller than everyone there, her hair a mass of tangled jata, her clothes the colour of mud, one hand raised and holding aloft a staff of dull black; the ebony had rubbed against her hand, turning her palms blackish. She offered a cursory salutation to the Parents of the World and to the Leader of the Ganas before turning to Murugan: 'Aha! The God of the Kurinji, how long we have waited to see you here, even though you appear to us up on the hill.'

She stopped in front of him, and her body began to tremble and shake, her eyes rolling in their sockets. She began to strike the staff on the earth in a staccato beat, and was soon whirling round and round, the lengthy locks of her jata swirling in a wide arc around her. A frenzied chant came out of her mouth, like the sounds of forest birds and creatures. She spun and stamped, stomped and chanted, shouted and danced. Father Shambhu jumped up, and beating on the udkukkai strung to his waistcloth, began to dance too, his steps following her beat. The crowd stood as if turned to stone. Ganesha smiled. How often did one get to see something like this? A wild woman dancing with a wild god; he beyond time, and she who lived her entire life in anticipation of just such a day. A day when her god, who appeared in the mist, in the flowers and creatures of the hills, and spoke through her tongue to his people, would sit in front of her, in his very person.

The dancers slowly spun back to stillness, and the oracle stood before Murugan, her ancient face turned to his. Her eyes went from him to Aambal, and once again, she shivered violently. Hoisting her staff and looking at the girl, she said, 'Beware, be aware that life is at stake, count the measures, do not slip and do not let the slip fall upon him.'

Aambal wanted to move away, but stood frozen. She wanted to disappear but here she was, already at the centre of everybody's attention because she had arrived there holding the hand of the boy god, and now, the oracle, their oracle, was telling her to … to do what? Keep him *safe*?

The oracle touched Murugan on his bare shoulder, on his cheeks, ears, eyes, the top of his head, and then she knelt to place her head on his feet. A change came over Murugan as she kissed each dark little foot—he was smiling, his body still. He touched the white jata on her head, lifting up a few of its tangled locks in his hand. He said to her, 'Rise up, ancient one, rise up; I have heard you speak to me all these years, I have spoken in your mouth and you have spoken in my ears, you are the cord that knots me to the mud of the kurinji lands. Go in peace and wait till the hills burst into bloom, I will come to you then. Go now.' Bending down, he kissed the top of her head. She stood up, her eyes blazing, and stick high in the air, made a sound that was half a peacock's quivering cry and half the triumphant trumpeting of an elephant. Then she was off, running back the way she had come—into the great hills that were many times the height of Pazhani.

Murugan was to join the school right away. Aasaan assured the boy's parents that he would be fine, and so they all left, and then the townsfolk left as well. Aasaan had not said anything about Paravani, so he just stayed. Murugan told Aambal with relief that he had been prepared to protest if his beloved peacock was asked to leave.

Aambal shook her head and whispered, 'Spoilt! Spoilt little godling.'

He giggled and said, 'He's my best friend, we are always together.' Aambal looked at him and he quickly said, 'And now, you're also my best friend.'

She smiled.

Aasaan took the little boy around and told him the rules of the place. That was the start of the next ten-and-a-half years in the lives of Aambal and Murugan. Paravani decided that the school was much too noisy for him, and it was awkward to just sit around there. So he went off into the forest. If Murugan wanted him, all he had to do was call out.

Murugan liked his new life. Running around doing things, lessons, cooking, watering plants, going to the river to bathe with the other children. He liked that Aasaan was just as stern and just as loving with him as he was with the others. Before long, his fellow students forgot their self-consciousness around him.

As the days passed, and the weeks, Murugan grew accustomed to the ways of the other children. In Aambal and Murugan's age group were four others, who would all turn sixteen around the same time and leave the kalari to return to their homes. There was Kuyili, whose grandmother was one of the oldest people in the village and had been their chief for many years. Kuyili's parents were travelling bards but she wanted to be a soldier, taking after her maternal grandmother, two aunts and an uncle, all warriors who had never turned their back on a battle. Then, there was the Chera prince, Perunkadungko, who would return to be crowned next-in-line to the throne. There was Nanjil, both of whose parents had been spies and died horrible deaths after their enemies fed them a poison resistant to the antidotes they carried. His grandfather had left him at the kalari, knowing that Aasaan could make the boy put his grief and anger to use in understanding what he wanted from life, and he had: he began to pursue the knowledge of poisons and antidotes, determined to become a healer. Also in the group was Neeli, whose parents lived in the rich-soiled basin of the Kaviri, growing rice and pulses, and weaving cloth from cotton that they travelled to Madurai to sell. Neeli wanted to become a teacher, and unlike the rest of them, she would not leave when they did, for Aasaan had agreed to take her on as an apprentice. Among the six of them, there was unstated acceptance and loyalty, and good-natured competition.

There was another, who visited once in six months, twice a year, in the first five years that they were at the school. Thennan—Aasaan's grandson, a fair-skinned, delicate-boned little boy. His parents, Nani and Arivalan, came from Madurai to leave him with Aasaan before they made the trek across the Vindhyas to sell their wares: leather soft as cloth for coats and bags, and pliant skins for drums of many kinds, for hairbands, neckbands and chest bands.

Thennan was different from the children at the kalari. His hair and body smelt fragrant and he spoke softly. The words he used were city words—his metaphors had temple towers, market lanes, pearls, rubies, granaries and suchlike. He went everywhere with Aambal and Murugan. They showed him how to climb the spreading arasamaram without getting bitten by fighter ants, and how to climb the 'sleep tree' without falling asleep, by biting on a bit of wild tamarind. He showed them how to pluck the marikozhunthu, crush it and rub it under their arms and on their wrists and necks, and how to make their voices lighter or heavier, or funny and screechy.

Thennan was a favourite with the younger children and with Kuyili's grandmother because he could sing. How he could sing! His voice fell into his listeners' ears and ran through their heads and bodies, making them want to join in or dance, and sometimes, to stand up and speak about battles and brave kings, or to whisper *Amma*, *Akka*, *Aththai*, *Paati* quietly as the tears bubbled inside their eyes. Whenever people praised his singing, Aambal and Murugan behaved as if they were the ones being commended.

But the year they all turned ten, Thennan stopped visiting. His parents had crossed the Vindhyas and settled in Magadha, for the trek became difficult when another child was born to them. Everyone missed him, but for Aambal and Murugan, it was as if something treasured had been taken away and hidden in a secret place. Sometimes Aasaan would get news of the family from people who had travelled to the northern lands. One year, Thennan's father, Aasaan's son, visited and brought gifts for all the children, beads and bangles, boxes of sweets, and for Aambal and Murugan, rolls of parchment and a stylus each. That night, they slept clutching their gifts, silent tears rolling on to their pillows.

At the kalari, Murugan was like all the other students: he sat and listened to the lessons, read aloud what he had traced out in the fine sand and spoke his defence or opposition to topics of discussion. Aasaan and all the grown-ups called him Murugan, and so Aambal did too, when they were with other people. But because she thought of him as 'Kandhan', sometimes that name slipped out of her mouth.

Aambal began to notice that there were evenings when she and the other children were occupied with games or gardening, but Kandhan sat under the peepal tree with Aasaan instead. At those times, Kandhan appeared to be teaching his teacher. When

Aambal asked him, he said, 'It's nothing, just talking Tamizh.' She felt left out, but her pride would not let her admit it even to herself. Occasionally, an old man would turn up. He was short and stout, with a protruding belly and thick white hair knotted into a bun at the top of his head. He would sit with Aasaan and Murugan.

When Aambal asked him who that was, Kandhan said, 'Akattiyan.' Aambal squealed, 'The one who wrote the *Akattiyam*? But he lives in Pothigai, how does he come here?'

Kandhan laughed and said, 'I suppose he flies or something.'

'On what?' Aambal demanded.

'On syllables of Tamizh,' he replied, laughing mirthfully.

She pinched him and walked off, muttering to herself.

Everyone that Aambal loved—her parents, her Aasaan and her grandmother, who could reel off the songs she had heard in her childhood—loved Tamizh. When she first heard Kandhan being called 'Tamizh Theivam', the God of Tamizh, she thought it was a joke. Then Aasaan told her the story of how Murugan had indeed made this language, 'which was the old made new', gathering its parts slowly and putting them into his belly, where they lay cooking for the equivalent of many thousand years of Bhu until he taught it to Kuru Muni, who taught it to others, who in turn took their learning to people across the lands of the South. As Aasaan described these marvels, she felt her heart skip and her chest swell with pride. For this boy, her friend, her best friend, was the god that the panar sang of, the god the oracles danced for, he was the god that the priests spoke of, but most of all, he was the God of Tamizh.

Sometimes though, when these images formed in her mind, the trees seemed to grow bigger and envelop the sky. The clouds covered the sun and the birds loomed over her, as if she were a tiny grasshopper, and the grass at her feet shot up, rising over her head. She felt she was growing smaller and smaller. She was smaller than a blade of grass, she thought, and Kandhan towered above her, an enormous banyan with ancient roots plunging through the red mud of her homeland. It was a strange feeling, for when they were studying, plucking fruit, watering plants or bathing, it wasn't like this: he was the slightly daft little boy, unsure of the ways of his classmates and of Aasaan and the villagers. The boy she had to instruct, sometimes secretly, in how to deal with the world.

Aambal shook her head briskly, as if she were tossing things out of it. She shut her eyes and said, 'Kandhan is my friend.' The sharp blades of grass scratched her legs as the wind blew, the giant birds shrank back to specks in the inverted cup of the sky. She shut her eyes and felt herself growing bigger, like a figure on the horizon that comes closer and closer. 'Kandhan is my friend,' she repeated, louder this time.

'Of course I'm your friend, Aambal.'

Kandhan! Where was he? Had he been here the whole time? Had he seen and heard everything she had thought? The little devil! She'd pinch him real hard. But where was he? She looked around, but he was nowhere to be seen. Silly! She was imagining things now.

One day, while they were clambering up a tree, Kandhan said, as if they had been talking about it earlier, 'Aambal, you are my friend. I gave up everything except Paravani and this staff of akil, when I left home. I left the world, then I found Pazhani, and Pazhani is my world, and you are the first human person to be my friend.'

Aambal looked away, she didn't want him to see her crying. 'Kandha, they say you love Tamizh more than anything else, is that true?'

He smiled and did not say anything.

So she asked again, 'Do you love Tamizh more than Pazhani? What about Paravani? And your Ammaappa and Anna? Do you love them less?'

Kandhan, his head going from side to side, his voice sing-song, mimicked her. 'What about Aambal? Do I love Aambal less than Tamizh, or the same, or more?'

'Uff, you're making fun of me. Wait, I'm going to come there and push you down.' She plucked a twig and chucked it at him, and he ducked.

It was after this that Aasaan told Aambal to attend the occasional sessions with Aasaan, him and Akattiyan, when the latter came to learn, and though she had a hard time keeping up with some of the conversation, she learnt many things that were not taught in class. And as she learnt more, she began to feel that perhaps there would come a time when she too would understand, just as well as they did.

When Murugan met Aambal, he felt something he had never known before: the thrill of being ordinary. To Aambal, he was a god only when she thought about it; in their everyday life, he was her friend, less clever than her in most things that they did together. He enjoyed the way she turned her serious face towards him and raised an eyebrow, asking, *Okay?* when Kuyili or one of the other children teased him, calling him 'little godling'.

Murugan liked being companioned; Aambal wanted to fill him in on everything, show him how to do things. If anyone laughed at him because he could not do something, Aambal told them off, but she would not let him be till he learnt it.

When his parents and others had left Pazhani after giving him into Aasaan's care, Murugan was not sad. There was a time when he would have been miserable, but Pazhani had taught him that he was different when he was all alone. And he now had a friend who was stubborn and clever and reminded him of his Mother: the same sharpness and kindness.

As time passed and Murugan grew older, things continued to shake their limbs and waken inside him, and he began to see more and more into all that his eyes fell on: what everything was becoming. When he first met Aambal, he heard the poetry resounding inside her. He heard secret numbers and charms speaking in whispers from the locked chest of Aasaan's memory.

Years passed, five and then another five, and he crossed his sixteenth year. Murugan had slowly been coming into himself, as rain comes into itself inside a cloud and begins to fall, fulfilling its own longing to mix with the red mud and rise inside the roots of plants and trees. During these years, Murugan often thought of that evening at Gauri Kund when Anna had told him the story of Creation, and of Surapadman. He would recall that he had asked, 'Why can't he be my friend?' On these occasions, he felt a vague disorientation, as if he was missing the nuance of a riddle. Sometimes he thought he felt flashes of realisation, but then they disappeared. He often reminded himself that this was a fight he could not lose, that now, though he no longer wanted to fight or best everybody, he had to win. That was what the waiting Asura wanted too.

Murugan understood that the Asura king had formed him as much as he had formed himself, with the conditions he had laid down: *the boy should not be all-knowing, though all knowing is inside him*. And it allowed him to enjoy feeling like everybody else, this feeling that he had to find his nature, and that there were things he still had to understand. He could turn his back on his godliness when he wanted to, and that was most of the time.

3

FRIENDSHIP

Murugan was son to the Parents of Creation. While he may not have awakened to all of himself, he had figured out how he could best fit into the life of the many worlds by the time he was five. For the most part, that meant he underplayed his godliness and gave free rein to his unlimited delight, his profuse affection, his vigorous stubbornness.

When he arrived on Kailasa, his powers were already fully formed: he could bring everything to a standstill, or burn it all up, and just as easily revive everything. Of his many powers, it was the faculty of hearing that was the most remarkable. The essence of things came to him unbidden, flowing into his ears as sound. He could hear the gait of what was inside each person, the rhythm that their bodies, hearts and mental faculties should step to, and the work they would do, if they were able to sense their own 'gati'.

When Aambal first appeared from behind the flowering kanakambaram, repeating to herself a line of the verse she had just heard, everybody else heard the line too. But into Murugan's ears there flowed the faint echo of the poems she could write in time to come. If she would. He also heard the sound of cymbals and the resound of a murasu. He understood that she would be important to him in the battle for which he was always in preparation for. He remembered this every day that he spent with Aambal.

Aambal's relationship with language was strange. Sometimes she just burst into verse and sang, clapping her hands for the beat. Or if someone bet that she couldn't make up a poem on something, she would scrunch up her face in anger and shut her eyes, and a poem would burst out of her mouth. The listeners would laugh with delight at having tricked her into making up a poem. But praise her for her skill, or say that she would grow up and become a poet, and she either ignored whoever had said it or walked away, snorting. In the time they were studying at the kalari, Murugan did everything to make Aambal take her ability seriously—tricks, threats, bets, bribes—and slowly, what she did to humour him began to thrill her too. She would take a jumble of images, add simile and metaphor, flavour with sound and spine with grammar, and create worlds of meaning that pleased not only her audience but also herself.

Between Murugan's persistence and Aasaan's careful grooming, Aambal transformed from an occasional versifier to a poet, aware of her strength and determined to make a name for herself.

In the years that they spent in the kalari, the fact that Murugan was not like the other students was largely forgotten. On occasion, however, as if according to a secret plan, he revealed to Aambal bits of his divine nature.

One day, Kuyili said that her family was going up to 'Velan's Hill' to deliver up an offering, and Aambal said, 'I have been up there only once, with my grandmother and parents, when I turned five. We walked to the holy hill.' She saw a strange smile on Murugan's lips and said, 'What, you don't believe me?'

He replied, tapping her back with the akil staff, 'No, of course I believe you, I was there.'

Aambal frowned. *What was he up to now? This boy, uff, he just couldn't be normal.* She decided to ignore him.

But Murugan wasn't done yet. 'And what happened?'

'Nothing happened. What will happen, Kandha, it was a temple, the oracle blessed us, we prayed and gave our offerings, and, and—' Aambal stopped suddenly. *How did he know, he wasn't even there.* 'Who told you?' she asked, glaring.

'Told me? Told me what?'

'Told you what happened.'

'You said nothing happened.' Little bursts of laughter spurted out of him now. 'If nothing happened, how would I hear about it?'

Aambal was watching his face, glowing with the white of all his teeth, the way he was grinning. Kuyili giggled, knowing that this would only end in one way, with Aambal lunging for Murugan and Murugan running off.

'So there *was* something!' Murugan was laughing away now.

Something had indeed happened on top of the hill of the God of the Hills, who danced on the tongues of oracles, whose eyes guarded the path of warriors and lovers and these lands where the purple kurinji blossomed once every twelve years. They had climbed for an hour-and-a-half through the thick forest, Father beating occasionally on the little tudi that he held, and Mother singing songs that praised the god for making the forest and filling it with animals and for holding his people close to his heart.

Near the top, where the thickets grew close together, their leaves curtaining what lay ahead, a stream pushed its way out from a crack in a rock. They could go no further without a sign that they had permission to enter. Before long, they heard a rustle and a brown-tailed squirrel paused, stared at them and scampered away. Aambal's grandmother folded her hands and said, 'He has given permission, let us go.' They picked their way through the thickets and tangled vines. If a twig scratched their skin, making it bleed, a leaf brushed against it, causing the wound to close. When they lost their way, some creature appeared and showed them a path hidden between bushes and thickets.

When they arrived at the top, in a thick grove of kadamba trees, there it stood: a little cave, a hollow on the side of the hill, over the moss-covered surfaces of which ferns and creepers ran wild. Fallen kadamba flowers had stained the moss red. Inside stood a lance, blackened with age, its tip blood-red from the kadamba flowers. The stem of the vel was twined with a garland of kadamba buds, around which nectar-hungry bees circled.

The family laid down their bundles. Aambal's mother took the tudi from her father and offered it at the foot of the vel, then all of them knelt and touched their foreheads to it. Grandmother opened the little containers of cooked rice and small portions of fish and meat, salted and dried forty days before this journey and flavoured with turmeric, pepper, cumin and garlic the night before they set out, along with millet and jaggery balls. Tearing off a large leaf from a plant, she placed everything on it, and added a few flowers that she picked from a bush. Aambal could not look away from the flowers, the vel, the offering. It was as if she had never been in a forest before or seen an offering, or heard her mother burst into song, or seen her father kneel and touch his head to the earth repeatedly. Something was different here.

Just then, Aambal saw *her* burst through the thickets, her matted locks swinging wildly, staff in hand. She strode in, all six feet of her, calling aloud, 'Vetri, vetri.' Her eyes scanned the visitors and fixed on Aambal. 'What do you have for him?'

The little girl pointed to the offerings and said, 'See.'

The oracle laughed, a soft, round laugh, like the rolling of fingers on the skin of a parai. 'No, what do *you* have?'

Aambal reached for her father's hand, and he said to the oracle, 'Holy one, this is our gift.'

The oracle laughed even louder, as if the hand that caressed the parai had slapped out a rough rhythm. 'No, she has something, and she cannot leave without leaving it here.'

The girl said, 'I want to go home.'

Father assured her, 'Shh, we will go home.'

Right then, there was loud rustling and a wild seval rose into the air, crowing—an arc of black and red that stretched through the air momentarily, a scarlet comb waving like a flag on a racing chariot. It landed near Aambal, touched its beak to her hand and disappeared. As it rose into the air, the girl's voice called out, 'Rooster red, rooster black, come to live on Velan's flag. Rooster black, rooster red, Velan's herald.'

The oracle shook her staff and called out, 'Vetri, vetri.' She reached over and touched Aambal's head with her free hand and said, 'See, I told you, you had something.'

That was what had happened. But nobody at school, not even Aasaan, knew of the incident. She asked him again, 'How do you know? Who told you?'

And Murugan said, 'I was there, and that was your first poem for me.'

Aambal said, 'You!' She grabbed a handful of his curly hair and tugged. 'As if! Liar! And that was not for you, it was for the Kurinji Kizhavan, the God of the Kurinji.'

Murugan sniggered as he darted away, and Kuyili laughed. Aambal remembered the touch of the rooster's beak, she remembered the way the oracle had insisted that she had brought something for the God of Hills. She looked at Murugan, who was looking away now, as if this conversation had never happened, and in his eyes was that look, as if he was straining to catch a faraway sound. She shivered, realising that she had, again, forgotten that he was not human.

'Aambal,' Murugan's voice pushed its way through her thoughts. 'Daydreaming as usual. You know that's what poets do, no? You have to admit you're a poet, otherwise no daydreaming for you.' And he was off before she could grab hold of his hair and pull.

They came unexpectedly, the three people on horseback. Aambal was on the veranda, lying in the sun with a day-old fever; Aasaan had taken the children to the river to bathe, while Kuyili's paatti sat with Aambal.

When they heard the sound of hooves, the old woman stepped out into the front yard. She did not recognise two of them, but the third was Akattiyar.

She said, 'Aasaan has just taken the children down to the river.'

The two people with Akattiyar, an elderly man and a younger woman, were both strong-bodied and tawny of skin. Aambal's eyes were on the woman. She looked to her like the idols of goddesses in the big temples. Her hair was braided into many strands and wrapped around her head, her eyes were long and shiny, she was wearing a waist cloth drawn between her legs and tucked at the back. A cloth went around her chest, binding her breasts.

When Aasaan arrived, he greeted them by name: Nakkeeran, Velliveethi. Aambal's hands trembled. Nakkeeran, the Grand Leader of the Great Assembly at Madurai, and Velliveethi! Who did not know Velliveethi's poems? Aasaan and the guests greeted one another with warm embraces. Aambal thought that, when they grew up and got separated and met again, she would embrace her friends like this.

The children stood around warming themselves in the sun. Aambal saw the three visitors' eyes fix on Murugan, and by the way he refused to look that way, she knew he was embarrassed. They did not turn away, as if they knew that he had to look their way eventually, and when he did, they folded their hands and greeted him with bent heads. Murugan grinned at them, as if he had just seen them.

The visitors joined the children and Aasaan for the afternoon meal: small chunks of meat and sweet potato cooked together with pods of garlic, green pepper, slivers of fresh turmeric, salt and a dash of roasted kayam, wrapped in leaves and cooked under the embers of a wood fire. To drink, there were pitchers of buttermilk mixed with roasted and powdered ginger, neem and sesame.

Before they ate, Aasaan asked Nakkeeran to 'speak to the food', and he smiled and in a voice that reminded Aambal of her grandfather, recited the little food-prayer known to all those who lived in the southern lands. The prayer praised the food made by the Great Parayan, who holds the parai close to his heart and dances through the fields, and Mari, the goddess who sends rain in the mouths of her parrots. It invited all beings to partake of the food.

Throughout lunch, Murugan studiously ignored the visitors, though they couldn't stop glancing at him. When the meal ended, Aasaan laid out mats for them in the shade of the trees and they fell asleep, tired from the journey. When they awoke, it was late evening. They sat with Aasaan as he supervised the children, and after dinner Aambal could hear them talking as she fell asleep. The next morning, as was the custom with visitors, the three taught the children one thing each: Nakkeeran taught them a new metre, Akattiyan taught them a way to bend one of the toughest rules about the metre, called the Unbending Ashoka Tree, and Velliveethi taught them how to work with androgyne verb variations.

The children were playing, and Aambal, who was feeling better now, was standing watching them, when Akattiyan came up to Murugan and said, 'Ayya.' The children laughed and Murugan went red. He said, 'Murugan, call me Murugan, or Kandhan, or,' he added with a smile, 'Guha.'

The sage was not disconcerted. 'Nakkeeran and Velliveethi want to speak with you. They have a favour to ask.'

The boy looked back at him seriously, his face settling into that look which made Aambal think of vast skies and the cave on the top of the hill. Remembering that Kandhan was a god made her feel a little left out. Was she always going to be left out like this, when she and Kandhan were in the company of other people?

Murugan noticed that many of the children had stopped playing and were watching. He fidgeted, his face flushing red, then he grabbed Aambal's hand and turning to Nakkeeran and Velliveethi said, 'This is my friend Aambal.'

The girl jumped back, but both Aasaan and the guests had turned to her. She snatched her hand from Murugan's grasp and hurriedly managed to put her hands together and bow. 'Greetings,' she said.

'And that,' Murugan continued, 'is Kuyili, you met her grandmother. This is Cheraman Perunkadungko, and this is Neeli.' The children, realising that they were going to have to greet the elders and who knows what else, quickly ran off to continue their games. Aambal was rooted to the spot because Murugan had her hand in a firm hold. She wanted to hear what they said, but she would have liked to be invisible.

'And what,' Velliveethi asked Aambal, 'do you like to study?'

Murugan answered in a voice unnecessarily loud, 'She makes up songs. Show them, Aambal, show them.'

Velliveethi nodded and said, 'Yes, recite something.'

Aambal wriggled and tried to look away, but Aasaan was looking at her. He said, 'Aambal, recite something.'

She muttered, 'Kandha, I'm going to kill you.' Then, turning to the older woman, who had heard the exchange and was smiling, she asked, 'What should I sing about? What language should I use: Tamizh, Vadamozhi or a Prakrutam?'

Velliveethi smiled and said, 'Tamizh, always.'

Aambal was happy, for though all the languages she had learnt from her parents and from Aasaan made her happy, Tamizh made her throat clearer, it made her chest feel wider and it made words pop into her head, like cotton popping out of ripe pods.

Velliveethi added, 'Sing about Tamizh.' Her eyes were on Murugan, whose lips had parted into a wide grin.

Aambal glared at him, then shut her eyes. Aasaan gestured to Akattiyan and the others to sit down; the other children continued playing and didn't mind them. Aambal's voice shook a little as she started. She kept her eyes trained away from both Murugan and the visitors, looking off into the distance. As she recited, it was clear that she was composing in the moment, and soon her voice grew stronger, the syllables of Tamizh ringing and resonating in the air. She spoke of the language transported in the heavy bags that its god had loaded on to the broad back of Kuru Muni. She spoke of how this god kept his eyes on those who spoke his language, and how he entered into the styluses and inkwells of poets. And how he waited to appear to his people as the elusive kurinji. When she ended with a line hailing herself, saying, *I have acquired only two of the ten poetic qualities and beg forgiveness for errors. Like the kurinji, my words are still young, and tended by my Aasaan, they will blossom in time*, the visitors smiled, and Aambal saw Velliveethi clapping Aasaan on the back. She felt happy.

Their eyes went from the little girl, whose words had recalled to them their childhoods, to the god, who was gazing at his friend with a look they envied. Murugan had been remarkably still as Aambal recited, and clapped loudly the moment she finished. He tapped his foot in the rhythm she had sung in and said, 'See, see! I told you!'

Afterwards, Aasaan drew Murugan aside and Aambal stood afar and watched: Kandhan was wearing his god-face. You would think he was made of wood—luscious, black-brown wood, saturated from below with red. Then Aasaan gestured to Aambal to come to them, and explained to her that the visitors had come to ask Murugan to go with them to the Great Assembly at Madurai. They wanted his help to solve a problem that Lord Shambhu had refused to help with. And Murugan had agreed, but he wanted Aambal to go with them.

Aambal's first thought was: Kandhan? But she caught herself, remembering the snatches of his godliness she had seen. He may be a little bit slow, he may not know that touching the iranaperi plant made you laugh and roll around like a mad person, he may not know the short paths from the town to the kalari, he may not know so many things that the other boys and girls knew, but Tamizh he knew.

Nakkeeran had been surprised when Lord Shambhu refused to come to the aid of the Assembly. He wondered whether the Lord was displeased with him, for he had come twice before, at the behest of Akattiyan. He had come, quietly solved the problem and disappeared, not even waiting for thanks. But this was different, he had said specifically that only Murugan could resolve this situation.

When the Assembly first started, its elders had a simple rule for selecting and rejecting poetic works. Poetry that was fit resonated, it opened and led the listener into a world where hidden and new aspects of the language and of poetic diction were revealed. If it offered nothing except the words, then it was unfit.

This process of selection gave rise to a set of guiding principles for poets, but as the seasons passed, it became apparent that these fluid guidelines had somehow coagulated into a template that more and more poets were fitting their words into.

With the result that they produced poems that could not be faulted by rules of composition, metrical requirements or any other formal poetic attributes, but they had nothing more. The elders despaired, and none more than Akattiyan, who felt responsible for the Assembly and the work it produced. He prayed to Lord Shambhu, who appeared in his dream and promised a resolution. True to his promise, the God of the Dance appeared at the Assembly, and he brought with him a slab of wood—a palakai large enough for a grown human to sit on. And he said to the Assembly that the palakai would expand as much as needed, but it would only allow those poets to sit whose poetry was worthy.

And so it was that many a poet was summarily unseated. The plank, which came to be called the 'Tamizh palakai', would shake and buck like a horse, and send those of dull words and little poetic skill flying through the air to land on the polished floors of the Assembly hall. The palakai became a good measure, and once more, poets were writing with vigour and discipline. They became like honey-drunk bees, intoxicated by the nectarine Tamizh that filled their hearts; they composed, transcribed and, in the rush to get back to writing, they deposited their completed manuscripts in a pile in the Assembly. To tell which was whose, or separate them by theme or by form, became a task that no one wanted to do, and was perhaps more than any one person, or two, or even a hundred could do. So, once again, Akattiyan called out to Lord Shambhu, and once again, the Lord promised to help. He appeared at the Assembly, this time in the guise of a wandering grammarian seeking his fortune. He proposed to the Assembly that he could tidy up the submissions if they were willing to employ him permanently. They didn't take him seriously, though they assented to him trying. But when, over the period of one night, he had separated the palm-leaf bundles by category and added extra leaves with the names of the poets, they knew that it was the Lord of Dance come to save them again.

This time, however, he had said no. Three poets, Kapilar, Nakkeeran and Paranar, had written three poetic works on Tamizh, and as was the custom, they each sat on the palakai with their works, and all three remained seated—all three were worthy. But the Assembly wanted one of them to be identified as the best. On other occasions, when such a selection was required, it was possible to make distinctions based on aspects like syntax, metre, metaphors. But this time, that was impossible, because no one in the Assembly could find fault in any of the three. The Lord told Nakkeeran that this was a problem that should be solved by the God of Tamizh himself, who was being schooled by Bogar. So, Nakkeeran sent word for Akattiyan and when he arrived, along with Velliveethi, they rode to Pazhani.

Murugan agreed to accompany them to Madurai, along with Aasaan and Aambal, to judge the three works. But, he said to Nakkeeran, 'I have a condition. If it is agreeable to you, only then will I accompany you. And the condition is this, that I will stuff my ears with soft cork, I will be blindfolded and I will not speak.' Nakkeeran frowned and opened his mouth to speak, but before he could protest, Velliveethi said, 'Yes, we accept your condition. We will understand by a sign that comes from you, what your judgement is.'

The next morning, they set out, Paravani carrying Murugan, Aasaan and Aambal, and the others on their horses. They arrived at Madurai when the sun was still halfway to noon and went straight to the Assembly. Murugan, the gleaming akil staff in one hand, a blindfold over his eyes, cork in his ears and his mouth shut, was led to the high seat where the leader of the Assembly sat. He ignored it, walking instead to the palakai, where it swayed gently in the breeze that blew in from the pond. The plank rustled and changed shape even as they watched, becoming a small square with just enough place for the little boy. It hummed softly.

Murugan saluted the Assembly, then raised his hands to his chest, in supplication to his brother, who was the beginner of all things. As the Assembly watched, the plank changed again, this time into a throne for the blind, deaf, mute boy clad in a single piece of white kora and holding a dandam in one hand. Paravani obligingly came and spread out his feathers in a giant fan of shimmering colours, causing the hundreds assembled there to gasp and clap. Aambal's eyes never left Murugan's face. She suspected that he could see through his blindfold, and sure enough, his face turned to her and the familiar smirk appeared.

The three poets read from their work. As Paranar read, tears trickled down Murugan's cheeks from under the blindfold, wetting it. The Assembly heaved a sigh, clenched their fists, what would be his reaction to the other two? Then Kapilar read, the boy's little fingers tapped his thigh, and tears seeped from under the blindfold. The audience could hardly bear the suspense anymore: what would be the reaction to the third? Then Nakkeeran read, and the boy shivered, the hair on his body stood up, and the tears flowed freely down his cheeks and his neck and onto his chest. Thus they found their winner. Akattiyan requested Murugan to take off his blindfold and to take the cork out of his ears, and speak to the Assembly. But he would do none of that.

Instead, he stood up, raised his dandam to make a sweeping gesture over the assembled people, and walked out. Aambal felt as if she was up on Pazhani hill on an evening when the winds blew in with a chill that made words rush into her mind, tumultuous like a mountain stream. It was only when she felt the tear drop from her eye that she realised she too was crying. She was glad that he could not see, this boy, he was going to now preen even more, *bah*! As her head rose, Murugan's head turned right towards her.

When they returned to Pazhani, it was as if the event had never occurred. Murugan went right back to being boisterous, loud, boyish.

When Aambal came to the kalari, Aasaan had known she would. Mother Parvathy had appeared to him in a dream, and the parrot on her wrist spoke: 'Wait for her, she will come to learn from you. Nurture her skill. You must find what it is, for she is to companion the Boy Weaponed with a Staff.'

Aasaan had found the skill: her way with words; it had not been difficult. What was difficult was to get Aambal to acknowledge that she had this skill. She would shy away, embarrassed, run off, impatient. It seemed like too much work and she did not like the attention. She could, if she wanted to, make up an antadi, twin lines or sets of four, that looped on and on, but ask her to recite or to compose, and she would shake her head and say, 'I can't.' But with Aasaan's gentle guidance and Murugan's aggressive campaigning, by the time Aambal was ready to leave the kalari, she was no longer shy about calling herself a 'poet' and acknowledging that she had enough mastery of it to work towards getting into the Great Assembly at Madurai.

Earlier, Murugan used to nag her: 'Aambal, sing a song' or 'Aambal, recite a poem'. His ask, worded like that, would only get a glare and a 'no'. But should he say that he was feeling sad, that he missed his brother or mother or the Matris, and ask if she would sing to him like they did, she would put her hand in his and repeat songs she had heard from her grandmother or her parents. And should he say to her that he bet she couldn't make up an antadi with twenty sets, all beginning with 'la', or one with every second line rhyming with progressing consonants, she would be off before he could finish, the words flowing out of her mouth, orderly but rushed, gushing as if from a wellspring. But should he say that she had a talent for words, like Kuyili with weaponry, she would just walk off. Over time, Murugan's persistent eliciting of the words, almost dragging them out of her mouth, worked. And as he watched from his cave on Pothigai, Ganesha was happy; Aambal's words needed to be masterful, for they had to guard the god of this language she loved.

There were some poems that Aambal made up, which were like distance markers on this journey of seeing herself as a poet. One time, Murugan had gone home to Kailasa and Aambal was walking back to the kalari from Kuyili's. She was humming to herself and trailing a stick behind her, striking with it, marking the beats. A loud whirring suddenly sounded, followed by a guffaw. Where was it coming from? She looked all around. Nothing. She recognised the mix of guffaw and giggle, of mocking and invitation, as Kandhan's. But where was he?

'Kandha,' she called, 'is that you? Where are you? I can't see you.' Then she called him by the name she always used when she was angry. Muruga. The Beautiful One. 'Muruga,' she called, 'Muruga!'

Again, the laugh. 'Here, here I am. Can't you see me?' More laughter. 'Call me,' he was telling her.

And she called, 'Murugaaaa, Murugaaa, Murugaa.' But there was no sign of him.

'Come on,' his voice came, 'not like that, with rhyme, rhythm and alliteration. Oh, and add a pun.' He giggled and she grit her teeth.

'I'm not a poet,' she said, stamping one foot, 'I can't.'

'Oh, don't be such a dullard. Of course you can, and if you're not a poet, how did you make up that dragonfly poem last week?'

'That wasn't a poem, Kandha, that was just fun.'

'Oh, really?' came his mocking voice. 'What was it then? A not-poem? Okay, call me in a not-poem, come on, come on, don't you want to see where I am? Or are you going to be dull and unspeaking?'

He could see she was getting furious. The pointing finger on her right hand was beginning to move, yes, there it was, tracing words in the air. He smiled. Murugan felt the import of what was going to happen, his eyes began to sting. *Good thing she couldn't see him crying, then it would be her turn to call him names.*

'It's fine, I'll go. Don't tire yourself thinking too much. You probably need to sit down and think and all that. Bye, I'm going,' he called out, and a whirring sounded in the air, tickling her ear and setting her teeth on edge.

She said, 'Uff, you think you're so smart, no? Well, I'm smarter than you, here's your poem.' And she proceeded to recite quick flowing words that spoke of how he may be called 'Guha' and be as dark and lonesome as that word meant, but when the fireflies of Tamizh left her lips and flew into his ears, he would become visible, because no one who cried could remain invisible, and he would be unveiled by his own language.

It happened in a flash. Before she had finished the last word, there was a gasp from him and a snapping as if of fingers. She saw above her, in the sky, a chariot drawn by two black steeds, as black as the mayi in her eyes, their bodies shining in the midday glow of the sun. Paravani stood at the helm, next to Murugan.

'Ha, ha,' he said, 'see! That's the first poem you've sang to me. Remember this day, don't forget that you said you couldn't and then you did.'

The chariot had landed by now. 'Come,' he said, 'let's go for a ride.'

She jumped on, joyous, and then they were soaring above the clouds. He asked again, 'How about one more poem? Don't you think this deserves a gift? For them,' he said, pointing to the magnificent steeds. 'For Kalam and Neram.'

'Kalam–Neram? Why are they named that?' Aambal asked, distracted by what the words suggested.

'Because the other two are called Kshema and Svasti,' he replied enigmatically.

'What are you saying? Always talking in stupid riddles. And I'm not reciting any more poems,' she added, pinching his arm, 'not another line.'

After the ride, Kandhan and Aambal headed for the kalari, while the chariot and steeds took to the air and returned to Kailasa, where they would remain till he grew up.

When they reached the kalari, there was someone waiting for Murugan. The visitor had been on his way to the kalari when he heard Aambal's recitation and stopped, noting the rhyming and counting the syllables, his fingers tapping out the beat on his ektara. He finished the last count—tricky, for it needed an unsounded space of insight, but her counting was faultless. She was the one! It came to Narada in a flash, he saw that not only did she have a way with words, but the words also had a way with her—*she was the companion.*

Narada knew without knowing why, that her sense of timing would at one time become a matter of life and death for them both. This knowing made it easier for him to approach Murugan, guilt over whose exile had been building in his heart, coating its muscle and cartilage. He wanted to be absolved, but did not know how to ask for forgiveness. He had never done it before because he had never been unsure about his actions.

The insight that came to him as Aambal finished reciting—he could offer that to the boy god and ask forgiveness. Narada followed Murugan, and though he had it all planned out in his head, the moment he was in front of the boy, who stood still, his eyes still, his hands and his breathing still, the dandam in his hand emitting the fragrance of akil, Narada's mouth would not open. How to ask forgiveness? And what was he asking to be forgiven for? He shook his head and said, 'Muruga, your friend has a way with words. She saw what was to happen before it came into being; the image of your tears filled her head, her words, before the tears filled your eyes.'

Narada did not usually share these insights that came to him unasked: he stored them away, for he knew the value of information. But he wanted, more than anything else, for the boy to look on him kindly, thank him and smile at him. He wanted to feel what others had said they felt when this boy acknowledged them: as if he had climbed into your ribs, hummed a lullaby to put himself to sleep inside your heart. When the sage finished speaking, Murugan smiled at him, he reached out and tapped his foot with the dandam and said, 'I am not angry with you anymore.'

On that day, Narada understood what Nandi had meant when he said, on the occasion of the competition, after Murugan had soared out of Kailasa on Paravani's back: 'Kandhan's affection can bend Fate and Death and Time.' A tremor started in Narada's eyes, tears rushed and plunged over the rim of his eyelids and tumbled down over his cheeks. He did not try and wipe them away, but stood there weeping, till his eyes shut and he dropped down to the soft mud floor of the kalari and slept, for the first time in his life. The sage had been created to bear witness to everything that happened in the many worlds, and he had never shut his eyes before. When he woke up, he understood why they said that Murugan gave you what you needed, in addition to what you asked for.

4

SETTING UP HOUSE

The sun rose and set, the seasons turned and the years passed, and it was time for Kandhan, Aambal and their four classmates to leave the kalari. They had all crossed sixteen, and completed the requirements of formal education; they had also learnt to read the elements inside and outside them. They knew how to speak and articulate in languages, to use their grammars in prose and verse; they also knew how to write apologies in the voice of silence, to edit and rework the scripts that they lived themselves into, and above all, they had earned the stamp of Aasaan's approval. When he said, 'You are fit', their hearts leapt, and when he placed his hands on their heads and spoke a blessing particular to them, their spines tightened, and they stood taller and felt stronger.

To Cheraman, he said, 'May the glory of your gentleness go before you and speak to the earth wherever your flag goes.' To Kuyili, he said, 'May the tiger and the leopard spirits guard your back and may the snake show you how to wait.' To Nanjil, he said, 'May the goddess of medicine, with her breastplate of leather, breathe in your fingers.' To Neeli, the future teacher, he said, 'May your words be armoured like the tortoise by the shell of understanding.' When it was Aambal's turn, he said, 'My child, may you attain the last of the ten poetic qualities.' And her mouth fell open, because the last time Aasaan had said anything about this, she was only at seven. To Kandhan, Aasaan said, 'May that which needs to melt, melt, and that which waits, may it mix and blend.'

After that, they went into the village to bid farewell to all those they had grown close to, and to purchase gifts to take back home with them.

Aambal was in a frenzy: she had so much to say to Kandhan. What were his plans? Could she ask him to go home with her? Would he be allowed to? She worried that he would forget her, she worried that she would not be allowed to even see him: at the school they were all equal, but what about the outside world? Would Kandhan even want to stay friends? And would he be allowed to? Even if they were friends, would she be able to remember to behave 'properly'?

Unexpectedly, Kandhan came to Aambal and said, 'I've taken permission, wrap up and come with me, I have to show you something.' When she did, Paravani was waiting, and Murugan asked, 'Front or back?' She considered: she was going to be scared, her fear of heights would shame her, better to clutch at Paravani's neck than Kandhan's back or waist and have him snigger … and in case she slipped, he could catch her if she was in front of him. *Oh, had she spoken aloud*? Kandhan was smirking.

'What are you sniggering for? I'll sit in front. I like to see where I'm going,' she said, and walked towards Paravani.

'Of course,' Kandhan said, his voice low and sweet, 'I know that; what else could it be? You're a champion of high flying, don't I know that?'

Aambal turned and lunged for his hair, but the sight of Aasaan watching them stopped her in her tracks. She muttered, 'You wait,' and climbed on.

Paravani sped over the clouds. The hills soon joined an unbroken range of mountains. The cold bit through Aambal's clothes and gnawed at her bones, the blood in her veins seemed to be freezing. She was shivering despite the thick upper cloth wrapped tight over her chest and around her waist. Kandhan, of course, did not feel the cold, having come from the highest mountain in creation. They flew due west and then south, over the thick forests towards Anaimudi, the rock face that rose into the sky in the shape of an elephant's forehead.

Aambal looked down, head swimming. These were sacred lands. The elephant-faced rock marked the regions where the hill people lived, lands so sacred that you could not set foot there without a guide and without the ritual forty days of prayer and rest. She smelt it, the grass and the flowers, the sharp, distinctive smell of the shola. What was that buzzing though?

'What's that sound, Kandha?' she shouted above the roaring wind.

And he shouted back, 'It's the bees; they've come for the kurinji.'

'But the kurinji will not bloom for two more moon cycles,' Aambal said, but Kandhan just laughed.

Paravani began to descend, wings sweeping against the wind. Aambal felt like her stomach would spill out of her mouth. She clutched at Paravani's neck and shouted, 'Kandha, Kandha,' and felt his arm around her waist, steadying her, his voice saying, 'Close your eyes Aambal, keep them closed.' She shut her eyes, and everything went blank, no light, no sound. The next thing Aambal knew, she was struggling to open her eyes. She could hear buzzing, rustling, popping, slithering. She opened her mouth to call to Kandhan and Paravani ... but why couldn't she speak? Her eyelids strained open. A little bit of light, blue above her, the sky!

Her head was heavy, and she had to exert herself to turn her head to the right. Kandhan was lying there, and the brown-green hill was now purple: the kurinji had sprung open, thousands of bees were buzzing around the flowers and circling Kandhan. They seemed to be flying through him, his ears, eyes, mouth, hands, chest ... his chest was bare. He was lying on his back, his long hair was untied and seemed to be alive with creatures. And the kurinji blossoms, had they flown through the sky and landed on him? Kandhan was draped in them, the pollen springing on their stamens. His hands held plants of kurinji, with their roots still encased in mud, as if they had simply risen and come to him. The hillside was moving, thousands of little creatures were rising from the mud in waves that washed over him. They were swimming into him, passing through skin and swimming out, as if there was a canal that went in and out of Kandhan, and these creatures—worms, bugs, bees, caterpillars, butterflies, dragonflies—were the water in it. Overhead, birds wheeled and called, and from lower down the slopes, bands of sure-footed tahr were climbing, and tigers, lions, elephants, wild geese were perched on rock faces, watching.

Aambal's mouth was moving. Kandha, Kandha, she could hear herself calling, but could he not hear her? *Aambal*, he said, *just lie still. I was waiting for you to wake up.* Aambal's breath stopped for a moment, what was she seeing? Kandhan was mud, these creatures were burrowing into and out of him, Kandhan's body *was* mud. She shook her head to clear it and looked again. He was not separate from the mud, grass, rock of the hill. It was like he and the mountain had merged, and he was transparent, and the mountain was transparent. She turned her head this way and the outline of the mountain slopes was inside Kandhan; she turned her head that way and his body was inside the mountain. Was she dreaming? Was she dead? Aambal felt as if she had turned to stone. She moved a hand to pinch herself when—

Yow, she yelled, as Kandhan's hand reached over and pinched her.

You're not dreaming, he said.

'What is this, Kandha?' she asked, her voice high and squeaky. Her heart flung itself against the barricade of her ribs, as if it would break through and escape.

Kandhan smiled and said, 'Aambal, do you remember you came here before? But you were there.' He pointed to the slope. 'And you could only climb till there. You would have stood at the edge of the kurinji, like at the edge of the sea.'

Aambal's hands unclenched. She had been right there, she recalled, the point from where you could see the slopes of all the mountain faces, purple with the kurinji flowers, their stems waving in the cold mountain breezes. Her father had hoisted her on to his shoulders and said, 'See how the hills have turned purple. This is the carpet for our Velan, the god with the vel, the god of our hills.' Aambal had been all of four then. Even the air and the sky had been purple, and the colour got into everyone's eyes, and they too had become purple. 'Kurinji-tinted, Velan-touched', her mother had said to her father, when Aambal called out, 'Amma, you're purple; look, Anbu is purple, we're all purple!' And now, after all these years, Aambal's eyes were full of kurinji-purple, and she recalled the name her mother had used. 'He is,' she had said, 'the Kurinji Kizhavan, the Hero of the Kurinji.'

Of course Kandhan would remind her he had been there! Aambal's irritation with her friend increased. 'He has to be in all the stories,' she muttered to herself. Her heartbeat was slowly settling down. The cold air caught at her nipples; she shivered and wrapped her arms around herself. Kandhan was sitting up now, and layers of little creatures fell off him and sank back into the earth, while more rose up from the mud, through the covering of thick grass, and streamed over him. The kurinji nodded, the bees circled around his head, hovered and dipped to touch his head or fly onto his lips. Paravani shook out his wings and began to dance.

The animals on the rocks called into the sky; the tahr ran along the rock as if it were even ground. Aambal felt the air growing still, the clouds slowing, she could feel her heart slowing. Her belly fluttered as if there was a shoal of tiny fish under her navel, and her head was beginning to feel cool, as if the mountain chill had blown through her skull and swept it clear. Now, something stirred: words! She heard 'kurinji' and 'slopes', then Kandhan was speaking, his voice like the humming of bees, the chattering of birds, like the roar of lions and tigers, the trumpeting of elephants, *he was talking to the animals.*

A fine drizzle fell, but the cold mountain wind froze the raindrops and they dropped with a tinkle like tiny shards of glass. Kandhan stretched out both his arms, and with a flurry of wings, birds of many kinds descended on him. In place of the little creatures, now there were toads, frogs, rabbits, deer, foxes and wolves, and these made way for the snakes swarming out from under rocks. A group of bright green snakes shot through the air, making Aambal cry out. Finally, herds of elephants that had climbed along the steep flanks of the mountain appeared over the slope. They knelt and trumpeted and poured over him waters they had carried from the lake inside the forbidden forest, which was home to them. Kandhan stood up, the akil dandam in one hand; he raised both arms over everything. There was a stilling, and then a sound like everything heaving a sigh. Paravani slowed and drew his wings back in, the clouds began to move along, and Kandhan said to Aambal, 'Come, let's go.' And she said, 'Yes,' though she had meant to say, 'Go where? Tell me what else you're going to do now.'

As Paravani ascended, Aambal looked down and saw that the purple had gone. The kurinji blossoms had closed back into buds.

They flew low over a mountainside, then Paravani landed and Kandhan got down. There came a mighty hiss, as a giant serpent sprung up, raising a giant hood. It rose up, the hood, a parasol over Kandhan's head. Kandhan bowed, and with folded hands said, 'Greetings, old one.' The snake hissed and the forest reverberated with the sound. There were more snakes all along the forest floor, and like the worms earlier, they too slithered up close, and Murugan raised his akil staff and spoke to them.

Then he took Aambal's hand—she clearly needed a hand—and led her into the forest, where the trees grew thick and close together, the rock faces were blackish green with moss and lichen, vines fell from trees, and the branches were all entangled. Paravani flew up into a tree and perched there. Kandhan stopped suddenly and said, 'Ah, here it is.' They were looking at a clump of rocks, one leaning against the other, a five-foot mound. At the base, there was a slight opening, maybe the thickness of a human hand. 'This is my cave,' he said.

'What? How do you go in? And come out?'

He laughed and pointed to the opening. 'Through there.'

She was scowling now. 'You have a trick to widen that?'

Smiling, he said, 'No, we have to narrow ourselves.'

'We? Count me out.'

'Alright, if you're okay to stay out by yourself, that's fine. The sun will go down in a while.'

Aambal looked around. It was getting dark, and what were all those sounds? Scampering, slithering, strange calls. 'Kandha, don't play the fool. I want to see too. I'm not scared, I can stay out here if I want to, but I want to go in, so show me how.'

Kandhan had flung off his head-covering and upper cloth long ago, his hair was hanging free. He pulled off the cloth around his waist and stood in a komanam, the strip of kora looped through the thick silver aranjanam chain at his waist and knotted at the back. 'You have to discard what you don't need.' His hand went to his waist, then he shook his head and said, 'Not this.' He looked at her and said, 'If you were not here, I would be naked.'

What could she discard? She wasn't going naked—she'd rather stay out of the cave. She looked at Kandhan, who smiled at her and said, 'Discard what you don't need.'

'Okay,' she said, and took off her shawl. 'Let's go.'

He asked, 'Are you sure you've discarded everything you don't need?'

Aambal looked down at herself, the red skirt and green blouse. That was staying, but her anklets, bangles, and the chain around her neck? She took them off and dropped them on the forest floor.

Even before she was done, he had slid through the small opening that was less an opening and more a crack. Only half his face was visible; that was how small it was. He said, 'Come.'

Aambal's hands itched to grab him through the crack and pinch him hard, but as if he knew, he moved back, his face out of reach. She said, 'Kandha, don't play tricks with me, how am I going to fit in there? You are a god, you can do all this.'

Kandhan's voice was serious when he said, 'Not a trick; anyone can do this—you just need to tell your body to narrow and take up less space.'

Aambal stared at the opening and shook her head. 'No, no, no, I can't. Kandha, if you're my friend, you won't do this to me.'

And then he was standing beside her, taking her hand and saying, 'Here, see.' He knelt and pulled her down. 'You go first. Close your eyes and imagine that your bones are fluid, as they are. The opening is not what you see, there is another that is of the same measure as the one who wants to enter. Fold your shoulders in, like the wings of a bird, close your eyes, empty your head, stretch it out as if it's the feeler of an insect, seeking.' His hand was at the nape of her neck. She shut her eyes and did as his voice directed. The rock felt soft, and when her head and shoulders and the top half of her body passed through, she was so taken aback that she opened her eyes and suddenly could not move. Kandhan said, 'Go in,' and she replied, 'I'm stuck.'

'You have to make the rocks let you pass,' he said. 'I can't do anything. I may be a god, but there are rules for these things.' She started to cry, and he put his hand on the middle of her back and said, 'Recite a poem, speak to it.'

Aambal opened her mouth to yell at him, but the words that had appeared and gone from her head on the slope of the purpled mountain were now on her tongue, sweet, so sweet that she didn't want them to leave. Tears stung her eyes as she heard her own voice reciting. She blinked at the sudden warmth as the rest of her slid inside the cave, Kandhan's cave, its concave ceiling and lumpy sides sparkling with hundreds of min-mini-poochi, their bodies glowing-unglowing-glowing, lit-unlit-lit-unlit.

Aambal wanted to ask Kandhan what was happening, but she said nothing, for when she looked at him, she forgot herself: fireflies perched here and there on his dark body, and it felt to her that she was looking at a stretch of night sky lit with stars. Kandhan stood there, his loincloth a bright patch, like a smile in the cave's black. In one hand, as always, was the akil dandam. It seemed to Aambal that it was not a staff of akil, but a man, his body resplendent and speckled with ash, coils of jata tumbling down his shoulders and back, and his arm around the waist of a woman as dark as he was pale. Aambal shook her head and heard Kandhan laugh.

'Aambal,' he said, making her sit down on the floor, which was warm, as if there was a fire somewhere below. 'Why do you think I brought you here?'

'I don't know, that's what I wanted to ask you—why did you bring me here?' She didn't say what she was thinking: that he had never shown her his godliness like this before, so why now.

'You're my best friend, Aambal, I can't hide from you, I am what I am. This is how everything reacts to me.' He was still holding her hand, and she said nothing because she had followed his breath as he spoke and sensed a pause, not a stop. Then he said, putting his other hand over hers, so that her writing hand lay between his two, like a pearl inside the twin mantles of an oyster, 'I wanted to show you the kurinji before anyone else saw it, Aambal.'

The fireflies crowded around to look at this woman who had sung the sweetest song they had heard in a long time, this woman who was dear to the one dearest to all living creatures. Aambal's eyes were on Kandhan, but her mind was back at the aambal pond, both of them diving and Kandhan screaming, 'Cold!' Everything that they had said and done together came rolling back into her head, her belly was still. *Something had changed.* She had heard the mountain flanks and the shola and all the little and big creatures speak. Aambal had heard their gait, felt their breath, it had gone into her ears and eyes and into her blood and bones, the very marrow, and it had taken her heart in its grip and opened its doors to leave something there. She could not see her own face, but the fireflies could, and so could Kandhan; it was like the hillside when the kurinji burst into flower all at once: it said *yes*, and *yes*.

She asked him, 'Kandha, what does all this mean? If you were here whenever the kurinji bloomed, how could you be a child when you came to the school?' But she knew what it meant and did not want to think about it—as if she could keep their friendship just the way it was, as long as she didn't think about it. And yet, it was something she had thought about before, something she had shoved down, submerged. Kandhan was God, he was everywhere, at all times. He was not prone to Time.

With the hunters, he was like them: roving, hidden, wild, with polished bones and wooden pins in his hair. He sat down with them and talked of the hunt, and as his father did, ate their offerings of meat and drank vigorous brews of aged flowers and herbs in honey, and of fresh palm toddy. He bent his head for them to decorate his neck and chest with the pastes of forest sandal, neem, and clay from the riverbeds. He sat still, humming aloud, while they knotted kadamba flowers into garlands for him. Sometimes, the old mothers untied his hair and combed it out and rubbed animal fat into it, and plaited it into many strands that fell down his back and bounced when he walked.

It was the hunters who gave him the name 'Velan' and 'Kurinji Kizhavan', and he owed them his allegiance. It was his duty to lead them to game, to fruit and tubers, to the heady nectars that fermented in flowers and on palms, and to paths that held their steps firm as they sped from approaching dangers and slowed them where rivers flowed or the trees were in bloom.

When the priests in the valleys lit their lamps and called to him in words taught and passed down, he went to them in spirit. When young women pined for him, hearing stories of his beautiful face, his golden speech and his cool embrace, he appeared to them, colourful cloths wrapped around his waist, his dark chest, on which hair curled like newly sprouted fern, covered with garlands of the red kadamba flowers, intoxicated bees spiralling around the blooms. And the women swooned against him, and spoke words that, when they woke, they would not remember.

He changed shape at will and joined the ranks of whoever called to him. She knew all this; her mother and grandmother, father, grandfather, everyone who lived in her beloved home by the sea knew this god. Was Kandhan really the one they spoke of? His eyes had not stirred from her face, and when she turned to him, he smiled. He was holding his breath, he was waiting. Aambal sat up straight and said, 'Vela.' Just the one word, then she placed her hand over his. And they sat like that for a while, disentangling their hands only when their wrists began to hurt.

Kandhan leaned back against the wall of the cave and tapped the stout stick twinkling with the scores of fireflies that had come to perch on it. Aambal waited. These were familiar signs, he was fidgeting, he had something to ask.

'Aambal, will you come and live with me?'

'In Kailasa?' Aambal's voice was squeaky and her eyes round. 'How can I? I'm human.'

He laughed and said, 'Not Kailasa, though humans do live there. Our Akattiyan, I met him there first. No, I mean here, in

Pazhani. I am going to live here, and I don't want you to go. I want you to come and live here and be my poet.'

Aambal's hands were at her chest now, she had to dam her heart's surge. She said nothing.

Kandhan said, 'And I want you to join the Great Assembly at Madurai. Don't you see, you have to? You must stay, you must come and live with me.'

'Live with you? In the palace?' asked Aambal, shaking her head. 'What about my parents? What about my family? My life?'

'How about if I marry you?' Murugan asked, and before she could open her mouth, he said, 'Wait, wait, don't say it. I'm rephrasing my question. How about if you marry me?'

'Muruga!' Aambal's voice was high. 'I don't want to marry anyone, and you're my friend, why would I marry you?'

At any other time, she would have called him daft and accused him of wantonly annoying her and it would have led to a scuffle, but Murugan was serious and so was she.

'Look at me, Aambal. Do you really want to go home? Do you not want to make your mark in the Assembly? You can't do that from your home. And I want you to be my poet and stay with me. How can you leave me and go? Will you be happy without me?'

Aambal felt as if she was back on that mountain side, the earth rising up around her friend and enfolding him like a cape. Something had happened to her there, something had changed inside her. She had felt like one of the sure-footed tahr on the slippery slope of the kurinji-covered mountain flanks, with the God of the Kurinji beside her. The mountains, the tahr, the snakes, the moss and lichen, they had all said something to her, which she struggled now to put into words. Had they said, 'Kandhan's poet?'

How could she imagine a life without him? She had spent most of her life with him, rarely separated for more than a day or two. Never once in all those years had they made plans separately. It was always 'we will do this', 'we will do that' and 'this and that we will not do'. She didn't stop to consider what her parents would say or do. 'Yes, Kandha, you are my friend, and I do want to get into the Assembly, and I also know that, without you, I will not be happy.'

Kandhan's breath came out in a sharp hiss of relief, his face stretched into a beaming smile. Aambal continued, 'But I will not stay in your house, I will find my own house.'

Kandhan laughed at this. Here she was, back to herself, bossing him around! That inflection in her voice was reassuring—it meant she was sure.

She said, 'God knows how you'll torture me if I'm there all the time. No, thank you.'

Kandhan's body slumped with relief: with everybody else he could be sure, but with her, he never knew what would come out of her head. His mothers had been right: *the answer had indeed been inside his heart.*

Two evenings before the ceremony of leaving the kalari, a day before he took Aambal up to the mountains, Murugan had climbed up Pazhani hill and sat there under the dark sky until day broke. He had gone up to find an answer that eluded him. He called on his Krittika mothers for help, and when they appeared before him, he said to them, 'Mothers, guide me, I don't know what to do. Tomorrow, after the ceremonies, everything will change; everyone will go their separate ways.'

And they said to him, 'Son, Karthikeya, Guha, Kumara, Muruga, Kandha, what do you want to do?'

He told them, and also why that might not be possible and how he felt. They built a fire on Pazhani, and in that fire, they cast flowers of wild tulasi, garlic and a pinch of pink salt. When the smoke came up, it entered Murugan's nostrils and filled his chest and burnt his eyes, and his heart speeded up. His blood began to sing and he felt as if he was swooning. They asked him, 'Kumara, do you see?' They did not ask, *what do you see.* He blinked, coughed and strained, and something in his chest snapped, a curtain swung open, to reveal a large stage. On that stage stood Aambal, her face serious, back straight, her hand holding palm leaves, and she was declaiming in Tamizh. As he heard the words, tears ran down his face, and he held his head in his hands and sobbed. His six mothers stood around him, letting him cry. 'I cannot do it without her,' he said. 'And she will not do it without me. But how am I to ask her, and what if she says no, what if—'

One of them put her hand on his head and said, 'Son, look in your heart and you will find the words.' And he had, and he did.

Aambal's parents had considered this possibility: that she would stay on with Murugan. They knew that he had set his mind on making Aambal attend to her skill with poetry; they knew, too, the ambitions that he had made her feel: she wanted to be among the best poets in Tamizhagam, she wanted to be in the Assembly. She wanted to write verses that made Murugan exclaim with pleasure and wonder, and praise her. But they were anxious: Aambal's father feared that the god might fall in love with her; her mother feared that Aambal was in love with the temperamental god.

They stayed on in Kuyili's grandmother's house, helping Aambal find a house in the village, and to organise the housewarming that Kandhan insisted she have. On the morning of the housewarming, he came to Kuyili's house with gifts for all of them. After he left, and they had all looked at their gifts—clothes woven and dyed in Madurai—Aambal's mother picked up her daughter's saree of deep green bordered with red, the pallu woven with peacocks, their feathers bursts of colour. She thought she had seen something. Sure enough, in the peacock feathers were alphabets in Tamizh, some of them embroidered in darker colours, and when she traced the letters, she read 'Aambal' and 'Kandhan'.

Aambal's mother pulled her close and asked, 'Aambal, have you lost your heart to him?'

'No, Mother,' she said steadily, 'but I love him. He is my best friend, and for him I will give up my life.' *And my God,* she thought, *the God of Tamizh*. She would not say that aloud, even to her mother and grandmother, whose clever fingers ground herbs and wove cloth and could also inscribe words, in this hardy language, onto palm leaves they had cured. And everything they wrote, they began with his name, Velan—standing at the beginning, vel in hand, both guard and judge.

'And he?' asked her mother.

Aambal said, 'He too, Mother, he too.'

Construction began on Pazhani. Murugan wanted his palace to be designed and built by his people, those who lived and worked in the town over which his hill stood guard. And so it was that Aasaan sent word for architects, masons, carpenters, metal workers, mirror makers, cloth merchants and so on. The hill was like a bustling marketplace, but with the discipline of a beehive: the foundations were rising quickly, and in the foothills, new storehouses were filling with all kinds of material. Murugan was up there every day. Kuyili's brother, Naran, had agreed to take on the overseeing and travelled up from Tanjai; Kuyili's grandmother took charge of the makeshift kitchens, where dozens of cooks were at their fires, cooking in batches for the workers who were taking turns to work and sleep.

The days were busy, and when Ganesha arrived unannounced, Murugan was in the middle of a great deal of work and noise. They walked around the site and Ganesha spoke with the workers and expressed his pleasure at the finesse of the design and the construction. He addressed them by name, the masons, brick-makers, carpenters, mestiris, architects: Paithu, Angai, Makizhvan, Moovan, Achira, Vazhuthi and so on, each one beaming at the praise from the god they invoked at the start of all that they did.

In the evening, as they sat together, Ganesha asked his brother, 'Kandha, what is the heart of your palace?' Murugan waited. The question had not been addressed to him, or to anyone for that matter; it was a word-hold for the storyteller into his story.

'Let me tell you the story of Surapadman's great city, Veeramahendrapuram,' Ganesha began.

The basic plan for all Asura cities was always the same: the homes, palaces, rest houses, assembly halls, places of worship, granaries, warehouses never occupied more than a third of the total land. The rest was pasture and wilderness. All structures had to have large windows and doors for light to stream in, and every building had a room that faced a street, the doors of which were always open for anyone who needed a place to sleep, work or live. The civic system took pains to ensure that citizens were not short of anything: good counsel, building materials, seeds for planting, funds, information, whatever was needed for living well. Education was compulsory and open, appreciation and expression of the arts was built into daily life. At the centre of each city were schools where astute teachers trained their students to ask questions. In the wilderness surrounding the city, rivers ran clear and animals thronged; the paths marked by their hooves closed up after them, leaving no trace.

The Asura, who craved knowledge, invited and welcomed into their cities beings from the other thirteen worlds, the seekers, the wise, the experimenters, everyone except the 'twice-born' from Bhu. The dvija were anathema to the Asura, for they could not bear how, through the ages, dvija men and women had stoked their greed for power and perverted the ancient laws that the Manava race had lived by: land, language, occupation and food for everyone.

When an Asura king built a city, it was intended to protect and also inspire its citizens. And, knowing Surapadman, it was expected that his city would surpass anything anyone had built. And indeed it did—it floated in the mighty sea, between King Dashagriva's Lanka and the southern coast of the Tamizh lands. It was named Veeramahendrapuram. The city appeared always to wear a blue halo, thought to be produced by the sun hitting the water's spray.

Surapadman had commissioned Mayan, the best architect in the fourteen worlds, to build for him a floating city, held down by a system of ballasts that would not only keep it afloat, regardless of the wind's velocity, but would also keep it gently revolving throughout the day. And for him, a palace from which he could look over the waters to the coast of the land known as Thiravitam and Tamizhakam, regardless of the island-city's spin.

Padmakomalai, Mayan's daughter and assistant, who was known for innovating on the old, took charge of designing specific sections of Surapadman's palace: the library, the courtroom, the study, the music room, the kitchens and stables.

That was how they came to be seated across from each other at a table, with parchments bearing building plans laid out in front of them. 'She asked him,' said Ganesha, 'like I am asking you now, "Where do you propose to locate the heart of this magnificent palace, around which the rest of it will fit like the parts of a body?"'

The light from the morning sun struck the metal weights that held the parchments down, and fell over the drawings. 'Where would you put it,' he asked her.

She said to him that it was his dwelling and his own heart should tell him where the heart of it ought to be, and what he would place in that room.

He said to her that she was the architect, and she could hear what the light and the air were saying about the rooms waiting to be built.

She told him that he should sit quietly and shut his eyes and wait till an image came into them, and that would be his answer.

Later that day, as the sun was setting, Surapadman sat on one of the temporary benches that had been set up here and there, on the island that the architects and artisans had constructed. He shut his eyes. The sound of the waves fell into his ears; on his tongue was salt. As the island turned soundlessly, he opened his eyes, and into them came the lights from the high towers of the fabled seaside town of Chendur. As he looked, the lights blinked, and he recalled an old ballad sung by a wandering musician, describing Chendur's waves as boats ferrying Tamizh between the Rakshasa and Manava lands. The library! That was the heart of his palace, his home. The library in which, on shelves of karpura wood, he would arrange his prized manuscripts—some inked by his own scribes, songs and poetry composed by his scholars and some by him, and yet others, copies of great works from across the worlds, including the mother grammar, the *Akattiyam*. The library would have a tower, as tall as the lighthouse towers of Chendur, and he would climb up there to look out over the rugged waves.

Padmakomalai smiled when Surapadman told her that he had followed her instructions and found an answer, and again when he told her what room he had chosen. Through the days of the construction, these conversations continued, and Suran found himself imagining going through the rooms. He saw their interiors, the windows through which light streamed in, and sometimes, spray from the waves. As he went from room to room, in his mind, there was someone beside him, who watched him silently, and in her hands was one architectural implement or another. And when she actually walked with him through the palace, pointing out how the work was progressing, her sight joined his, and the whole world seemed better balanced and better fabricated to him. He had fallen in love with her, but of her feelings he had no idea. He could not ask her, for that would be inappropriate. If only his sister Ajamugi were here.

Far away, in the land of the Gandharvas, Ajamugi heard his wish in her heart and appeared in Veeramahendrapuram.

Ajamugi observed Padmakomalai's work, and she saw how every line she drew, every instruction she gave her workers, spoke of how well she had come to know Surapadman. In the days that followed, Ajamugi and Padmakomalai became friends, and Ajamugi hinted to her friend her brother's feelings, and Padmakomalai made it clear that she held Suran close to her heart. Thus it was that Surapadman married the one who had shown him to recognise what his heart wanted from this fabulous palace being built for him. The wedding was conducted on the day of the moving-in ceremony, and all of Veeramahendrapuram rejoiced. The fireworks on that day, it is said, could be seen as far as Chendur.

'Chendur,' Murugan repeated with a faraway look in his eyes, remembering his visits to that town by the sea. The red of its soil gave it that name, the red mud that turned your hands red when you scooped it up, and turned your feet red when you walked barefoot.

Ganesha touched his brother's shoulder and asked, 'What is the heart of your palace? Where will you place it and what will it embody?'

He clearly did not expect an answer, for he got up and pulled Murugan up and said, 'Go sleep now.'

His brother's words resounded in Murugan's ears, and when his chief architect, Nanthiya, came to speak to him the next day, he asked her, 'How come you haven't asked me where I want the heart of the palace to be?'

She smiled and said, 'You have already told me. You said, "Libraries and kitchens and rooms to sleep, these are to be well laid out and luxuriously fitted. The Assembly hall—let it be spare, large, with perfect acoustics." Is that not the heart of your palace, the room where your poets will read?'

While the construction was in progress, Aambal was to go to Pothigai and apprentice herself to the 'Mother of Tamizh', the Kuru Muni who had carried the infant language at his breast, nursing it with all his attention and care. Aambal expected her time with the sage to be one of rigorous and active study. Instead, it was a time of quiet, of introspection and practise, for Akattiyar said to her, 'A language is learnt by comprehending its syllabic, word, sentence and meaning-making structures, but a poet needs its gestures of intimacy. And for that, you have to be still, approachable, intimate.'

Every day, Akattiyar sent Aambal out onto mountain paths, so she could observe carefully her surroundings. Like the ferns that were still dew-damp and not just green, but of a colour for which you might find the words if you watched so keenly that there occurred a concord of poetic sight, language and nature. He said to her, 'Go to the ledge, look down into the precipice, and be ready to fling yourself down unless you find one verse, one line, one phrase or one word that rings true.'

In the course of her days there, Aambal was surprised at how easily she settled into a new pattern. The tempo of her breathing slowed to the easy rhythms of the mountain and its creatures. She understood that this was a time to let fallow the soil inside her, which she had tilled and ploughed and cropped and weeded all these years. The days passed, and Aambal began to hear, as Akattiyar had said, the words that waited in all things, and the Kani men, women and children who lived on that mountain, who had neither script nor grammar, seemed to know this, for they said to her, 'You can sing now.'

Akattiyar called her to him and handed her a bundle of palm leaves, a stylus, an inkwell full of indigo ink and an instruction: 'Write about the Lord of Pazhani. About his love for this language that sweetens the heart, sharpens love and speech, and which, in this time, has given you the last of the attributes of poetic attitude.'

Aambal returned to Pazhani after Murugan and his retinue had moved in and he had the time to set up a daily routine with her. He began to groom her for reading at the Great Assembly. He expected Aambal to arrive at his doorstep every morning, on time, before the court began its daily functioning, to read to him the poems he had asked for the previous day.

They settled into this schedule, and among the early morning sounds on Pazhani, there would be his voice exclaiming in praise, annoyance, censure or instruction. He was a tough taskmaster and sometimes Aambal felt he was being excessive, but then she would remember how harsh and unbending were the rules of the Assembly, and how strict Nakkeeran was in upholding them. So she wrote, rewrote, edited and reworked, she read and practised, and as the days passed, she felt the strengths of her work growing and its weaknesses reducing.

Murugan saw this maturing, and he said to her that she was climbing up the hill at a time when her head was light and ready to compose, that she should work at home, through the day, and he would come down the hill in the evening to go over her work.

The villagers grew used to the sound of Paravani's giant wings flying towards Aambal's house, and to the occasional sight of the poet and the god strolling through the streets towards the market, to the shops where parchments, styluses and inks were sold.

At court, both the older, more experienced poets, as well as those who arrived from the towns, began to compliment Aambal's poetry. Murugan ensured that Aambal always had a few perfected poems to read whenever an occasion arose, at court and otherwise, and soon, people began to talk of her and her work.

Aambal now consciously began to plan and prepare for reading at the Assembly: she moulded her voice, practised standing straight, looking into the distance and keeping her face impassive. She had heard, with dread, of poets' undoing in the Assembly; overtaken by nervousness, their faces contorted with disappointment, they blabbered or went mute. She did not want that to happen to her. She would not let it.

Being allowed into the Assembly to read was not easy; being selected to be a member, and to keep that position, meant constant hard work and innovation in one's poetry. She was not afraid of hard work, but she had to get in first— Nakkeeran was a stern leader, and he could be curmudgeonly. If he thought that Kandhan would try to interfere in her getting in ... *she should warn him about trying to influence the old man.* But was she ready? She often asked herself that, because reading there was not simply a matter of being an effective poet: it was about fitting in, about keeping to the rules, about being impressive without losing popularity. It was also about being able to live in Madurai, the sophisticated, wealthy city that drew poets, scholars, patrons and kings, like a well draws the thirsty.

One evening, Murugan appeared at the door of her house with a bag for her, and said, 'Be ready in the morning, we are going somewhere.' When she opened the bag, she found a dark red cotton saree from the Chettinad country, and a blue blouse. On the pallu were leaves of green, and there were little buds of orange all over the body of the saree. *He was going to be bedecked, like at his housewarming on Pazhani. She should also wear jewellery. For she was going with him, and as his poet, she should appear to care about how she looked.* She had worn no jewellery since the day she had dropped her anklets and chain on the forest floor. She considered asking for the loan of some jewellery from her neighbour, when she noticed that there was still something in the bag. It was a little pouch with silver anklets and a silver chain with matching earrings, beaded and strung with silver leaves and sparkling green marakatam.

The next morning, Murugan appeared wearing a white veshti, a light-blue upper garment, ornaments of aquamarine and pearls, and an indigo shoulder cloth. In his hand was the akil dandam, viridescent as always. He took one look at her and said, 'Oh my, look at you. Thank you, Aambal.'

She pursed her lips and said, 'Yes, I know you don't like my "poet clothes" when we are meeting other people.' Then, remembering that she had no idea what was in store for her, she asked, 'Where are we going anyway?'

'To the Assembly,' he said casually.

Aambal's breath snagged in her throat. 'The Assembly! Why didn't you tell me?'

'Because you would have stayed awake and looked terrible, and your panic would have stopped you from reworking the last stanza of the poem you're going to read today.'

'Read?' Her voice touched the upper scales. 'What? How? Now? Like this? Oh no, I can't.'

The smile on Murugan's face grew wider, then he became serious and said, 'Today is the selection of poets who can apply for inclusion—if you are selected, and you have to be, Aambal—you will read there once a month for twelve months and become eligible for enrolling in the competitions for induction into the Assembly.'

'But today,' she squawked. 'Today? I'm not ready; I'm not prepared. You should have told me.'

'You are ready,' he answered. 'What do you think this last set of antadi was for? The one where you've spoken of me as the sun and my devotees as ants hatching in my warmth? That's what you will read.'

As it went, however, Aambal stood up in the Assembly and read her poems, and received as much applause as the best of them. At the end of the day, Nakkeeran, his white beard flowing, his white hair knotted at the nape of his neck, his white veshti and upper cloth sparkling, rapped his stout, gold-band-decorated walking stick on the floor for silence. He announced the names of the twelve, chosen from among a hundred, who were being invited to come back for the next twelve months. Aambal's name was also included. Nakkeeran then disbanded the audience, asking the chosen few to remain. He invited Murugan to say a few words as the patron of the Assembly—this was the first time that Aambal was hearing of it. But now she realised how awkward her position was, and his too. *Was that why he was always so demanding in his assessment of her work? Was that why Nakkeeran was so critical, testing her more than the others? What did he think, that Kandhan wrote her poems? Bah, she didn't like the old man very much.*

Thenceforth, Aambal had to write what Murugan commissioned, and also for the Assembly readings, and the demands of each were so different that sometimes she found her head being stretched in opposite directions. Murugan wanted to hear her voice speaking about the language he so loved, or about him. He wanted her to find metaphors drawing from the world in which she lived, with its insects, trees, people and flowers; its alphabets, music and dance. He sometimes said, 'Forget the rules, make your own.' And when she did that, it was like she was back up there, on Pothigai: she found words in unlikely places.

The Assembly, on the other hand, not only had themes for its monthly readings, but also specified every last thing: metre, number of verses, line-break schemes. In the end, the constant switching made her quick with her words, like on her feet. She could land without falling and spring up lightly, and she could stand in her poems, endlessly waiting for the words to roll in over the horizon and break over her palm leaves. And of all the poets at court, it was Aambal that they called 'Murugan's poet', though there were other poets better than her, more accomplished, more famous.

Unknown to her, Murugan entrusted Aambal's elderly neighbour, Nalayani, with ensuring that she changed out of her customary white kora clothes whenever she had a reading at the palace or at the Assembly. At the Assembly itself, Aambal could not get over the feeling that Nakkeeran was grilling her, hoping she would trip herself up, which she did not. *What was wrong with him?*

Nakkeeran, in turn, was annoyed that the taciturn god, who had been an infrequent presence at the Assembly and its monthly readings, never missed a reading now. In the old man's eyes, it was not befitting for the patron, to behave like this. *What was wrong with him?*

Murugan could see Aambal bristling at the comments Nakkeeran directed at her, but he said nothing. The old man had never been secure in his office because even before he took over, its Founding Father, Akattiyan, had said that it was time a woman led its work. Murugan was also aware that Nakkeeran could never attain the ease of versing that Velliveethi or Auvaiyyar possessed, because they, in a way that only women are capable of doing, tossed to the winds all considerations of weight and impact, and their unchained words soared and poured.

In Nakkeeran's head, all these thoughts compounded when he observed the way Murugan's eyes never left Aambal's face when she stood up to read, and the way he nodded his head, in time with her voice, or the way Aambal always looked at Murugan before she began. And he certainly didn't approve of the way they sometimes behaved—like undisciplined children! He had seen Murugan grab her hand when he talked to her, and one time, Nakkeeran had seen Aambal pinch the god's arm and loudly say, 'Don't be a fool, Kandha.' *To the God of Tamizh!* It was all too much, he thought. *But who could he say this to?*

Pazhani hill was a beehive of activity. Visitors thronged to the great palace: scholars, poets, horse traders, farmers, cooks, storytellers, oracles who rarely came down from their posts in the hills. Murugan's classmates came, Cheraman Perunkadungko, now king of his lands, came with a train of his attendants; Kuyili came from the north, where she had fought in wars that made even the fearless quake.

The palace kitchens never closed and the cooks worked in shifts. The dining halls were open all day to feed those at court, people who climbed up the hill of wisdom so they might find answers to their problems, or the townsfolk who often wandered up to attend the poetry readings or proceedings at court, or just to eat on the hilltop, to sit in the dining halls as the clouds passed by, looking in through the large windows.

Nothing escaped Murugan's eyes or ears. He had seen how his parents, though distracted by their passion for each other and for their work, never left anything unattended—even the business of the competition; he now understood how much attention had been given to it.

The part of his life at the palace that he liked best was the readings in the Assembly hall. His poets read every day, then they spent time examining the poetry in order to sharpen and make it more subtle, and more beautiful. Every day, he went over Aambal's work. Sometimes he gave her a verse to be done in an evening, at other times, ten to be done in a week or a hundred in a month. Her head would often spin at these demands, but then all that she had learnt in her training with Akattiyar would come back to her, she would calm down and she never failed to complete a task—whether it be a single verse, a decad, or ten decads.

Thus the days passed, until one day, Ganesha arrived, unannounced, just as a poet was reading. Murugan sprang to his feet and ran to his brother, embraced him and sat him down on the throne, taking up position beside him. He understood why his brother was here: the time had come for the battle, with the one he was born to fight.

Ganesha sat through the readings, more thrilling today for the readers because the Divine Scribe was in their midst and listening with rapt attention, offering suggestions in his smiling voice and gifting each poet with a silver stylus at the end of their reading.

'It is time, Muruga,' Ganesha said later, as they relaxed after the afternoon meal. 'Time for the battle. Appa and Amma want us to go to Kailasa to meet the Sura—it's going to be a tedious process, you know that. So, prepare yourself.'

Murugan felt his heart both sink and soar. This was the encounter that he had waited so many long earth years for, the battle that everything and everyone who had taught him was preparing him for. He felt regret that this life he was leading—full of goodwill, mingling with the residents of his beloved Pazhani town, the long hours of poetry and editing—was going to change. But there was the thrill of finally meeting this exceptional warrior that anyone would be honoured to fight but who had chosen him for a combat that all of creation was invested in. But before all that, this meeting. It was going to be difficult, both the meeting as well as the return to Kailasa. *It would be nice if Anna was with him.*

Ganesha laughed and said, 'Yes, Kandha, I will go with you. To Kailasa, to the meeting, and then back here, where I shall remain till the battle is over.'

Murugan heaved a sigh of relief. Kailasa, he thought, shaking his head, *what it did to me.* Warm clouds rumbled outside the window, reminding him that he had his own home now: Pazhani, the hill of wisdom.

5

SURAPADMAN

Never had there been one like him, and never would there be another: few beings in all the fourteen worlds matched the glory of Surapadman. Of the mighty Asuras, he was the best; of warriors, he was among the handful that could stand against the Three. Wherever he went, he conducted himself with great care and consideration for the ways of the world he was in and the beings, among whom he was. He had a way with things that made it evident he was seeing them in all their potential glory, for Surapadman, like all the Asuras, looked past circumstance and status to the rasa indwelling in everything.

He was also beautiful. Even Manmatha appeared to be full of flaws, which had been corrected in Surapadman. His eyes were dark pools that made you want to lean closer and look at your own reflection; thick curls of hair, combed back from a high forehead, tumbled down his neck and over his back, on which the sinews stood out like veins of rock down a sheer cliff face. His waist was like a jeweller's knot—delicate, but hinting at its own strength. And his face had the sheen of deep brown palingku stone carved out of the sides of mountains; his nose angled down to his lips, like the slender body of a trumpet, the nostrils flaring like a trumpet's bell. His thick moustache, perfumed with vetiver or satakuppai, ran the length of shapely lips the colour of the evening sky, and curled up at the corners like twin sentries. Sideburns spread past the translucent shells of his ears on which ornaments dangled, striking against his neck and shoulders when he moved, down his jaws, like black-woolled sheep along the flanks of a very steep hill.

Surapadman's chest was like the door of an unbreachable fortress: those who looked on it felt safe. He was like a banyan basking in its own shade. And, just as no one can look away when they see a snow leopard between iced-over boulders or observe the white wool of the kasturikamalam dissolving into and sealing an open wound, so too, eyes that fell on him hesitated to blink, let alone turn away.

Thus was Surapadman, born to the magnificent Surasa and the venerable Kashyapa, from whose loins all the living things in the fourteen worlds had been engendered. The story of Surapadman's birth makes eyes widen, the heart race and hair to stand on end.

After Kashyapa was chosen by Brahma to couple with seventeen of Daksha's daughters, and they had given birth to all the beings that the Creator, Brahma, had imagined, including the Sura and Asura, he retired to live on Meru. Kashyapa was tired of his virility and of the pleasures that a virile body could enjoy and impart, and on Meru, he created a web of magic that let no one and nothing enter or leave. Many, many moons came and went. He stopped taking note of time's passing, and by and by, his ears forgot the sounds of the world he had left behind, of language and speech. He abandoned himself to the heaving and resting of nature, like a child in its mother's lap, and he felt the time had come for him to merge into the particles of mud and dust, and the wind of Meru. But then, Surasa appeared. And everything changed for the venerable, almost-renunciate Kashyapa, and for creation itself.

It was not difficult for Surasa to locate Kashyapa's dwelling, to get past the traps he had set; it was as if there was nothing in her path to Kashyapa. She was a few feet away from him when her voice broke into his thoughts: 'Greetings, venerable Kashyapa, I wish you well.'

He turned and his eyes did not widen, as the eyes of most men did, when they looked at her. Her frame was sturdy like the trunk of a fully grown tree, her limbs were like branches firmed and browned with every passing season. Even when she stood still, her body seemed to sway, like leaves do when the wind touches them. She stood, her legs slightly apart, her feet at an angle to each other, her lower body as still as a tree trunk and the upper body like its branches. You could not look away because you felt that now a bird would start from its darks, now you might catch sight of flowers or fruit.

Surasa was the daughter of the Asura king Asurendran. She had arisen from deep inside the Vast, where water and fire changed one into the other, where the waves swirled and changed into fire before falling back—and like the fire inside water, so was she.

Shukracharya, the Asura's guru, took charge of Surasa's training. She mastered what she was taught with joy, and the more she learnt, the more she wanted to know. When the training was done, she understood what her guru had been teaching her: everything carried inside it a story of itself, and it also carried within itself the ways in which this story could be edited.

By this time, Surasa had grown into a strong-limbed, long-eyed, fearless and articulate young woman, whose lips were always slightly turned up, as if ready for a laugh. Surasa had many skills, but the greatest of them was riddling: she seemed able to look into space and see hidden there conundrums and possibilities that had never come to life, and they came to her, as to a lover, saying, *love me, show me to the world*. In time, her fame became such that Mothers Parvathy and Lakshmi took to visiting her, or inviting her to visit them, and the three of them would riddle away, laughing, making bets, removing their ornaments and handing them over to whoever won. More often than not, it would be Surasa.

Riddling was not a matter of asking a question and getting an answer—a good riddle stirred up threads of events that could have happened but never did, a good riddle made language turn and do things it was not used to doing, a good riddle made the riddler feel as if she was rearranging the very universe. And it made the one who was being riddled feel as if they were being shown the very secrets of creation.

One day, Shukracharya called her to his side and told her, 'You are going to give birth to children whose glory is foretold. Like you, they too have arisen out of the deepest part of the Vast, and of all of them, one will be glorious beyond compare.' He then advised her how to get to Meru, where the venerable Kashyapa lived in contemplation. 'Go to him, and know this, that when he fathers the first of these children, he will feel as if he too has been born anew, for such is the glory of that first one. He has, after all, come to reveal the secret that sits at the heart of Time.'

Shukracharya reminded her not to underestimate Kashyapa's mood—one of denial and resistance to all things, especially pleasure. He reminded her also that the sage had only heard the language of nature in a long time. Lastly, the old man warned Surasa that she had to prevent him from turning his back, not just on her, but on the language of her riddles.

When Surasa approached Kashyapa and expressed her desire to join with him and bear children, he turned her away, saying patiently and courteously that that part of his life was over. Unfazed and unabashed, she explained that no other man would do, since no man came close to him. 'Your eyes can see inside and outside of every creature that has life, for you are the progenitor of all life. Your speech is that of animals and birds, of the wise snakes, the curious centipedes, the sturdy-willed foxes, and everything else that has life. I want to bear children with these qualities.'

Kashyapa did not interrupt her; her speech was pleasing, her voice reminded him of the wind striking against the stone face of his home. When she finished, he said, 'Surasa, I will not change my mind. I can see that you do not want to try and seduce me with song or dance or any of those things, and I am grateful for that. I am moved by the clarity of your vision, but I cannot change my mind now. Please leave me.'

Surasa, who knew that the sage would not let her go without offering her food, and that he would remember to do this not if she stayed but if she left, bowed and turned to go. As she took her first step, Kashyapa, as if suddenly remembering something, said, 'Surasa, wait, I cannot let you go without offering you a meal.'

They sat across from each other, partaking of the meal that Kashyapa had made for them, and Surasa was making a riddle in her mind, one that had the spirit of the great mountain and of this man who had come here to forget his past. 'Revered Kashyapa,' she said, 'I wish to express my appreciation for this meal you have put together for me—the tender rabbit meat, these mushrooms, these juicy bamboo shoots, this atthi dribbled with wild honey, and this palm toddy. Let me offer you, in return, a riddle that I have only just conceived.'

Kashyapa had been prepared for her to ask again, to try and persuade him, but this he was not prepared for and could not resist. He told her to go ahead.

Surasa then asked Kashyapa, 'What is the thread that ties you to me, without yet being a thread?' As she spoke, it seemed to Kashyapa that the air was weaving a cover around the two of them, because for the first time since he had come here, the chill winds of the mountain invaded his skin, marched through his blood, stomped through his bones and attacked the marrow. He needed warmth, and his whole body was scrambling towards the fire in Surasa's chest. Kashyapa did not want to end this moment. He shut his eyes and thought about what she had said. What tied him to her but was not a thread? What was it? All he could imagine was the thread of her breath, scented with the honey and toddy that they had partaken of, the thread of her voice as it drummed in his rib cage, arousing the dancers there, the thread of her fingers undoing the knot of his hair, the thread of their limbs.

He could not find an answer, and it is said that when she told him what it was, his heart stopped and his hair stood on end, and he was deluged with a desire to join with her and to produce children who could ask and answer riddles. He wanted there to be many more like her and like him. By this time, Kashyapa was aroused and he stretched out his hand and held hers. They embraced, the athletic Surasa and the beautiful Kashyapa with his deer eyes, his pale skin, its splendour like dull gold, his lean legs and slender fingers.

Their passion reached its peak in the first quarter of the night, when the white moon shone bright, the lotuses opened their faces to be kissed, the chakravaka birds greeted each other, and the night winds brought with them the fragrance of night jasmines. His seed rushed into her womb and joined with her own seed, to form into a child who swam out of her birth channel, now open and flooded with birth fluids. The boy flowed right into the hands of his father and immediately attained full growth, standing tall, his mahagani-hued skin glowing under the moon's ivory light, his eyes glowing like embers, his hands folded, his voice hailing his mother and his father. He was named Surapadman. As they stood, mother, father and firstborn, there emerged from the venerable Kashyapa's sweat 40,000 bright Asura, women and men, who grew to full stature within a few matras.

With Surasa, Kashyapa was aroused in a way he had not been with any of his many wives. He was filled with an ardour that made him joyous, and perhaps for the first time, he allowed himself abandon. The wind ran over his body like a feather. Surasa lay beside him, one leg tossed over his thighs, her head on his shoulder, her fingers caressed his ear, his neck. The hoots of owls rang in the air as they woke and flew out into the night, the moon shone bright, and Kashyapa was filled with the desire to mate as animals do. So, first they took on the form of lions, and Singamugan, lion-like, his hair spread around his head like a lion's mane, was born, and again, 40,000 mighty Asura emerged from the sweat pores of Kashyapa. Then the couple took the form of elephants, and Surasa gave birth to Tarakasura, and a further 40,000 Asura emerged from Kashyapa's pores.

Pleased, pleasured, satiated, they lay in each other's arms. They knew the time had come for Surasa to return and for Kashyapa to leave his flesh-and-blood form. She turned to him and said, 'You gave me a meal and invited me to eat with you, you took my riddle in the spirit of a gift, you joined with me, giving me pleasure that filled my body, and joined with my life to make new life. There is but one thing we have not shared.'

That was when she asked him to make a riddle. Kashyapa wondered if she was freeing him from his only remaining obligation: to language. They say that he lay in her arms, his eyes looking up, and as an owl sped past, slicing the ivory disc of the moon, the riddle came to him. And he asked and she heard and pondered, and it eluded her. The air seemed to grow warmer, and she began to sweat. She sat up, kissed him, giving his lower lip a playful nip. She mounted him and paused a moment, straddling him, her hands on his shoulders, her knees at his waist, her eyes on his face. Her body bore down on his, then pulled back, and as she lifted and thrust, she repeated the riddle, and excitement gripped his loins, it swirled in his throat, making him call out. Then her voice spoke the answer and his seed fountained out, filling her, flowing towards her womb. And thus was born their daughter Ajamugi, a forest spirit, like a sliver of moonlight tinged with gold. She tumbled out of her mother, laughing, and stood before her parents, fully grown, her eyes long and dark like her father's, and her skin, like his, golden and translucent. This time, from Kashyapa's sweat, there poured out 80,000 Asura, golden-skinned, delicate of body and bright of eye.

Kashyapa blessed his children and bade Surasa farewell, and she went back to her home, her kingdom. From the pores of his body, light wafted out and dispersed like pollen. It spread into the air, dropped to the earth, fell on leaves and flowers, and was swept up by the wind of Mount Meru into the casket of its womb.

The three sons of Surasa and Kashyapa built their cities and settled down, while their sister, true to her sprite-like nature, led a nomadic life. She went from one thing to another, her heart delighting, and her feet, like her father's, always bare, headed towards new destinations, accompanied by men and women who could sing and dance and play instruments. And Time continued to pass through the many worlds, in each stepping to a different gait.

A long time had gone by, 1008 earth years, and Surapadman had travelled through the universes again and again; he had learnt and taught, written and edited, he had fought and made truces, he had given and received, he had loved, wooed, married and birthed children. He had tracked down every secret mystery he sensed or dreamt of, or been asked to solve. Happy and having lived to the full, he now missed the home he had left. He wanted to return to the deep, dark, billowing surge of the Vast.

He hoped Murugan was ready. He had heard of all that had happened to him: schooling, moving to Pazhani, the grand palace with its fabulous library and court poets. He had heard about all of it, and now he waited.

Before taking his Asura form, when Surapadman had still been a lusty billow, he had one day felt an impulse to surge forward into the endlessness of the waters of the Vast. And when he did, he felt the presence of something, and when he understood what it was, as if in acknowledgment, tremors sped through the Vast. He was swept up and tossed high; he surged, splintered and fell back into the turbulent waves. He understood that he had been chosen to set into action a cosmic drama. Then and now, he did not know how it would end, or if it would even end. But till it ended, he would remain in his Asura body, bound to his Asura nature. The ending depended on Murugan.

Surapadman knew the secret of the boy, but the boy must understand it, only then would the cycle end, and only then could he go back home. He had devised the drama, he had cleverly put together its action, its movements were hinged on conditions that he had stipulated, but of its end, he had no clue. No one did. Not even the only being in creation who could manifest that ending.

Surapadman sent a crisp message to his Sura brethren, addressed to their king, Indra. *He was going to take over the work of creation*. He wrote, 'Your Creator god does his work of creation with half-attention, and what is created remains half-perfected.' He went on to say that he felt this had gone on for too long, and of how, when the son of Shiva and Parvathy jailed Brahma and took on the work himself, all of creation had sparkled and rejoiced. But then, he was asked to return the job to Brahma, who for a short time had seemed inspired by the boy's punishment, but that had not lasted. 'I am out of patience,' he wrote, 'with the creator's laziness, his incompetence, and the only solution is for me to take over the work of creation myself.'

When Surapadman's message reached the court of the Sura, Brahma quaked. It was true, Surapadman would do a far better job. He imagined the Asura king lingering over each creation, exploring its potential and finding the best form for what he made, like a poet labours over the syllables, words, lines, sentences and stanzas of verses, waiting as its sound and sense shift, until it settles into its own best posture. But an experimenter could not be given the work of creation—he would upset the balance of things. The created worlds were meant to be inhabited by imperfect beings who sought perfection. Surapadman knew this, of course, and he knew too, that were he to actually be given this thankless task, he would turn it down. It was merely a device to get the gods agitated and run to the Three, who would know that the time had come. They would summon Murugan from his home on Pazhani.

That is what transpired. When Murugan and Ganesha arrived, and all the Sura were assembled, Indra formally stated that he had come to ask the Parents of Creation to send their son, Karthikeya, to combat with the Asura king Surapadman, who was threatening the very order of existence with his ludicrous proposition. Murugan's eyes went to Brihaspati as Indra was speaking. He saw that the Sura guru's eyes were on him: they were both recalling Skandagiri and Indra's tone then.

The formalities were tedious and Murugan sat through it all silently, until Indra said in his petulant voice, 'We should attack right away. Karthikeya cannot be defeated. He is the son of Shambhu and Parvathy.'

Murugan jumped to his feet and said, 'I have accepted this task at the behest of my parents, and that was a long time ago. I will do it, but whether I cannot be defeated or can, is not what we should be talking about now. I would like to follow the dictates of diplomacy: a message received necessitates a message returned. Let us send a messenger to the court of Surapadman.'

When he saw that Indra was about to protest, Brihaspati stood up and said, 'You speak wisely, Karthikeya; it is but right that we try words before weapons.'

Murugan smiled, turned to the court and asked, 'Who better than the king of diplomats, Veerabahu, for this mission?' He was met with cheers of agreement.

Thus it was that Veerabahu transported himself to Veeramahendrapuram, turning invisible as soon as he landed on the floating island. As he walked along its wide streets, he looked around in appreciation.

Unknown to Veerabahu, Surapadman was watching him in the large crystal in his assembly hall, along with a large number of courtiers. As Veerabahu landed, with what he had no reason to doubt were silent steps, his footfall resounded inside the assembly and the Asura assembled there laughed. If the 'invisible' Veerabahu had seen himself in the crystal, he would have seen an old, tiny scratch on his armour plate, and he would have been abashed. There he was now, stepping over the cobbles, passing along the wide tree-lined approach to the assembly hall. He must have been pleased with himself as he passed one armed guard after another, who ignored him because they had been told to pretend they could not see this man.

Inside the assembly, he snapped his fingers and turned visible, a smirk on his face, which quickly disappeared when he saw himself in the crystal face. He stumbled, then turned to the throne. When his eyes settled on Surapadman, they widened: perhaps he had not expected the Asura king to look the way he did—like a noble banyan throned in its own shade, eyes guileless, his demeanour indicating welcome and respect. Surapadman now stood up. He held his hands out and hailed Veerabahu, 'Hail, oh brave, noble son of Shiva and Parvathy, ambassador of Karthikeya, welcome to Veeramahendrapuram.'

He descended a few steps from the raised platform on which his throne sat, and came towards Veerabahu, who, feeling like a child caught stealing, said nothing. He had planned a grand entry to show the Asura who he was, what he could do, but here he was, exposed. So, instead of doing what his diplomatic finesse would have prompted him to do—walk towards the Asura king, extending his own arms and greeting him, he stamped his foot and an enormously tall throne appeared, high enough to touch the ceiling, and in a trice, he was seated on it. Surapadman's head rose, like smoke rising from a fire, wafting, graceful. He smiled at Veerabahu, folded both hands and said, 'Wise Veerabahu, you did not need to bring your own seat, we had one prepared for you.' When he gestured, another throne sprang up, taller by a hand's span than the one on which Veerabahu sat.

Veerabahu's skin went cold, his eyes burnt, his tongue was thick in his mouth—its feathered lightness, which could talk the thoughts out of even the most logical heads, was gone. The Asura king made a sign and the sounds of nadaswaram and tavil flowed through the assembly; a group of musicians had begun to play. As the sound of their instruments slowed and dimmed, the voice of the court bard rose up over the hanging lights, speaking of the valour, wisdom and discretion of Veerabahu and wishing him success and good sense. The subdued titter that stirred among the rows of Asura may not have been Veerabahu's imagination. When the song was over, Surapadman spoke again: 'Noble Veerabahu, if you will come down and share a meal with us, we would all be happy.'

Veerabahu had by now come to his senses. He caused the magical throne he had created to shrink, and as soon as he got off, it went up in smoke. With folded hands, he greeted everyone in the assembly and said, 'I greet all those present here, and am humbled by your welcome and your hospitality. I would be honoured to accept your invitation.'

So they shared a meal, and then Veerabahu rested. In the evening, at court, he was asked to speak. Veerabahu announced that he had brought word from Karthikeya, Lord of Pazhani, in response to King Surapadman's decision to take on the activity of creation. Karthikeya, reported Veerabahu, had said that the great Asura should not take on this task, for he was an experimenter whose search was for truth and potential, while a creator's task is to keep the chain from rolling to a stop. When he was done, Veerabahu turned to the Asura king with folded hands, inclined his head, and sat down.

The king thanked him and stood to speak. 'I have always done what I came to do, which is to bring out the best in everything and everyone, and I cannot ignore the fact that Lord Brahma's creations are deficient; they are poor versions of what they could be, if created with insight and care.'

Veerabahu understood what was being communicated to him. He bent his head and shut his eyes, imagining the battlefield. When Surapadman was done speaking, Veerabahu communicated the next part of his message: since battle was inevitable, Karthikeya had left it to the Asura king to decide the location and the time of the battle.

Surapadman was silent for a few moments, thoughtful, then he spoke, naming the place and specifying a day and time.

Veerabahu bid the king and his court goodbye and flew back to Indra's court. It was what was expected—nobody had imagined that Surapadman would take back what he had said, or that a battle could be avoided. When Veerabahu relayed the day, date and location for the battle, cheers and applause rang out. Only Ganesha noticed that Murugan frowned and soon left the court. He called Paravani and took off into the skies in the direction of the Krittika stars.

6

MAHASENA

The air of Pazhani bristled at first: what was this? The boy and the mantle of stillness he wore were soothing, making up for the centuries of burn that the hill had endured, and now this? A few days later, the bristling turned to a stretch, a straightening up and a swagger: warriors moved across the hill, women and men from around the worlds, their bodies toughened through discipline and practise, their minds uncluttered. It was impossible not to be drawn into the rhythm of their marching, the music in the sounds of their weapons swinging and striking.

Ganesha had flown back to Pazhani with Murugan after the battle deliberations were done. The twelve Matris, led by Dhumi, who had been Murugan's mentors and bodyguards from the day he arrived in Kailasa, arrived soon after, followed by Veerabahu, who came with his eight siblings, warriors who were together known across the worlds as the Nine Brave Ones. They were Veera Kesari, Veera Mahendra, Veera Mahesvara, Veera Purandara, Veera Rakkadha, Veera Marthanda, Veera Anthaka and Veeradheera.

The story of their birth is both sad and amazing. Mother Parvathy, after she left her parents and came to live on Kailasa, missed her friends and sisters terribly, especially when Shiva went off to hunt or aid his disciples. One day, she took nine gems—

ruby, pearl, yellow sapphire, garnet, cat's eye, diamond, emerald, coral and blue sapphire—from her anklet, and created nine women as lovely as the gems: Manickavalli, Muthuvalli, Pushparagavalli, Gomedagavalli, Vaiduryavalli, Vairavalli, Maragatavalli, Pavalavalli and Neelavalli.

They went with her everywhere, except when she was with her husband in their bedchamber or up in one of the caves or inside some forest, engaged in long-drawn love games. One day, they were seated in the garden, threading flowers, the nine women and Parvathy, laughing and talking, when Shiva emerged, fresh from a bath, his lower body draped in a wet swathe of cloth, hair tumbling down his chest onto his flat belly and along his hips and thighs, his eyes shining. The nine women looked at him and desire surged in their chests, and in their guts and loins. Shiva turned and smiled at them, and taking nine leaves of tulasi from a nearby plant, he made nine men, their faces shining, their bodies firm and healthy. The nine women lay with these men, and each of the women became pregnant.

When Parvathy saw this, she was filled with bitterness and could not bear the sight of the nine women. As for the women, the thought of giving birth when they knew that she longed to birth a child, stopped their pregnancy and kept it from ending. They grew heavy and burdened by the babies growing inside them. Every little movement was painful. Their husbands could not bear their suffering and went to Parvathy, begging her to go to the women. At the same time, the women went to Ganesha and begged him to intervene for them with their friend. Knowing his mother, Ganesha advised them to go to her themselves. When the women set out, they met Parvathy on the way, coming to them. She asked their forgiveness and they hers. She blessed them that they would give birth to nine fully grown men, who would be considered the children of Shambhu and Parvathy, as the nine women and men were a part of them. She also promised them that these nine children would be companions to a younger sibling whose birth was awaited by all of creation, and that they would be known forever as his generals, messengers and trainers.

Veerabahu was the eldest of them. Born to Manickavalli, his skin had a ruddy sheen, like that of the brilliant ruby. Each of his brothers glowed with a tinge of the jewels from which their mother had been born. They also gave off the fragrance of the tulasi from which their fathers had been made. And now they were here, to fulfil their destiny as companions and generals to their brother. They would take their positions in the army, along with the twelve Matris, and they would jointly train the soldiers and draw up plans for battle formations, offence and defence.

Veerabahu was going to train Murugan, not so much in the mechanics of warfare, but on how to stay focused. He feared that Murugan would look at Surapadman and see the man who had authored compendiums on animal sounds or on the minerals found in Patala, the one who repaired Ravana's Rudra veena and taught the secret of Time to the Apsaras, or any of the many things that Murugan so admired. That would be disastrous, and had to be prevented by all means. To Veerabahu, there was a clear solution: keep Murugan's mind from wandering, remove all distractions. This meant that he was to be prevented from meeting wandering sadhus, musicians, grammarians, poets, even the oracle, and most of all, his friend Aambal, 'Kandhan's poet'. Didn't they have some foolish agreement that she would compose through the day and he would revise with her every evening? That had to stop at all costs. Veerabahu summoned Murugan and said to him, 'You must not leave the confines of the palace, and most of all, you must stay away from visitors, you must not meet your friend Aambal.'

Anna had already cautioned Murugan: 'Kandha, they are your elders, and they give much importance to discipline. Be courteous and do as they ask. They are your battle generals and they know what must be done.' So, he merely asked Veerabahu for permission to go and tell Aambal. If Veerabahu knew better, Murugan's voice would have told him right away that a plot had been hatched, but he only heard the polite voice asking permission.

In her house in the town at the bottom of the hill, Aambal was upset. Kandhan hadn't come by in four days and he never went away without telling her. Where was he? Why hadn't he said anything? He was so annoying, and now, she couldn't write, read or edit—wherever she looked, he was there, sniggering. She should go to the palace and ask where he was, even though the thought of his housekeeper set her teeth on edge. The man would look at her disapprovingly, shaking his head, and only then would she look down and realise she was wearing her home clothes. But if Kandhan did not turn up today, she would go.

Then he was there. He stepped off the peacock's giant back and walked towards her, his face serious, and with none of his customary swagger, the akil dandam horizontal in his left hand, his arms pressed close to his body. *Something was wrong. What was it? Her parents? Her sister or brother?*

'Kandha! Where have you been? It's been four whole days … why can't you just be like normal people, send word—' Her voice broke off. His face remained serious. She looked at Paravani, who looked away. Her breath caught. 'What is it, Kandha? What's happening?'

He took both her hands in his and began to speak. He described everything that was happening: the meeting, the decisions, the message sent by Surapadman and the one sent to him, the decision to go to war, the forces that had arrived on Pazhani, and finally, what Veerabahu's conditions were. He did not tell her where the battle was to take place. *Not now, not now, she would not take it well at all.*

Aambal heard only snatches of what Kandhan was saying, her thoughts were aflutter, like parrots in fields, scattered by the clutter of rattles. *The time had come.*

She knew of the condition of the great Asura and the conditions of Kandhan's birth. She also knew that Kandhan could lose the battle. He had told her, 'If I lose my concentration and forget what I have to remember, I will lose. If I don't recognise the thing I am supposed to, then too I will lose.' He would not die of course, he could not die, but it would mean that something that was meant to happen would not happen because of him.

'You're going to stand against King Surapadman and his brothers? But why do you have to be shut away for seven days?' *Was no one allowed to see him? His brother? His peacock? His friends, the Gandharva twins? The twelve Matris? Why only her? Didn't kings take their poets to war with them? Why hadn't he told them that she would be his war bard, that her words would resound like a por murasu, rousing his spirit?*

Aambal felt as if someone had pushed her hard and she was flying through the air, unable to fall or stand or fly. She would have liked to scream, to tell Kandhan's brothers, 'Kandhan has been my friend since we were five, and in all these years, I did not distract him. If anything, I've steadied him.' All the years of her life appeared before her eyes. She heard Kandhan's voice asking her to give up her family and her home, and live with him and be his. And she had, hadn't she? Had she been delusional when she made that choice? Had the hills, the hill creatures and the purple kurinji been warning her when she thought they were hailing her as Kandhan's poet? Maybe they had been saying, 'No, no, no, don't be Kandhan's poet.'

Aambal could feel the rage sparking. This was not fair, and she wasn't going to let him get away with passing the blame. She wasn't going to let him go without teaching him a lesson. She wanted to hear him say, *Aambal, you're my best friend, I need you. Come to the battle with me.*

She shut her eyes and willed herself to drop to the ground, pleased with the thud when she fell. It sounded real! She lay still, the anger and the dread of the impending battle keeping her from laughing. Kandhan was on the floor by her side, shaking her and saying, 'Aambal, Aambal, wake up.' She lay still, and he called again, sounding panicky, 'Aambal, Aambal, get up.' *Good! A few moments more and he would cry, and then he would talk.*

'Aambal,' she heard his voice through her thoughts, 'Aambal, you're my best friend. I need you. I want you to come to the battle with me.' She reached out and pinched his arm, and he jumped. 'Ouch! What did you do that for? Why did you pinch me, you stupid poet?'

'Just in case you felt you had to kiss me or something. Take this, and this.' Then she was pinching him, and they were laughing. Eventually, the god took leave of his poet. She said, 'I will not sleep in all the time you are on the battlefield, even if I am not allowed there. My eyes and ears and my words will always be by your side.'

The god smiled and nodded. *No, she would be there, beside him, his best friend, his war bard.*

Veerabahu started Murugan's training, while his eight brothers began training the warriors, mostly Sura and other ganas who had come from one or the other of the fourteen worlds or whose homes were on Kailasa.

That Murugan would be so well-behaved was not what Veerabahu had expected. He said never a word in disagreement, and he was so focused on the workouts and the training that the older sibling heaved a sigh of relief. The days passed and nothing changed, and then, on the fifth day, it happened.

Aambal, who had sworn she would not go to the palace, stormed in there with the combined fervour of a forest full of elephants running from a forest fire.

Witnesses said they saw a bird disappear at the same time as the flames began to spark. They knew it was not Paravani, the great peacock, Lord Murugan's mount. This peacock was small, its wings only a fraction of Paravani's wingspread. But they were sure it was a peacock that they had seen starting up into the sky from Aambal's rooftop at the same time as the flames began to soar out from the windows and the chimney.

Aambal was crossing the fields that lay between her little house and the leather works. The smoke rose up like a black cloud, but it was the smell that came to her first. She knew that smell, it was the smell of fire feeding on wood and thatch, and the dry leafy smell of palm leaves catching fire.

She felt a sudden dread and began to run. As she ran, her feet took on the strength of giants, the wind thundered inside her chest, and from her belly a wail spewed up. Aambal crossed the fields and ran down the lane that led to her house and saw what she had feared before she got there: it *was* her house. The little house that Kandhan has organised a housewarming for, the house where she had sat every day, writing verse after verse, waiting for Kandhan to come and read them. The house where she kept, bound with indigo thread, bundle upon bundle of palm leaves and parchments. This was the house inside which she had left the last verse in the hundred that she would submit to the Assembly as soon as Kandhan's battle was over and he returned. But most of all, this was where lay, weighted down with pebbles, the first five of the poems that she had sworn to write every day of Kandhan's training and of his battle days: the poems that she had promised her friend would be like a charm around his body, like guards at the doorway of his life. And now, they were burning in there, inside her house. How could she have been so careless? What did this mean? Had she put Kandhan at risk? Is this why Veerabahu had said, *No Aambal*?

The crowds parted as she broke through. She rushed blindly towards the burning house. They grabbed her and held her back; she raged, shouted and screamed. The sky was black, as if thousands of ravens were flying in close formation. 'It's the palm leaves,' some said. 'Must be all that ink,' others said. 'It was her life, so much work, all wasted.' 'Poor thing,' they said, 'hope she doesn't go completely mad.'

'She's calling on Our Lord of Pazhani, but he is training for the battle. He can't come down here and we cannot go up there,' they said.

Aambal felt as if all her alphabets were running helter-skelter inside her, as if they had mutinied. She could feel javelin thrusts, sword cuts, and elephants trampling the life out of her, and she ran away from the attack, her hair streaming behind her. Her upper cloth soared away. Someone picked it up and held it out to her, then ran after her, holding it out, but she ran on, unaware. She raced up the steep face of the great Pazhani hill as if it was flatland, shouting his name: 'Kandha, Kandha, all gone, it's all gone, your poems, the poems for the Assembly, everything gone! Kandha, where are you, where were you when my house burnt down?'

Aambal headed straight for the gate, and the guards, who knew her well enough, didn't stop her. However, when she came to the great door, on the other side of which Murugan was practising hand-to-hand combat with Veerabahu, who was calling out directions, the guards called to her to halt. When she did not heed them, they had to grab her. It took four of them to stay her, but she continued to scream and wail. They all heard her voice. Ganesha looked at Mushika, and they smiled at each other. Veerabahu did not pay attention because he was concentrating on his younger brother's lunges and parries, though he must have heard it too. And Murugan? Of course! How could he not? This was Aambal's voice.

She stretched and strained against the eight hands restraining her, and eventually broke their hold and rushed inside, screaming his name: 'Kandha, Kandha, Kandha'. Her eyes were red, her voice was like the sharp keening of birds mourning the death of one in their flock. Paravani continued to sit, his wings close to the ground. A hush fell on the training warriors and over their trainers, over the masseurs and the physicians and the drummers. Over everyone. All eyes were on Aambal. Those who knew her understood that something terrible must have happened—for all that the Lord of Pazhani was her friend and her fellow student, she was usually decorous, calling him 'My Lord' or 'Lord of Pazhani' or 'Lord Karthikeya'. She may sometimes pinch him or tug at his hair, but those things she did quickly and quietly, and was rarely caught. They had never seen her like this. Those who didn't know her may have thought her mad or perhaps maddened by the Fates, who had chosen her as an oracle. *That* they had seen before.

Veerabahu had turned when he heard the sounds, but Kandhan kept practising, as if he was so focused that nothing could distract him. The older brother made an impatient sound and turned back to directing Murugan's mace blows. He expected that someone would stop the woman, but her voice only grew louder. Veerabahu leapt down from the platform on which they were standing, the practice area, and ran towards her, having lost his equanimity. Who was this woman? Why was she here? Didn't she know that Murugan, commander of the great army going to battle with Surapadman, was practising and needed focus? What did she mean, bursting in like this? How dare she!

He approached her and raised a hand. 'Stop, stop there.' Aambal turned her face to him, and those who were there say he staggered, only for the blink of an eye, but stagger he did. His mouth opened again to stay stop, or perhaps he was going to chant a spell, perhaps he was going to leap into her path or throw a magic rope around her. We don't know because at that moment Murugan was there, between his poet and his general, between his best friend and his brother, between the woman and the man. Murugan said *Aambal* and, like a candle near a fire, her shoulders slumped, her mouth closed, and tears running from her eyes, she fell against Murugan's chest. He held her.

Veerabahu stood rooted to the spot, tears running down his cheeks. No one had ever seen Veerabahu cry, because he had never cried before. They stared, perhaps some sniggered, his brothers may have been embarrassed, for they were the Immoveable Warriors.

'Aambal.' Murugan's voice was low, but it filled the air and echoed. He took one of her hands and repeated, 'Aambal.'

She looked up at him and said, 'Kandha, everything is gone, it's all gone, burnt. My whole house, burnt.' Her hands clutched his arms and shook him.

He smiled at her and said, 'No, nothing's gone, look there.'

Paravani, who had been making such a show of keeping his wings close to the floor, now opened them. There, on a stretch of indigo silk, were neat bundles of palm-leaf manuscripts knotted with indigo thread, inkwells and styluses. Her eyes widened, her face cleared like the sky after a storm. She stuttered as she said, 'Kandha', and in that word there was chiding, gratitude, and a hint of the familiar threat: I will deal with you later.

Veerabahu understood now why they called these two inseparable, and why the woman named for the timorous blue lily was called 'Murugan's poet'. He asked Murugan what he wanted, and his brother said, 'She must go into the battle with me, she will be my war bard. Surapadman's might is not just his valour or the strength of his army and weapons. It is also in his words. I need a poet to shield me from the attack of his words.'

That was how it came about that Aambal was allowed to go into the battle with Murugan.

Ganesha sighed. *One more thing out of the way.* He knew this had been planned before either Kandhan or Aambal was born, Kandhan brooding on the rim of his father's third eye and Aambal at the opening of her mother's birth channel, with Time gently holding back its folds till Murugan had taken birth before pushing his companion out.

Veerabahu embraced his brother and held out his hands to Aambal. When she put her own in them, he said, 'Aambal. Aambal, war bard to Karthikeya. Here, take this.' Waving his hands in the air, he pulled out a pair of cymbals cast in bell metal and tapped them, one against the other. The sound fell over everyone and everything there, reminding them of the war that awaited.

Aambal felt Ganesha's eyes on her. Kandhan's brother, the Guide of All Creation, he who had been lovingly brought to life by the Mother of All Creation. He had his mother's eyes, long, stretching towards his elephant ears as if to leap out of his face, like the black carp that leapt into the fields in Chendur.

Chendur. Chendur! *Chendur by the sea, from where you could see the two fabled islands: Sri Lanka and Veeramahendrapuram. Chendur! That was where the battle would be fought. Chendur. Her home, the place where her family had always lived.*

Ganesha nodded. *Yes*, his face said, *yes, your home, your Chendur.*

Aambal shivered. Her fingers tingled as if they had been plunged into a sleeping lake. She clutched the cymbals lest they slip out of her hold. What if she died? Her parents, her siblings, how would they bear it? What if something happened to Kandhan? Aambal shut her eyes. *Nothing would happen to him, nothing should.* The words of the oracle came back to her: '... count the measures, do not slip, and do not let the slip fall upon him'.

She held out the two metals discs of the cymbals and struck them. Everyone stopped what they were doing. Murugan moved back to give her more room. Aambal began to recite, loudly, in the amplified, throwy voice that bards used when they were performing a martial metre. It began with a warm-up gait, like the heart's walk, two-one-two-one-two and moved into a swift march. The warriors struck the ground or their shields or their chests with their weapons and called aloud, 'Vetri, Vetri, Vetrivel, Viravel; Viravel, Vetrivel.'

Through their training and apprenticeship, warriors are taught to master all weapons, but they know that eventually they will find the one that becomes an extension of their own will. They may not discover their connection to this singular weapon themselves: their aasaan, the oracle of their land, a parent, friend, sibling, lover, spouse, sometimes even a passer-by or a creature in a dream might tell them what it is, or bring it to them. And when the warriors hold the weapon meant for them, they feel the weapon returning the grasp. Sometimes, a name for the weapon will swing into their head, like the swing of the weapon itself—true, sharp.

Surapadman's weapon was a sword brought to him by his mother, Surasa, who appeared in court soon after the details for the battle had been fixed. He was not surprised to see her, knowing she would come, for it might be the last time they met in this world. His three siblings also arrived with their armies to join their eldest brother. Ajamugi came too. She would take part in the battle, though war wasn't something she was inclined to. When Surasa arrived at the court, the four siblings were pleased to see her, for she had been reclusive, often spending long periods of time on Meru. Shukracharya too welcomed his one-time student with special warmth, for he knew the importance of the gift she came bearing for Surapadman.

Shukracharya announced to the court that the Queen Mother had brought the weapon with which their valorous king must go into battle. The weapon, he announced, was a sword. When Surasa drew it out of its copper scabbard, the sword rippled with a fiery light; it looked like condensed fire. Its sparks pierced the ribs of the warriors in the room, awakening there the timeless drummer who beats out the call to valour. She handed the sword to Surapadman, who took it and laid it, and his own head, at her feet. She blessed him and announced to the assembly, 'This is Maya. And in the hands of your king, this will be equal to the weapon of his opponent, the mighty Karthikeya.' Those assembled there raised a lusty cheer that rushed out of the courtroom, out over the island, over the waves of the mighty sea, and sounded in Chendur, on the other shore.

Surasa also brought from Meru two steeds white as snow, with arched backs, muscled flanks, glowing tails, and foreheads marked with stars. One night, she had been woken from sleep by the voice of Kashyapa, who said to her, 'Go to the western slope of our home, and find there two horses grown from seed I spilt when I joined with you. They are called Kshema and Svasti, and will carry our firstborn, Suran, to his desired goal.' There was no talk of victory or defeat, or of valour. Svasti, benediction for well-being, and Kshema, welfare. Surasa smiled. *Kshema, was it?* Fitting, since it was to Karthikeya that these steeds were carrying Suran.

Murugan's two steeds were night-black, and like Surapadman's, they also embodied the paradox inherent in all creation, in all work: that which a thing can *become* always pulls away from that which it *is*. These steeds had been given to him while he was still a child by his aunt, the Goddess of Fortune. The names of Murugan's war horses were Neram and Kalam: Time and Duration.

Murugan's weapon, the vel, was brought to him by his brother, the Lord of Beginnings. Like Surapadman, Murugan received his weapon in court and in the presence of his entire army.

'This weapon,' Ganesha announced, 'is the Shakti Vel, it holds the blessings of the Mother of Creation, Shakti herself, and is equal in every way to the Maya of our worthy opponent, King Surapadman.' Rousing cheers rang out as Murugan took the vel from his brother. He would not be taking the dandam to the battlefield. Murugan knew that the green akil dandam was not for warring. He would leave it with Anna for the span of the battle.

Like the two who would lead their armies, their soldiers too picked their weapons and made ready. These may not have been their best weapons, maybe they hadn't found those yet, but this would be their best battle: it was not always that warriors could go to a battle with such glorious commanders on both sides.

Thus, Surapadman and Murugan waited to march towards Chendur, which was getting ready for the armies, for their leaders, and the great battle. Aambal's parents and her siblings also waited. They knew that she was to accompany Murugan, who because he now carried the vel called Shakti was called Shakti Velan. They feared for Aambal: she might be struck by a passing arrow, a mace, a spear aimed at Murugan; they knew too, that she could lose count of the beats of her cymbals as she recited verses to spur Murugan on or focus his attention. And that would be fatal for him, for the battle, for all of them. Although they were afraid, they were proud of her. When her siblings wanted to run to her side, their parents said, 'No, she needs to be alone now. We will not meet her till the battle is over, unless she asks for us.'

The thought of Chendur clouded Aambal's thoughts. It was where she had been born, and where she had come back to, all her life. It was where she had watched and learnt from her parents; it was her home.

Kandhan had visited with her many times before, but this time, he would not visit, he would not speak. Nor could she. There could be no meeting with families or friends before a battle, and speech was forbidden.

Chendur waited, along with its people, the roll of waves sounding a constant refrain. What would its red soil say, if it could speak? Might it tell tales of unknown times, when other battles had been fought here, the blood spilled then, turning it red forever?

The gods and their forces arrived in Pazhani with their guru, Brihaspati; their king, Indra; his wife, Queen Sachi; his son, Jayanta and daughter, Devayani. Mayan, with his heavenly architectural implements, had arrived a few days earlier and, in a few blinks of the human eye, constructed grand buildings to house all of them. When their use was done, he would dismantle everything and pack it all, like betel leaves, betel nuts, spices and lime, into a chellapetti-sized box.

The formality of war dictated that Indra request Murugan to appear at the court, albeit makeshift, and present him with the title of 'supreme commander' of the armies that would march against Surapadman. Both armies comprised of a mix of ganas, but there were no Sura in the Asura army and no Asura in the army of the Sura.

Murugan would go to the court, accompanied by his bodyguards, advisors, generals and war bards. The occasion demanded that someone had to welcome him formally and bestow upon him the title. Brihaspati was fraught with anxiety: what if the speaker was unable to invoke and amplify Murugan's greatness? What if he took offence? And because it was Murugan—whose disdain for insincerity of speech was well known, as were the stories of the fury with which he had once attacked Indra for daring to stand in his way—Brishaspati was all the more nervous.

The Sura guru considered long and hard before settling on a speaker. He rejected most of the gods right away, they were too low in the hierarchy. He considered their commander-in-chief, the brave Garjana. She was a remarkable warrior and Murugan would be pleased to hear her speak, but she was one of few words and the occasion required some oratorical flourish. Apart from the warriors, the people of Pazhani had gathered in the thousands to witness the occasion. Indra's speech would be expectedly florid, Jayanta was a nervous and graceless speaker, and even the queen, usually an articulate speaker, was now nervous. Ah! But of course!

Devayani. She had the oratorical flair to hold everyone's attention and impress the young man whose love for fine speech and poetry was well known. Devayani, the foster daughter of Indra, sister of Jayanta, raised and tutored by Airavata, who himself was a great speaker and scholar. She was perfect.

Murugan set out from the hill to meet the gods. The temporary court at the base of Pazhani was a thrum of activity. The roads were lined with soldiers, and chariots waited by the side. The townsfolk had all turned out to look at the young god, who was clad in armour that glowed like the sun, the brass and copper of it polished and shiny, his long curly hair oiled and knotted up on top of his head. In one hand he held a vel, its long metal handle and its leaf-like face gleaming. Occasionally, he raised it in acknowledgement of people calling out 'Viravel, Shaktivel.'

Trumpets sounded, drums beat, Indra's bards' voices rang out in eulogy of Murugan, whom they addressed as 'Karthikeya, Bahuleya, Kumaraswamy, Arumuga'. When he stepped through the doorway, with the bards reciting, 'Hail, Karthikeya, Mighty Lord of Pazhani, Hail, Hail', women and men rose in their thousands and took up the chant. The warriors raised their weapons high over their heads and the chant swelled. 'Hail Karthikeya. Hail the mighty Vel.' Murugan raised his own weapon in response.

This was the first time Devayani was seeing Murugan. *So this was the handsomest man in all Creation?* He was smiling and nodding at the rows of people who stood to greet him as he passed. His eyes had caught the smile on Devayani's face. *This was Indra's daughter.* He had heard about her. Her scholarship and understanding of the language of all things, especially four-footed beings, was legend across the worlds. His chest stretched under the armour; his steps slowed.

Murugan went first to Brihaspati, hands folded in greeting, one hand curled around the stem of the vel. When he spoke, the ever-calm Sura guru felt his heart become so tumultuous that he thought everybody could hear it.

The boy was saying, 'Guru of the gods, most revered Brihaspati, my greetings to you. I have accepted the request you sent on behalf of the gods to whom you are guide and preceptor. Here I am, tell me what I may do.'

Brihaspati's ears felt cool, his eyes felt as if they had had a long rest and were now ready for work. He took the young man's hands and held them. In his heart, he wanted to kiss the dark, sinewed hands. He said, 'Karthikeya, Lord of Pazhani. We are honoured by your presence. On behalf of the king, the queen and everyone gathered here, I welcome you.'

He then formally presented Murugan to the king and the queen, leading him up the steps to where their thrones were. That over, he led Murugan down, to the empty seat beside his own, with Devayani on his right. He said, 'This is the princess Devayani, and that is Jayanta, whom you already know.'

Murugan folded his hands and said, 'Theivanai, in our land, that is what we would call you.'

'Theivanai,' she repeated. 'Theivanai.' It was pleasing, the 'th'.

The assembly was still standing, and Murugan's eyes went to the army chief, Garjana, who raised her sword to him. Murugan acknowledged her with a nod of his head and a smile. His eyes returned to Devayani, who was looking at him with a smile on her lips. *Those eyes! What was she thinking?* She nodded and smiled. *Were his lips smiling?* He wanted to smile, but it felt like his whole body was standing still. He wondered if Aambal could see him. His eyes scanned the crowd.

Brihaspati nudged him to be seated. When Murugan sat down, everyone fell silent. They had no idea who was to address him and introduce him to the court. They too knew the importance of the task—to please the visitor without fawning, to describe his greatness to the thousands gathered and impress on them that the fight he was leading them into was worth staking their lives for.

Brihaspati signalled to Devayani, who smiled and stood up. Indra and Sachi sighed in relief, and all who knew the power of her speech, they too sighed, then settled back in their seats. Jayanta was relieved that he wasn't to take on this task, and his chest swelled with pride in his sister.

At a nod from Brihaspati, Devayani turned to Murugan and said, 'Greetings, son of Shiva and Parvathy, Lord of Pazhani, welcome to the assembly of Indra and Indrani. As instructed by the revered Brihaspati, and on behalf of all those gathered here, I greet you and thank you for accepting our invitation.'

Murugan stood. He looked towards the royal couple on the raised throne, then at Garjana, and then the assembly. He nodded, smiled and sat down. His ears tingled. Her voice had the strong resonance of a perfectly cast bell, and it made him want to shut his eyes and doze off, so that it could rouse him.

Devayani addressed the gathering, turning this way and that, so all those gathered there could see her. She spoke of how the Asura king was threatening to capture the task of creation and of his refusal to give up, despite requests from the gods. She went on to say that he had chosen war over accord, and of how he had, even before the event, let it be known that there was only one person he considered worthy of combating with—the mighty Karthikeya, Lord of Pazhani.

She described Murugan's valour, and that of the great army he would lead. Her words were met with rousing cheers and shouts of 'Vetri, Vetri'. She turned to Murugan, addressed him as 'Vetrivela', Warrior Armed with the Victorious Vel, and said, 'You whose very name is Victory, whose shoulders are the mighty beams that hold up the twin balances of Time and Death, you are yourself a mighty army. May you lead these warriors to a matchless battle, the likes of which will never be known again.'

Facing her audience, her hands in the air, she called out a verbal salute to the god who stood beside her: 'Hail Karthikeya, Hail Senani, Hail Mahasena.' As she came to the last name, her head turned abruptly towards Murugan.

As each of the god's names resounded, the people assembled there rose and cheered, their voices amplified into a single resonant chant, joined by the beings in all fourteen worlds. Murugan stood, his ebony face warm, his chest leaping beneath his armour, his eyes fiery; their battle cries fell on him like the royal garlands, ensigns of their dynasties, that kings wore to battle. His eyes scanned the crowd for Aambal, and he caught sight of her white clothes amongst the shiny armour of warriors and the bright colours of the townspeople. He was filled with impatience to be on horseback, rushing to battle. He raised his vel and from his lips there came a war cry, 'Arogara-Arogara', which was answered with a cry of 'Vetrivel, Viravel, Viravel, Vetrivel' and a loud clanging of weapons by women and men as impatient as he was, to set off to battle, with him commanding them.

Devayani waited for the clamour to still before she approached Murugan. Garjana walked up too. In her hand was a sword sheathed in a scabbard of decorated leather. She unsheathed it and handed the sword to Devayani, who took it in both hands, and raising it to the assembly, proclaimed: 'Invoking the blessings of the Remover of Obstacles; the blessings of our Guru, Brihaspati; and the good wishes of our King and Queen, Indra and Indrani, I hereby appoint you the supreme commander of our armies.' More cries of 'Mahasena, Karthikeya, Mahasena' rang out. She then handed the sword to Murugan.

Garjana gave the scabbard to Murugan with a smile which he didn't seem to register, for he did not smile back. Everybody sat down again. All thoughts of battle, of armies, and of the people who sat around him faded to the back of Murugan's head. Why had Devayani stuttered when she called him 'Mahasena'? Had he imagined that she was going to say something else? It was as if some insight she herself had not expected had taken hold of her speech, her tongue, which she only managed to shake off in the last instant. She had said 'Maha' and then, instead of the tongue ascending to the roof of her mouth and settling there parallel, without touching, for the hissing out of the 'Sa' of 'Sena', it had touched the roof, and he had sensed its vibration, as if to make an 'rrr' sound. He had heard it, hadn't he? He wasn't imagining it? What was it about Devayani that made him hesitant? If Aambal were here, she would have brought him back to his senses, with one of her pinches.

He knew it was said of Devayani that she could hear the gati, the gait that every creature holds in its heart, the secret sound of the particular rhythm of life inside each creature. Had she heard something? What had she heard from inside him? What was the name that had inadvertently sprung to her tongue?

Murugan could not ask her, and she would not tell him. She couldn't. Nobody could tell him the secret of his birth, his self; he had to uncover it himself—this was Surapadman's condition. He would have to find for himself what she had sensed. What was it? What was he? What was this other name? *Maha*, he knew it was Maha, *Great*, but Maha what? She had called him the Great General, Mahasena. But she had seen that he was also something else.

His thoughts bounded back to the present when Aambal's voice rose over the crowds and fell into his ears. He had not realised that she had been asked to stand up and recite verses in honour of the warriors. He was glad to see her, still far away but visible. She was reciting to the accompaniment of her cymbals, the ones that Veerabahu had given her, but he was hearing the voice that had hesitated over his name. It fell over everything and echoed back, reveberating: *Mahasena, Mahasena, Mahasena.*

When she finished, a sea of hands, some with weapons, some not, rose into the air, waving in rhythm to shouts of *Mahasena, Mahasena, Mahasena, Mahasena, Mahasena.*

Murugan only heard half the name: Maha, Maha, Maha. Taunting him, the broken name ran amok in his head. It dashed to and fro, certain that he couldn't catch it; it ran at him and dashed away, like an impudent child who is secure in the knowledge that it will not be punished. Like a battering ram, it knocked against the rampart of his chest, and his ribs groaned but held fast. He willed it to break through, to break through the wall behind which he knew was the final lesson—the riddle in the syllables of his name.

The mood of the warriors—his warriors now, his army—was calmer, more settled, looking past the fervour of the moment to what awaited them, the place, the time and the event. They were calling to him by another name now: Chenduran. They were hailing him as the Lord of Chendur.

Perhaps the answers lay there, in Chendur, he thought, as he turned his attention back to where he was right then: the foothills of his home, Pazhani.

ACKNOWLEDGEMENTS

I owe thanks to many.

First, to my student Manjari Chandrashekar, for (unwittingly) becoming the reason for this book being a trilogy, rather than a single, with a gift she brought for me.

To my uncle Jinan, for spontaneously deciding to fund some of the research needs of this book and for checking on me, without fail.

To my middle child, Gauri, who read drafts, discussed ideas, and kept me going during a year-and-a half of anxieties, lows, doubts. *Your spirit is in this book.*

To my eldest, Paru, for making me feel supported, and for the courage of her choices. *Some of the women in this book have your traits.*

To my youngest, Sathyavak, whose passionate labouring at 'Andhakara Records' was a rare happy thing in this terrible time. *This book is dedicated to you.*

Much appreciation for the music of Sanjay Subrahmanyan, which, as another writer has said, seems on occasion to take you by the hand as you're listening and writing, and to lead you.

Gratitude to my dear friend, Sudhir Kakar, for his interest in my work and for the constancy of his affection.

To my editors Karthika V.K. and Ajitha G.S, many thanks for letting me take my time with writing blocks, and for their affection for the characters of this book. Working with them on editing the manuscript has, without a doubt, helped me to shift from poetry's unruliness, which I suspect is my natural element, to the disciplined coherence of prose. In the process, my understanding of editing has grown in both quantity and quality. It is a pleasure, always, to work with Karthika and Ajitha—they are sharp with the work and warm with the author of the work!

Finally, for the God of Tamizh, the mercurial, trickster god, who stirs my imagination, fuels my work and makes me what I am, all of my life.

Theivanai

PART TWO OF
THE MURUGAN TRILOGY

KALA KRISHNAN

a prelude

Ganesha sat looking out to sea. The waves rose and plunged and broke in a flurry of lacy foam on the sands, still warm, though the sun was halfway across the western sky. The waves of Chendur were greeting him. Chendur, he thought, its name, like its soil, red.

Mahasena, Lord of Chendur—the name suited his brother very well. Most names did: Kumara, Karthikeya, Skanda, Kandha, Muruga, Guha, Senani, Mahasena, ah, Mahasena. His fingers traced the letters on the sand as he repeated that last name. He stopped after 'Maha' and silently mouthed something, even as his finger traced and quickly smoothed it over.

He sighed and leaned back, resting his weight on both arms. His eyes sprinted across the waters to the lights of Veeramahendrapuram, dipping and bobbing on the waves. The blue hue that gave it its name, so distinct by day, was hidden in the gold of its lights. Veeramahendrapuram. Ganesha smiled. How many would recognise Surapadman's sport with the semantic resonance of 'Mahendra'? *How many would know that he was saluting Mother, whose skin was the colour of Indraneela, the blue of that jewel often called Mahendraneela? One day, a poet would describe her as 'Maahendraneela dyuti komalangi'.*

The language of that song, the same as that of the magnificent work Ganesha had scribed—it was beautiful without doubt, but he had had a surfeit of it, of its rules and grandiosity. Now it was Kandhan's language, the old tongue revived, that delighted his ears and surprised him with its variations and its love for its god and itself. He hummed under his breath, *'Vaaraan-di, vaaraan-di, Pazhanimalaiyaandi.'* He comes, here he comes, sister, the mendicant from Pazhani. How did it go? Something about a—Ganesha's head snapped up in surprise. What had he just seen? He tried to call the image back, but it was hazy—had he really seen it, red, black? Ganesha shook his head, what was happening? He was all-seeing, he should be able to see. With shut eyes he concentrated, but nothing. A footfall distracted him, making him turn around, and Surapadman stood there, a smile on his lips, his hands folded in greeting.

'These waves,' he said, 'I never tire of them. They come to Veeramahendrapuram from Chendur, and then return to Chendur.'

'These waves come to Chendur,' Ganesha replied, smiling, 'from Veeramahendrapuram, and then return to Veeramahendrapuram.' He began to rise and the Asura king helped him up. They strolled along the seashore.

Ganesha was anxious. Tomorrow, the battle would begin, and it would not end soon. He could not see what would become of it, because that becoming was not yet formed. As 'Mahasena' did, so would the future become. They walked together quietly. Surapadman began to hum, *vaaraan-di, vaaraan-di* … What comes after that, he asked Ganesha.

His mind still trying to bring back the image that had slipped away, Ganesha asked, 'What?'

Surapadman repeated his question, 'What comes after "*vaaraandi, vaaraandi*", Anna?'

Anna! Only Kandhan called him that, and yet, in Surapadman's voice, it sounded familiar. He filled in the line and they moved on. The sky was growing darker, the wind from the sea cooler, and soon, the two armies, camped at two spots on the opposite ends of Chendur's beach, would eat their evening meal and go to sleep.

'Will he?' Suran's voice broke the stillness.

Ganesha replied, 'I don't know.'

They walked in silence for a while, their footsteps in rhythm with the sound of the waves washing in and out, in and out. Ganesha said, 'It's time to go.'

Surapadman said, 'Bless me and bless him.' He embraced the elephant-headed god and said, 'I take leave of you now. I pray that your brother sees.'

They turned and went towards their respective sides. Ganesha would not take part in the battle. He had a tent near those of the bards and musicians who had travelled to sing about this battle, songs that would pass through generations and join the river of songs about the encounter between Surapadman, King of Veeramahendrapuram, and Mahasena Karthikeya, Lord of Chendur.

To be continued ...